A REASON TO BE

Sharon Francis

Copyright © 2024 Sharon Francis

All rights reserved

The characters and events portrayed in this book are fictitious. Any similarity to real persons, living or dead, is coincidental and not intended by the author.

No part of the book may be reproduced, or stored in a retrieval system, or transmitted in any form or by any means, electronic, mechanical, photocopying, recording, or otherwise, without express permission of the publisher.

Cover design by: Megan Saunders

CHAPTER 1

The sultry voice of Ella Fitzgerald crooning about dreaming a little dream was the only sound in the room of the hospice. Audrey was enthralled – music was a simple pleasure which, at this point in her life, were few and far between.

She sighed as the needle reached the centre of the record, clicking and clunking as it returned to its stand. 'Heavenly. If I popped my clogs now, I'd die happy.'

'Gran, don't!'

Audrey turned her head on the pillow to look at her granddaughter, sitting nearby. Daisy's hazel eyes swam with tears, and it saddened Audrey's heart. She was resigned to the fact she was dying; she wasn't resigned to leaving Daisy virtually alone in the world. They'd always been there for each other, and Audrey had assumed Daisy would be nicely settled when the time came for her to go, maybe with children of her own, but it wasn't to be. She patted her granddaughter's hand. 'Daisy, Daisy, Daisy.'

Daisy pulled her hands away and wiped her eyes, sniffing and blinking rapidly.

Audrey winced as she turned to address the other person in the room. 'Finn, give us five minutes, will you?'

He stopped tidying well-wisher's cards on the shelf and, spotting Daisy's demeanour, smiled and straightened his tabard. 'I fancy a cup of tea. Can I get you guys anything? A sandwich? Biscuits? Large glass of gin?'

Audrey shook her head and waited until he'd left the room. 'Now then, Daisy.' She patted the sheet, encouraging her granddaughter to replace her hand where she could reach it.

A Reason To Be

Daisy gave one last wipe to her cheek before doing so.

'That's better.' Audrey grasped it gently. 'Now, you do understand, don't you? You know I've not long left.'

'Yes, but I don't like it when you say it like that, like it's nothing.'

'Would you rather I was burying my head in the sand?' She let her head collapse on the pillow. 'Look, this has been on the cards for months and I'm ready. My affairs are in order, I've said all I need to say to the ones I love, and I feel blessed. A lot never have the chance to set things straight.'

'I still think you should let Mum...'

'No, no, no. I don't want the fuss and bother. She'd feel duty-bound to come over from America and take charge and I can't be doing with it. Let's be honest, me and your mum are like strangers these days and I can't be watching my p's and q's when I'm going to meet my maker.' Audrey took a ragged breath; the long speech having drained her of energy. 'Besides, I've left a letter for her, in the drawer there.'

Daisy's head swivelled toward the bedside cupboard.

'And there's one for you too, but it's to wait until I've gone, mind, not the next time I nod off. I know what you're like, opening your presents on Christmas Eve.'

'Gran!' Daisy's tone was outraged.

'Don't deny it. You've the patience of a flea, and you know it.' Audrey felt herself drifting away. 'Now, go and clean your face and send that boy back in. He's only hovering outside, for all his talk of tea and gin.'

Whether it was due to the medication, which kept pain at bay, but stole pockets of consciousness too, or because she was so near her time, but Audrey had the strange sensation of floating free of her body. She was suddenly aware of her sleepy figure lying below, as if her inner being was in the top corner of the room, looking down. She could see Daisy and Finn exchanging words outside, away from her hearing. As Finn re-entered the room, Audrey crashed back into the shell on the bed.

'Audrey? Are you ok?' Finn's voice was gentle but concerned.

She coughed and opened her eyes, and saw him physically relax. 'Still here, lad. Don't you worry.'

'Can I do anything to make you more comfortable before I go off shift?' He checked a watch hanging from the pocket of his uniform shirt, then let it drop.

'I'm as comfortable as I can be.'

He flicked old wrappers and tissues from a table next to the bed, into a bin.

'You could do something for me though.'

His face crinkled into a smile which lit up his blue eyes. 'What's that?'

'Keep an eye on madam there, will you? She's struggling.' Audrey grimaced as she shifted her shoulders. 'I think it's harder for her than it is me.' She was slipping again; she could feel it. Her eyes wanted to close, and no amount of effort would keep them open. 'I know there are rules, about fraternising with patients and families and suchlike, but I'll be gone, so they won't apply anymore, will they?'

He moved in close as her voice faded, and straightened her pillows. 'I'm sure she'll be fine, given time.'

Audrey forced a final bolt of strength into her tone. 'Yes, but she'll need someone close by for a while, and the two of you have gelled so well these last few days. Can you do that?'

'The hospice offers support to families where they can...'

'Oh, I know all that. I've read the leaflets, but I'm asking you. What she needs is a... a big brother figure, someone to keep a watchful eye on her, and I've a feeling you'd make a really good big brother.'

Finn looked at her sharply and drew back, his brow furrowed.

A Reason To Be

Audrey sensed she'd struck a chord. 'You've been here, so she already knows you. It'll mean more than some stranger passing her tissues.' She didn't have time for niceties. 'Can you do that for me?'

He nibbled at a fingernail. 'If you really think it would help...'

'That's that then.' Audrey relaxed. 'Now, stick on some Sinatra, will you? Something sexy. Let a girl have sweet dreams, even if she can't have the real thing.'

He smiled and sorted through the selection of records propped next to the player.

Daisy returned as the music started and Finn turned to face her, leaning back against the wall, his voice low. 'She's one of a kind, your grandma.'

'You can say that again.' Daisy chuckled. 'She wants "Fly Me to the Moon" played at her funeral as the coffin goes out.' She rolled her eyes. 'Thanks for sorting out the turntable, by the way. Gran's always loved her music.'

He waved away her thanks and sat on the other side of the bed.

Daisy watched. 'I thought you were off home in a minute.'

He shrugged. 'I've nowhere to rush off to. I thought I'd hang around and listen to the music.'

Her heart lightened a little. She sensed the end was nearing, and dreaded being alone when the final moments came. 'I didn't have you down as a fan of big band?'

'Listen to anything, me. Except opera. Even I've got my limits.' He winked. 'Tell me more about your gran.'

As the pair chatted quietly, Audrey observed from her spot on the ceiling. It was such a peculiar feeling, being in the scene, but also apart from it. She wondered if it was a privilege of the departed, to be able to observe those left behind, or perhaps this was merely an interim thing before her final journey. After all, down on the bed, her chest rose and fell in rhythm, so she was still alive.

She watched as a rattle attached itself to her respiration: saw the panic in Daisy's eyes, the determined air of calm in Finn's response. A desire to comfort the child sent her down to her body briefly, but once there, she was too weak to even open her eyes and she soon drifted back up to her vantage point. From here on, Daisy's well-being was out of Audrey's hands, but she felt sure her granddaughter would be ok.

Daisy's stomach clenched as Audrey's breathing became impossibly shallow, so light it surely couldn't sustain a living body. 'She's going.' Her hand flew to her mouth. 'I think she's going.'

'She's comfortable and she's not in any pain.'

'I know.' Daisy choked a sob. 'The thing is, through everything, she's always been there. I don't know how I'm going to manage without her. How will I cope?'

Finn smiled. 'When people pass away, the memories are still there. Just because she's not physically here, her wisdom will stay with you, but you'll hear her voice in your head, instead of out loud.'

'What if I don't, what if I can't hear her?'

'You will.' Finn thought for a moment. 'Like now. What would she say to you about what's happening to you both today?'

'I don't know. I don't know what she'd say.' Anxiety had its grip on her.

'Give it time.'

Daisy closed her eyes tight, swallowing down her alarm, and a thought occurred to her. 'She knew I'd be like this. She knows that when I panic, I can't think, that's why she wrote me a letter.'

'She did?'

'Yes. She told me earlier. It's in the drawer, for after she's gone.' Daisy put a hand to her chest. 'It'll tell me how to cope, I know it will.'

'There you are, then.'

Daisy pulled open the drawer and found two envelopes, one with her mother's name on it and another for her. She held her letter in both hands, like a precious stone. 'She's still here, but should I open it?'

'That's up to you. If you think it might help you, open it now. If you'd rather wait, then wait. There's no right or wrong.'

She ripped it open, desperate for comfort.

The letter was short, hand-written in her grandmother's neat print, but even so, Daisy couldn't decipher the words through tear-filled eyes. She struggled over the first few lines then thrust it into Finn's hands. 'Will you read it to me?'

He took it and opened the paper out carefully.

'From there.' Daisy pointed to where she'd reached on the page.

'Ok.' He cleared his throat and began to read. '*Of course, you'll be sad. We couldn't have meant so much to each other and you not be, but it will pass, and it's alright for it to pass and for you to be happy. I want you to know I'm content although, of course, I would have loved to be with you longer. I have always had a belief that we're put on this earth with a job to do, and I'm certain I've done the job I was put here to do, so it's right and good for me to move on. I know you've been struggling with finding your path for the future recently, but I believe the same for you, that you're here for a purpose and, though you may not know what that is yet, that's ok. In time, you will recognise it, and you'll find your own peace. Trust yourself, have faith in yourself and be kind to yourself. Being your granny has been the biggest joy, and my heart has been filled with love for you from the moment you were born. Your loving grandmother, Audrey.*'

When Finn looked up, Daisy's face was frozen in shock.

'What is it? What's the matter?'

She took the letter from him and stared blankly at it before dropping it in her lap.

'You see? She wants you to be happy.'

'But how can I be, now?' She waved the sheet of paper. 'After this?'

Finn frowned. 'I don't understand?'

'She says we all have a job to do.'

'Yes, and when the time is right, you'll know what yours is.'

Daisy stood up and the letter fell to the floor. 'I know. I heard what you read.'

'Then what's the problem?'

She squeezed the tight muscles at the back of her neck, her mind flitting from one thought to another: her messy childhood; the muddle her life was in currently; the void which would now exist without her gran; a completely unmapped future, and it all seemed to align disturbingly.

'The thing is, something happened when I was younger, something huge. But I never told Gran about it: it had to be kept secret.' She paused and stared at him, heart pounding in her chest. 'I think I've already done the thing I was put here to do. I've already fulfilled my purpose. But, if that's true, it means the rest of my life is completely and utterly pointless.'

A Reason To Be

Audrey had smiled as Daisy opened the envelope ahead of time - the girl would never change. She felt sure the letter would bring comfort, and perhaps it was a good thing Daisy hadn't been able to wait, as it meant Audrey could now share in the moment. But Daisy's response was not at all what Audrey expected, and she watched in horror as her granddaughter's agitation grew, and it seemed there was nothing Finn could say that would make a difference.

Audrey tried to explain, shouting into the ether, but the scene continued below. Her frustration increased, until she could see no alternative but to go back and guide Daisy through her misunderstanding. Earlier, all she'd had to do was think herself back into her body and instantly she was there, but now, despite summoning all her strength to return to the bed, nothing happened. She closed her eyes and gritted her teeth, willing a movement, but still nothing. However, as she relaxed from the intense effort, she found herself sliding away, as if through a tunnel, the figures of Daisy and Finn becoming ever more distant.

Glancing over her shoulder, Audrey saw a light coming towards her. 'No,' she shouted, every fibre of her being rebelling against the inevitable. 'Not yet.' But no matter what she did, she continued to slide. 'Just five minutes more.' Clenching everything, she tried to heave herself in the opposite direction. There was a brief pause, but the strength to hold on to it ebbed away and she slid away once more. Stretching out a gnarled hand, she reached for the shrinking image of Daisy, but there was no stopping and her eyes closed in defeat. Any hope she'd had of resting in peace was torn to shreds.

CHAPTER 2

Audrey's eyes were closed and her mind fuzzy, but she couldn't shift the uneasy sensation of being somehow in the spotlight. The last thing she remembered was Dean Martin serenading her, crooning that she was nobody 'til somebody loved her, as she lay in the bed at the hospice. His smooth tones, and the knowledge she was indeed loved, had soothed her into sleep, but now there was no music, although there was a low hum of conversation going on somewhere just out of earshot. She tried to home in, but it was too indistinct and, eventually, curiosity drove her to look.

'What in the name of …?'

A few feet away, two women clung to each other, eyes wide with alarm, as they observed her. They wore matching uniforms, smart skirt suits with pretty, printed scarves knotted at their necks, but that was the only thing about them that matched. One was white, blonde, slim and middle-aged, while the other, younger, black and rather larger, gave off an air of being far more approachable. It was the older of the two who took the lead.

'Audrey? Can you hear me?' The woman queried in a slow Texan drawl. She released her colleague and straightened both herself and her outfit, before edging forward. 'Are you with us now?'

Audrey peered at the woman. In the few short days she'd spent in the hospice, she hadn't seen anyone like her. 'Where else would I be?'

'Indeed.' The woman tidied a lock of hair back into an otherwise neat bun, then clasped her hands in front of her. 'And have we finished making a hullaballoo, do you think?'

Audrey's eyes narrowed further, completely confused, all was quiet as far as she could judge. Something entered her peripheral vision and she turned to see a group of young men in ski gear, settling into a circle of seats around a small table not far away, and realised she was no longer in her hospice bed. 'What the heck...? What's going on here? Where am I?'

The blonde woman stepped back at the rise in Audrey's voice and held up her hands, palms facing in Audrey's direction. 'Now, let's try and maintain a dignified level of noise and behaviour, shall we? There's no need for any more physicality.' She straightened her jacket again. 'We've had quite enough of that for one day.'

Audrey took umbrage at the woman's implication. 'I don't like your tone, madam, whoever you are. How dare you come in here casting aspersions? I've never resorted to violence in my life, and I don't intend to start now.' She glared at the woman. 'No matter how driven to it I may be. Now, on your bike.'

'Well!' The woman shot upright in shock, but before she could reply, her colleague stepped in.

'Grace, why don't you go and get Audrey a glass of water while me and her have a little chat.' She turned to Audrey and smiled. 'Is that alright with you, darlin'?'

Audrey would normally have retorted that she was nobody's darling, but the young woman's air and cheeky cockney accent was disarming, after the other woman's haughtiness, and she gave a short nod in response.

Grace sniffed, stuck her nose in the air and stomped away.

Her colleague smiled and shrugged, leaning in confidentially. 'Don't mind her. Grace likes things done a certain way. She doesn't have much room for emotional stuff.' She dropped into a seat alongside Audrey and picked up her hand, stroking it gently. 'Now then, I'm Blessing, and I think you've probably got some questions for me. Am I right?'

Audrey's gaze travelled beyond Blessing's figure, taking in a scene full of strange individuals and groups, in all manner of attire, dotted around a cavernous room of chrome and cream leather furnishings, resembling a huge airport lounge. 'Blessing.'

'Yes, Audrey.'

She met and held the younger woman's gaze. 'I think my meds might need adjusting.'

'No, darlin'. You're not on any meds now. You've gone past that. You're in the next place now, my lovely.' Blessing patted Audrey's cheek. 'Do you understand what I'm saying?'

Audrey pursed and unpursed her lips as she considered the matter. 'Dead, am I?'

Blessing nodded and winked at her.

'Don't tell me this is heaven, for goodness' sake. I was hoping for something a little more exotic.' She took a sharp intake of breath as a thought struck her. 'Unless I'm about to fly off somewhere fancy. Is that it?'

'No, no, sweet. You've got the wrong end of the stick entirely. This isn't heaven. This is sort of in between.' She paused, giving Audrey time to absorb what she was being told. 'No, this is Limbo.'

Audrey grasped her cheek with one hand. 'Oh, my giddy aunt.'

Blessing retrieved the hand and stroked it again, soothing, reassuring. 'It's alright, my darlin'. Don't believe all the bad press.' Shifting in her seat, she looked around for Grace. 'Where is she with that water?' As there was no sign, she returned her attention to Audrey. 'This is only temporary, a pit stop, if you will. People come here when there's a bit of unfinished business, so we can sort it out, and they can move on to where they belong.'

'But I don't have any unfinished business.'

A Reason To Be

'That's not the impression you gave earlier, you were in a right two and eight. You put the right willies up Grace. She's not used to that sort of thing; I can tell you.'

'But, I haven't. I knew I was going to die, and I was ready, more than ready if truth's told. I can't remember anything "unfinished".'

'Hmm, well, give it some time. Sometimes things get muddled when you arrive here. Ready or not, the shift can be a bit of a shocker. Spiritual trauma makes you forget stuff.' Blessing shuffled in her seat. 'Ah, here comes Grace. Water can help, rehydrates the brain cells. It'll all come back to you as you adjust.'

Grace didn't appear any more welcoming than she had before but Audrey decided perhaps she couldn't blame her, under the circumstances. Grace handed the glass of water to Audrey, and she downed it in one, keen to get the bottom of why she was in Limbo. She looked at Blessing. 'I don't feel any different. I still can't remember.'

'Blimey, sweet. It's a glass of water, not a magic potion.'

'Do I take it we have memory issues?' Grace's face showed no glimmer of a smile.

'Can't remember a thing, bless her.'

Audrey, confused as she was, didn't like to be on bad terms with anyone. 'I do apologise if I embarrassed myself earlier, Grace. I normally wouldn't dream of making a scene. I hope we can put that behind us.'

Grace huffed, but the tension in her shoulders dropped away. 'Well, I guess we can, extreme circumstances and all.' She sat in the chair the other side of Audrey's own. 'While the water does its thing, think back and we'll see if we can't jog your memory. What's the last thing you can recall?'

Audrey chewed her lip as she thought. 'The hospice. Music playing – Dean Martin, my absolute favourite.' She winked at Blessing. 'A pleasant young male nurse, plumping my pillows. My granddaughter, teary eyed. Floating away and feeling peaceful. That's it, calm and peaceful. No unfinished business.' She shrugged.

Blessing turned to Grace. 'Could there be a mistake? A misdirection?'

Grace retrieved what looked like a mobile phone from her pocket and tapped at it, then swiped from one page to another with her finger.

'Anything?' Blessing tried to peer over the top of the screen.

'Nope, all present and correct. She's booked in for a review with the big man today.'

Audrey looked from one to the other waiting for an explanation. She didn't like the sound of being reviewed by anyone, let alone the "big man", whoever he was. 'The big man?' She gulped. 'Do you mean *the* big man?'

Grace caught the tone of Audrey's question and looked up, a glint to her eye as she doused a smile. 'Oh, Audrey. There is only one big man around here.' She looked over Audrey's shoulder. 'And here he is now.'

Audrey glanced around, a wave of anxiety washing through her, but no one stood out, although there were a lot of strange people, in odd outfits, who she wouldn't have considered ordinary in her previous everyday life. There was a small group of girls in dance costumes, pom-poms tied at their wrists, and a mishmash of young men in a variety of sports gear, a footballer, a rugby player, and someone in leathers, with a helmet under one arm, but nobody she considered fitted the bill for the "big man".

A middle-aged gent, in navy tailored trousers and a pin-striped shirt, sleeves rolled up to the elbow, sidled up beside them and stopped, pulling a clipboard from under his arm and a pencil from behind one ear. 'Is Audrey Macgill around here somewhere?'

Audrey stared at the stranger, trying to figure out his place in proceedings.

'This is Audrey Macgill.' Grace got to her feet and smiled a crooked smile at the older woman. 'Audrey, this is the Spiritual Ombudsman.'

CHAPTER 3

The ombudsman placed a lavish tick on the paper on his clipboard and faced Audrey with a grin. 'Well, hello there, Audrey. Very pleased to meet you.' He dipped his head in a miniature bow. 'How can I be of service?'

Audrey looked blankly at him. 'I have no idea.'

He looked from Grace to Blessing and back again.

As Grace gave a small shrug, his shoulders slumped, and he rolled his eyes. 'Really?' He huffed. 'We really need to do something about our system. This is going to completely throw off my schedule for the afternoon, you know?'

Blessing chipped in. 'She can't remember leaving anything unfinished, so she says. Can you, Aud?'

'Not a sausage.' Audrey confirmed.

His face dropped and he leaned against a pillar, pulled out a tablet computer from behind his clipboard and tapped at it with a stylus. 'Let me see if there are any clues here.'

The three women watched expectantly, but his frown only deepened as he clicked his tongue while he read.

'Anything?' Blessing was the least patient among them.

'Hmm, no.' He swiped the screen left, then right and back again. 'Actually, it's quite odd.'

'How so?' Grace seemed equally intrigued.

'Well, the last scene while she was alive, quiet as a lamb, nothing going on whatsoever. Then, the first scene here, she's more Tasmanian Devil.' He glanced at Audrey askance. 'I wouldn't have believed she had it in her.'

'I am here, you know?' Audrey scowled.

'Indeed. Sorry.' He tapped his pen against his teeth. 'It's almost as if there's a missing link.'

'Tasmanian Devil! Missing Link! Any other insults you want to throw at me?'

'I didn't mean you.' He tutted. 'I mean there's something missing between the two scenes, but I can't understand what. Generally, one moment a person is alive and the next, they're dead, like crossing an invisible line. There's something I'm not seeing.'

Blessing pulled a face at Audrey. 'Here, sweet, it looks like you're an anomaly. We don't get many of them around here.'

The ombudsman grunted, continuing to study the screen. 'No such thing. I just haven't managed to identify the glitch, that's all.'

Grace chipped in. 'Maybe, if you let Audrey see the footage, she could fill in the gaps. Something sure got her riled up down there.'

The ombudsman grimaced. 'I'm not sure about that. Protocol doesn't generally allow for individuals viewing their own demise. It could have unforeseen implications.'

'She's already technically dead and halfway to the afterlife. I can't imagine the implications could be any more serious, could they?' Blessing queried.

'Hmm. I don't suppose they could. What do you say, Audrey? Do you want to give it a go?'

Audrey shrugged. 'I suppose, if it'll get me out of this place.'

'Right you are then.' He pressed a number of buttons on the tablet then crouched in front of her, his back to her, so she could view the screen over his shoulder. 'How's that? Can you see alright?'

Audrey patted herself down. 'I don't have my specs.'

'Oh, no. You don't need specs here, sweet. Give it a try without.' Blessing patted Audrey's arm.

Peering intently, the fuzzy image gradually cleared, until Audrey could see it perfectly sharp. 'Oh, my! I haven't been able to see that well for years.' Her focus shifted. 'Ahh, that's my granddaughter, bless her.'

'And there you are.' The ombudsman said, looking back at her. 'About to breathe your last, and.... That's it, you're gone. And now, it switches to the view from here, and there you are kicking and screaming and punching poor Grace in the midriff.'

Audrey was horrified. 'Oh, my! Grace, I am sorry.'

Grace sniffed. 'All water under the bridge.'

'I have to admit I'm baffled,' the ombudsman said. 'Totally flummoxed.'

They sat in quiet contemplation for a few moments.

'Might I ask something?' There was something not right about the scenes of the end of her life, though Audrey wasn't sure what it was.

'Ask away,' the ombudsman offered.

'Can you turn up the volume? Can I listen to what Daisy and young Finn are talking about?'

'If you think it might help.' He increased the volume.

Once again, the scene showed Audrey lying still in the hospice bed, while Daisy and Finn chatted. Daisy was relaying a funny story of when Audrey had been short-changed by the butcher and stood at the till, warning all his other customers to triple check their change, until he agreed he'd made a mistake and coughed up.

'Young whippersnapper.' Audrey chuckled. 'He won't try that trick again.' She paused. 'But that's not right.'

'I'm sure it was probably a genuine mistake on his part.'

'Not the butcher,' Audrey snapped. 'The conversation my Daisy was having with Finn. That was way before I turned up here. I remember listening to her telling that story, and then there was another one about me and my friend winning the bingo, then another about when she visited me when she was little, before she moved in with me. I didn't snuff it until way after this.'

'Hmm.' The ombudsman grunted. 'That's not what it says here, but... Wait a minute, this timeline's all over the place.' He tapped and swiped the screen, reading and rereading the data he was seeing. 'Hmm.'

'It's an anomaly, ain't it?' Blessing reached around Audrey to prod Grace. 'I told you it was an anomaly.'

'On this occasion,' the ombudsman interrupted. 'You seem to be correct. I can't make head nor tail of... What's this?' The swiping and tapping began again, then he dropped his arm down. 'You went wandering, didn't you?'

Audrey looked from one face to another and back again. 'I don't know what you're on about.'

He got to his feet and paced three steps away and back. 'What is wrong with people these days? In the old days, they were quite happy to follow the usual flow of things and stay put until their time came and then go where they were supposed to go. Now? Oh, no. They're off wandering all over the place, creating all manner of havoc.'

'I haven't done anything, honest.' Audrey held her hands up in denial.

'Oh, yes, you did. It's all recorded, you know. You can't do these things and think no one's going to notice.'

Audrey leaned over and whispered to Blessing. 'I don't know what he's on about. Do you?'

Blessing grimaced. 'Beats me, Aud.'

The ombudsman halted, took a deep breath, and looked Audrey straight in the eye. 'You, good lady, had an out of body experience, and don't bother trying to deny it. You toddled off to the top of the room to watch yourself as if it were nothing more than a jolly little outing, as if there were no rules to these things. No wonder my job is so complicated these days.' He huffed and put his hands on his hips, staring away from the group.

'Did you do it, sweet?' Blessing whispered to Audrey.

A Reason To Be

'Me? No!' Audrey didn't think so, but as the idea percolated, certain images cleared in her mind. 'At least, not that I recall… Hang on.' It was beginning to come back. 'Do you know, I think I might have.' She clicked her tongue. 'I'm sorry, I had no idea it was against the rules. In fact, I don't even know how it happened. One minute I was on the bed and the next on the ceiling. I didn't plan it or anything.'

'Ignorance is no defence.' The ombudsman sniffed.

'Well, in this case I think it should be. I couldn't help it and I certainly didn't do it intentionally.'

Blessing interceded. 'Never mind, Aud. I'm sure he understands.' She turned to the ombudsman. 'Don't you? You understand Audrey meant no harm?'

'I suppose, but just for once it would be nice if we could stick to a timetable, that's all.' He huffed. 'Oh, well, there's nothing for it. We'll have to get to the bottom of this mess somehow.'

'Sorry.' Audrey didn't like being the cause of so much fuss. 'And how exactly do we do that?'

'Only one thing for it.' He shrugged. 'We're going to have to examine the out of body footage.'

CHAPTER 4

Grace rose to her feet in one fluid movement and cleared her throat. 'Well, that's my cue to leave. Blessing, I would imagine you have work to do, too?'

'What, and miss a good gander at an out of body experience? Work'll still be there in half an hour.' She nodded at the Ombudsman. 'Come on. Let's have a shufty.'

Grace shook her head and strutted away.

'What's her problem?' Blessing asked, wide-eyed.

The ombudsman shrugged. 'Grace is old school. Doesn't agree with the whole "out of body" thing.' He waggled two fingers on each hand as he said, "out of body". 'I'm not fully au fait myself, but, you know, modern times.' He settled into the seat Grace had vacated and began to read his tablet.

'You're all acting as if this is something I chose to do but, I'm telling you, I had no say in the matter,' Audrey insisted.

'Yes, well, what's done is done.' He pursed his lips as he read. 'It all seems straightforward, actually. The data is on the same channel, but at a slightly different wavelength. Here we are, look at this.'

They crowded around the small screen, but all that appeared was a blur of colour.

'Blimey, surely that can't be right?' Blessing screwed up her eyes as she studied the image.

'No, it is.' He moved the tablet further away and then brought it towards him again. 'You have to let your eyes go slightly out of focus and then try to look through the screen rather than at the surface.'

'Ooh! Like one of them magic eye picture thingamebobs. Let me try.' Blessing leaned in over the screen and stared intently. 'Oh! I've got it. Is it a unicorn on a rainbow?'

The ombudsman raised his eyebrows. 'No, Blessing. We're reviewing Audrey's missing segment, not some childhood fantasy playground.'

'Oh, yeah.' Cowed, she squeezed back into her chair, allowing Audrey to get a good view .

'I can't make head nor tail of this.'

'Here, let me help.' The ombudsman held up a finger a few centimetres behind the screen. 'Now, focus on my finger.'

Audrey followed his instructions.

'Good. Now, keep looking at it. Keep looking at it...' He gradually dropped his finger behind the screen. 'That's it, pretend you're still looking at my finger, but now you're looking at the footage.'

The picture suddenly became clear and crisp. Audrey recoiled in her seat in surprise, but soon settled forward again, taking in the distinct image of her granddaughter and Finn. 'That's them. I can see them.'

'Good, good. Progress.' He settled back, holding the tablet steady in one hand, while operating it with the other. 'We don't need to watch the whole thing; the last few minutes should be ample. I'll skip to the good bit.'

Audrey would very much have liked to see the entire recording, to spend more precious time watching her beloved granddaughter, but felt she probably shouldn't push her luck. She had caused enough trouble already.

'Hmm. Well, this is two minutes to go, and everything seems to be in order, all calm and collected. Whatever it was, it must happen soon. Let's see.' He pressed play, and the figures began to move.

Audrey inhaled sharply. 'Oh, yes. I'd completely forgotten. The little madam opened my letter ahead of time, and I'd told her to wait until after I was gone, the rascal.'

The ombudsman looked askance at her. 'Annoying, isn't it, when people don't stick to schedule?'

She ignored the jibe. 'I shouldn't have been surprised. She got her patience from her mother.'

They continued to watch.

'Oh, bless. I hate to see her upset. I'm so glad Finn was there for her. Look, he's reading it out.' Audrey knew the letter by heart, and her mouth formed the words almost before Finn could say them aloud. She sighed, 'I wanted to give her some comfort after I'd gone.'

'What a lovely idea, Aud.' Blessing had given up trying to watch the screen but was listening intently. 'I bet it cheered her up no end.'

A bubbling began in the pit of Audrey's stomach as a niggling feeling grew, that the letter hadn't cheered her granddaughter, but instead had had the opposite effect. 'No. It didn't.' She gripped the ombudsman's arm as panic took over. 'It didn't help. It didn't help at all.'

As they watched, Finn stopped reading and Daisy's negative reaction became clear.

'I was trying to tell her she'd find her way in the world, that she shouldn't try and force herself to fit some imaginary mould, because I know she worries about that. I know she's got this idea everybody else knows exactly what they want to do for the rest of their lives, and how they're going to do it, but she doesn't yet. I was trying to tell her to slow down and let life happen; there's no rush. But… but…she's missed the point. She's got it all wrong.'

'She's certainly taken a very individual view of things, but not to worry, when she revisits the letter later, with a clearer head, no doubt she'll realise she's got the wrong end of the stick.' The ombudsman stopped the footage and flicked a cover over the screen, then tucked the tablet under his arm.

'No, she won't. I recognise that look in her eye and once she's made her mind up, there's no changing it. For some reason, she now thinks the rest of her life's a waste of time, and it's all my fault.'

'Now, now, don't fret. There's very little we can do about it after the fact. We just have to rely on Daisy's common-sense prevailing, given time.' He patted her hand. 'Anyway, it's nothing for you to worry about. As recently departed, you can put all that behind you and go and enjoy the benefits of the afterlife. Blessing, can you make the arrangements for Audrey to move on, please?'

'Course.' Blessing pushed herself out of the seat.

'Hang on. You can't be serious.' Audrey gripped the arms of the chair, as if she feared they would tear her away immediately.

Audrey's raised voice had drawn the attention of onlookers in the cavernous hall, and a general hush had fallen around them. The ombudsman leaned in to reply. 'Now then, Audrey. My records show you've done an admirable job keeping that young granddaughter of yours safe and well for years, but now it's time to let go. You need to let Daisy make her own decisions and, may I say, her own mistakes. There's absolutely nothing you can do about this situation.'

'There must be. There must be something. There's no way I can go and rest in peace knowing I've somehow set my lovely girl on the wrong path.' Her voice grew louder, and more interested faces turned towards them. 'No way on this earth... or this planet... or, or whatever this place is.'

The ombudsman coughed and held out his hands, palms down, trying to calm her. 'Audrey, Audrey, Audrey. Let's not air our dirty laundry.' He paused while she pulled herself together. 'My good lady, you must understand, there is no going back, which means there is nothing whatsoever you can do to change things. You may as well accept the fact and move on. I have every faith that Daisy's situation will come good. This is just a blip.'

'A blip?' Audrey so wanted him to be right.

'Yes, a blip. Nothing more.' He relaxed a little, possibly sensing he was wearing Audrey down. 'I'm sure in a few short days this will all blow over and Daisy will move on and look forward with a new sense of purpose.'

'I'm not so sure.'

'Trust me.' He smiled. 'I'll keep an eye on Daisy's movements for a short time, to be sure, but I have every confidence she'll be right as rain.'

'You really think so?'

'Absolutely.'

Audrey sighed. 'Well, in that case, I might as well hang around here and keep an eye on Daisy's movements too. I certainly won't be able to rest until I know she's alright.'

'But... Hang on...'

'That won't be a problem, will it? I mean, if you're watching her, surely I can too?' Audrey was not to be moved.

The ombudsman recognised the same air of determination she'd had when the butcher short-changed her. 'It's quite irregular.'

'I've never been one to follow the pack, and it's a bit late to start now.' She smiled at him. 'So, how do we do this? Do you have to get that computer contraption out again?'

He peered at her but had no argument. 'No, the computer is for the past or the future. The present is a completely different matter.'

She raised her eyebrows in question, but waited for him to continue.

'For the present, we look through a window on the world.' He shrugged. 'You'd better follow me.'

CHAPTER 5

Without thinking, Audrey got to her feet to follow the ombudsman, then immediately grasped at his arm for support. It had been a while since she'd been able to bear her own weight and suddenly finding herself independently upright scared her.

'Steady on there, Aud. There's no fire.' Blessing rushed to her aid.

'I can walk!' She let go and tested her own strength, tentatively stepping from one foot to another, arms out in case she should suddenly find herself off balance.

'Course you can, darlin.' Blessing watched as Audrey became more daring with her movements, progressing from baby steps to a lively jig. 'Good here, ain't it?' She chuckled.

'It most definitely is.' Audrey, breathless at the unusual exercise, placed a hand to her chest and inhaled deeply. 'Ooh. I've come over all unnecessary.'

The ombudsman interrupted. 'If you ladies are quite finished, perhaps we could get on with the task in hand.' He held out an arm. 'Audrey, come along with me. Blessing, can you let Grace know we're going to viewing room three.'

'Oh, can't I come too?'

'I think Audrey and I will be able to manage, thank you. I'll call you if we need you.' His tone was firm.

Blessing headed off across the centre of the room, chin on her ample chest.

Audrey accepted the ombudsman's assistance, and they strolled around the perimeter, bypassing the seating areas and most of the other occupants. Only a few stragglers stood close to large picture windows, overlooking an outside area she'd previously given no attention to.

'You get a reasonably good view of the world from here,' he said, pausing for a moment and pointing downwards. 'But it's very general and non-specific. Good for passing the time, like a large-scale soap opera, but in your case, obviously there's a particular person we're interested in, so we have to use a viewing room, but it's not far.'

She let go of his arm and pressed her hands against the glass, captivated by the view. The world appeared far away but, as she focussed on one spot for more than a second, it was as if the ground came up to meet her and, all at once, she could see people talking, laughing, and going about their business, as if she was right next to them. 'It's amazing.' She blinked, breaking the connection, and moved her gaze to another area. 'Truly amazing. Where is that place?'

'Well, we cover all four corners of the globe, of course, but I think that particular area is…' He tapped his chin. 'Oh, yes, that's Norwich. My personal favourite is fourth window from the end on the mid-section.' He pointed over his shoulder, then recaptured her arm, urging her onward. 'Fantastic views of the Serengeti. If you time it just right, the sunset is… what can I say? Magnificent.'

They approached a set of swing doors and he moved ahead slightly to hold them open for her. She followed in silence, the weirdness of what she was witnessing, leaving her unable to do anything but follow his lead.

'Almost there.' They continued along a carpeted corridor until they reached a door marked with a chrome number three and, again, he opened it for her.

A Reason To Be

The room was small, but the far side wall was completely made from glass and, immediately in front of it, was a long breakfast bar and a couple of low-backed stools.

'Here you are, Audrey. Take a seat and I'll set things in motion. Can I interest you in a cup of tea?'

'Does the Pope wear a funny hat?' She paused in her attempts to climb onto the stool, which was far too tall for her, and sighed. 'Everything's better with a good cuppa.'

He smiled, filled a couple of cardboard cups from an instant machine in the corner of the room and slid it in front of her on the breakfast bar, where she'd finally settled onto her perch.

She took a sip and grimaced. 'I did say a good cuppa, mind. Anyway, what happens now?'

Sitting next to her, he lifted a panel set into the top and fiddled with dials hidden there. 'All I need to do is enter the right grid reference, then we can check in on your granddaughter and see what she's up to. I suspect she's seen sense by now, and all this will be a wasted exercise.'

Audrey harrumphed. 'If it sets my mind at rest, I would say it's anything but a waste. Eternity is a long time to be worried about something, you know.'

'I suppose I can't argue with that.' The ombudsman gave a brief nod. 'Anyway, it's all done. She'll appear any minute now.'

'Where should I be looking?' asked Audrey, squinting at the glass, waiting for something to happen.

'Give it a minute.'

The picture cleared, and they found themselves only a few feet away from Daisy and Finn who were walking along a deserted pavement in the Spring drizzle. The youngsters were both subdued, their heads bowed.

'Oh, my!' Audrey reached a hand towards her granddaughter, but was stopped short as skin touched cold glass. 'It's like they're in the room with us.'

'Yes, the quality of the images is very good. It's down to the high resolution and non-reflective coating on the display interface.'

Audrey looked blankly at him.

He tipped his head to one side. 'The quantity of pixels per square millimetre? No? Never mind. Yes, it's like they're in the room with us, but I can assure you, they're not. They're on a completely different plane. This is merely an observation platform. There is no way for communication to occur between us and them. You do understand that?'

'Got it.' Audrey was just pleased to see her special girl again. 'What are they saying? All I can hear are the seagulls.'

'They're not saying anything at the moment. Try and be patient and listen carefully.'

*

Daisy kicked at the floor as she walked, stubbing her toe on the rough ground, but it was good, as it overrode other negative feelings coursing through her. She heaved a bag containing her grandmother's belongings up onto her shoulder.

'Here, give that to me.' Finn unhooked it from her and pulled it up onto his own.

She felt bereft without the weight of it and was reminded of what it contained and why she was carrying it. She shook her head, trying to dissipate the moisture in her eyes before Finn noticed. She'd done enough crying for one night, and now they'd left the hospice, she didn't want to do any more for a while. Her emotional well was dry, and her tear ducts needed a break.

He noticed anyway. 'You need to go home and get some sleep. You must be tired.'

'I suppose. I don't feel anything much, except that my whole life is completely and utterly pointless.'

'That's not true.' Finn tried to reassure her. It wasn't the first time the topic had come up since the reading of the letter and he was struggling to know how to make her see things differently. 'I really don't think that's what Audrey was trying to say to you.'

'I know what she was trying to say, but she didn't know the facts. If she did, she would have realised my best bit is already over. If I've already done the thing I was put on this earth to do, what's the point in me now?' She threw her arms up in a flamboyant shrug.

'You're just feeling lost because of your Gran passing on.' Finn shook his head. 'You've got years and years yet and you're bound to do loads more important stuff.'

'Years and years of emptiness. Years and years of pointlessness.' Daisy stopped and ran her fingers through her long brown hair, dragging it back from her wan face, making her look fragile and vulnerable.

Finn studied her for a moment then nudged her with his elbow. 'No. Even, if the idea about each person having one job to do was correct, what could you possibly have done that would outshine everything you might do in the future?'

She turned to face him. 'It's a secret. I promised I'd never tell anyone, and I never have, and I never will, but it was big.' Her brow furrowed as she thought about it. 'Very, very big.'

Finn took her arm, urging her onward. 'Well, in that case, I'm going to have to take your word for it for now, but I'm pretty sure, once you've had a sleep, you'll see things differently. Come on, let's get you home.'

She obeyed, moving forward a few steps then stopped. 'But I don't want to go home. Gran isn't there.' Her voice was a whisper.

'I know you don't, but you've got to sometime, and the longer you leave it the harder it gets.' He slipped his arm around her. 'Trust me, I know.' He continued along the path, Daisy being propelled by him. 'I promised Audrey I'd make sure you were alright, so I'll see you home, safe and sound. Come on.'

Daisy allowed herself to be led away. 'She did love me, didn't she?'

'Of course she did. You know that.'

She smiled a sentimental smile. 'Yes. I do.'

He followed her onto a bus, which had pulled in ahead of them at the bus stop. Urging her into a seat near the front, he stood alongside, providing a barrier between her and the rest of the passengers. An elderly woman, sitting the other side of her, eyed them warily.

'She looked after me for ten years, you know?' Daisy gazed up at him, eyes glistening with tears. 'Gave me everything I could possibly need.'

'I know she did.' He rummaged in his pocket for a tissue and handed it to her. 'And you paid her back by looking after her at the end. You're bound to feel a bit lost now she's gone, but there's still more for you to do. Once you're rested, you need to sort out the funeral. Give her the send-off she would have wanted.'

Rather than wipe her face, Daisy pulled at the tissue between her fingers. 'I'd forgotten about that. There'll be so much to organise.'

'There will.' He paused. 'But I can help, if you like?'

'Would you? I don't even know where to start.'

'We'll sort it together.' Finn smiled. 'There, you see, that's a role only you can do, so you've already found another reason for you to be on earth.'

'I suppose.' Daisy gave a small nod. 'But once the funeral's over, then what?'

Finn's tone was adamant. 'Well, then we'll see what's next, but there will be something. I'm one hundred per cent certain of it.'

'Hmm.' She leaned back in her seat and closed her eyes.

*

Audrey frowned, thinking about the interaction she'd observed between Daisy and Finn, leading up to her granddaughter, now alone, falling into bed. 'What was she talking about? Doing something big that's a secret? What does she mean?'

The ombudsman shrugged. 'I couldn't tell you, I'm afraid.'

A Reason To Be

'You mean it is a secret?'

'No, I simply don't know. And before you ask, no, I can't look it up. It's Daisy's business, and I can't access her past files without a jolly good reason. And you being interested isn't classified as a jolly good reason.' He nodded at the screen. 'If you keep watching, no doubt all will become clear in due course.'

Audrey smiled at the sleeping figure of her granddaughter, her dark hair spread across the pillow. 'I don't mind. I could watch her like this for hours.'

'I daresay you could,' he muttered. 'But some of us don't have the luxury of eternal rest stretching before us. I'm going to move things along and fast forward.'

'How can you do that if we're watching the present as it happens?'

The ombudsman sighed. 'If you don't understand the science of high-resolution images, I'm certainly not going to waste my time explaining temporal shifts. We'd be here forever. Just take it from me, I can move things along. Come on, pay attention. Let's see what Daisy's up to after her nap, and hopefully it'll bring all this silly nonsense to a close.'

CHAPTER 6

Daisy was examining her pallor in the mirror when Finn knocked on the door. She thought about not answering, expecting a well-meaning neighbour, and not feeling up to facing them. But then he shouted through the letterbox, and she rushed to let him in before Morag from next door got involved.

'I was beginning to worry.' Finn was weighed down by a bulky carrier bag on either side, and swung them ahead of him towards the kitchen, without waiting for an invitation. He shivered as he passed her. 'It's chilly out there this afternoon, but at least it's stopped raining.'

'Come in, why don't you?' Daisy knew he was being nice, but part of her just wanted to wallow in the misery she was feeling and begrudged his help. She watched him march right past her. The fridge door was open, and he was packing things away by the time she followed him through.

'Have you eaten?' Glancing over his shoulder, he took in her pale, drawn features. 'I thought not.'

'I'm not really hungry.' She shrugged.

'You may not be hungry, but you've still got to eat.' His eyes slipped to her crumpled clothing, the same outfit she'd been wearing last night at the hospice. 'Go have a shower and I'll knock something up.'

A Reason To Be

She stared at him, as if his words made no sense.

Finn took her by the shoulders, turned her round and carefully walked her to the bottom of the stairs. 'Go on. Shower. You've got twenty minutes.'

It seemed easier to do as she was told than muster an argument.

Against all expectation, Daisy's body reacted to the stimulation of the heat, the scent of citrus shower gel and the power of the jets on her skin and, although a heavy sadness still lay across her shoulders, her head felt clearer. A salty whiff of bacon floated up the stairs and, despite the complete absence of an appetite, her stomach growled.

Finn was setting two places at the table. He pointed at a chair. 'Sit down. I'll be right with you.'

She shuffled into the seat and leaned back to watch him buzzing around the kitchen, juggling plates and pans, a tea towel thrown over one shoulder. He returned, hands full, and placed a plate of steaming food in front of her, before edging around to the seat facing her.

Daisy eyed the food, undecided whether to be impressed or disgusted by the fried egg, slightly charred sausages and bacon, and toast.

Finn was already wielding his knife and fork but paused briefly to urge Daisy on. 'Come on. Get it down you. We've got things to do and you'll need the energy.'

She attacked a sausage with a fork. 'I don't want to do anything this afternoon.'

'I know, but there's a lot involved with arranging a funeral and it's probably best to kick things off as soon as possible. You won't be able to properly relax with all of that hanging over your head.'

The reality of the situation hit her anew. Daisy dropped the fork and placed her head in her hands. 'Oh, Finn. I can't face it. I just can't. It's too much.'

Finn reached across the table to pat her arm. 'It is a lot, but you can. Remember, only you know what Audrey wanted for her send off, and you want to do her proud. We'll do it together. We can make a list and tick them off, one task at a time. Before you know it, we'll have it sorted.' He withdrew his hand. 'But first, come on, eat.'

She could tell he wasn't going to back down, so she huffed and retrieved her cutlery.

As she put the first forkful into her mouth, he gave a small smile. 'Well done. Now, I want to see that plate completely empty.'

'Yes, sir,' she muttered, but her jaw followed orders and chewed obligingly. She guessed this was what it would be like to have a brother.

*

The ombudsman downed the dregs of his coffee, before twisting in his seat and launching the paper cup into a bin on the other side of the room. 'I must say, Audrey, you certainly chose a good candidate as guardian for your granddaughter. Finn is taking his responsibilities very seriously. If anyone can get Daisy back on the straight and narrow, it will be that young man.'

'I know my granddaughter,' Audrey replied, shaking her head. 'And it's not a job for the fainthearted, keeping her in line, I can tell you. I did the job full-time for years.'

'The voice of experience, eh?' He grimaced. 'How did that come about, Daisy living with you?'

She shrugged. 'Lizzy, her mother, my daughter, didn't have time for her. Too busy with the career to take care of her own child.' Audrey said the word "career" like it was a swearword. 'Gallivanting all over the shop. It started with me having Daisy to stay in the holidays, then weekends, then while Lizzy attended conferences here, there and everywhere. Then came short-term contracts in the US, except these so-called short-term contracts got longer and longer, until she was pretty much living in America. Now, of course, she does live there, literally, and has done for a decade.'

'And Daisy's father?'

'Fly-by-night. Didn't hang around for the birth, let alone anything that came after. Don't know what Lizzy saw in him, but then, me and Lizzy were always on completely different wavelengths.'

The ombudsman tipped his head. 'It's a good thing Daisy had you then, Audrey, if I may say so.'

'I suppose. The arrangement suited both of us. I gave her a roof over her head and food in her belly, and she was company for an old lady in her twilight years. I was glad to have her.' Deep lines formed on her brow. 'It rankles with me now though, that I've left her to her own devices. I wish I could have stuck around 'til she was properly settled.'

'It wasn't to be, Audrey, and besides, you've given her a solid grounding. With the right encouragement, I'm sure she'll come good in the end.'

'You may be right.' Audrey sighed in contemplation. 'But I'll be happier when I see it with my own eyes.'

CHAPTER 7

Before they'd finished eating, the doorbell began a rendition of Greensleeves, and the door handle rattled. Daisy dropped her fork and made a grab for Finn's hand to stop him in his tracks. 'Shh,' she hissed.

'What?' He stopped talking, and eating, and stared at the panic on Daisy's face.

'Quiet.' She glanced over her shoulder towards the window, as the bell began a second chorus, then dived behind the sofa. 'Quick. Get down here.'

'What?'

She took a moment from peering past the cushions at the window, to turn to him. 'Don't just sit there, move.'

'I don't…'

There was a sharp tap at the glass and a high-pitched call. 'Yoohoo! It's only Morag.' She did an exaggerated point in the direction of the entrance. 'The door's not on the latch.'

'Oh, hell. She's seen you now. Why didn't you move?'

'Sorry,' he muttered to Daisy, as he waved at the elderly woman gazing through the curtains. 'Who is she? Do you owe her money or something?'

Daisy sighed and rested her head against the back of the seat. 'It's Morag from next door.'

A Reason To Be

He waited for further explanation.

'Now I'm going to have to tell her about Gran.'

'Well, she's going to have to be told, isn't she?'

'I know, but I didn't want to have to do it today.' Daisy wiped her forehead with a desperate hand. 'I thought I'd leave it for a day or two, until I feel ready.'

'Yoohoo!' The call came again. The woman clearly wasn't going away.

'It's only putting off the inevitable, you know.'

'I know, but her and Gran were like besties. They were constantly drinking tea together, and crocheting doilies, and gossiping about the WI. She'll be all weepy, and sympathetic, and... huggy. I can't be dealing with that today.'

He stood up and ran the fingers of one hand through his short-cropped blond hair. 'Do you want me to get rid of her?'

Daisy's eyes widened in momentary hope. 'Would you?'

'If that's what you want.'

'Oh, yes. Yes, please.'

He waved again at the woman and walked towards the door.

'Only, don't tell her, or you'll never get rid of her.'

He stopped in his tracks. 'How can I...?'

The doorbell rang again, and Daisy urged him on. 'Quick, before she remembers the spare key.'

'Oh. Ok. I'm going.'

Finn opened the door, but the woman seemed undeterred by the appearance of a stranger and barged straight into the lounge.

Daisy had adjusted the cushion, so she could see but not be seen from the hallway, but at this turn of events, threw herself flat on the floor.

'Hello, young man. I'm Morag, from Tamarisk, next door to the left. Has she been sent home?' The woman craned her neck to look around. 'Is she in bed, bless her?'

'Sorry?' Her strong Scottish burh meant he had to concentrate to understand her as he shuffled round, preventing her from going further into the house.

Morag planted her feet and glared at him. 'Audrey. I mean, I take it you're the carer.' She leaned around him, as if considering darting past to the upper floors. 'They said she wasn't long for this world, but she's made of sterner stuff than any of them give her credit for. I said to her last week, before they took her in, I said, "Audrey, my dear, I'll be seeing you back in your own front room before you know it". And I was right, wasn't I? Well? Can I see her?'

Taken aback by the barrage of words, Finn was no match for the woman's forthrightness. 'No. No, you can't.'

'Asleep, is she? Shall I pop back in half an hour? I've a batch of cherry scones, fresh-baked this morning. She's always loved my cherry scones. That'll perk her up no end.'

It was impossible for Finn to follow Daisy's instruction not to tell the woman when put on the spot like this. 'No, you can't.' His shoulders sagged as he accepted defeat. 'I'm sorry, but she passed away. Last night.'

Morag's hand flew to her mouth as she gasped, clearly unprepared for the truth.

'I am sorry to tell you like that. It must be a shock, even though she was so poorly.'

'A shock, aye.' She gripped his arm for support. 'Of course, I knew it was bad, but Audrey was such a stalwart. I thought she'd see it off. I never thought…'

'No, I'm afraid not.'

A fresh thought seemed to come to the woman, and she straightened up abruptly. 'What about the wee one? Daisy, how is she? Is she here? She'll need support, poor lamb. Her and Audrey were like peas in a pod.'

For a moment it appeared she'd make another break for the stairs in search, but Finn intervened. 'She's ok. Upset, as you can imagine, but…'

'I should go to her.'

'No, it's alright. She's...' He floundered around for a reason to stall her. 'I think she might be in the bath now. I'll let her know you called though.'

'I owe it to dear Audrey to keep an eye on the lass.'

'That's very kind, but it's alright. Audrey asked me to spend some time with Daisy, help her through these first few days. I've got it in hand. Don't worry.' He gently ushered her towards the exit.

'Well, if there's anything I can do, don't hesitate.'

'Thank you. That's very good of you. I'll let Daisy know.'

She stepped outside. 'And, if you want me to spread the word, at the WI and Knit and Natter and down at the shop. They've all been asking after her, you know.'

Finn blocked the gap. 'That's very kind of you, but I'm sure Daisy will let everyone know in due course.'

A whispered response came from behind the sofa. 'Let her tell them.'

Finn cleared his throat loudly to cover the sound, before saying, 'Actually, Morag, I think that would be a great idea. It'll give Daisy one less thing to worry about, what with sorting the funeral and everything else.'

She patted his cheek, smiling. 'You leave that to me then, lad. Let Daisy know, she can rely on me.'

'I will. Thanks, Morag.'

He closed the door and leaned against it, sighing with relief.

Daisy stood up from her hiding place, hands on hips, scowling. 'So, Gran set you up as my minder, did she? She really didn't think I could cope on my own?'

His eyes widened at her words. 'Well, no, it wasn't like that.'

'You see? Even Gran thought I was a waste of space.' She shook her head and marched past him and up the stairs.

Like a rabbit caught in the headlights, Finn watched her go.

Audrey held her face in her hands, mouth open as she watched the scene. 'That wasn't my intention, at all. I just didn't want her to be alone.' She let her hands fall away and shook her head. 'You know, we lived together for years and barely had a cross word. You'd have thought we'd understand each other better, first with my letter and now with this, but she's taking everything the wrong way.'

'That's the problem with the written word, it's difficult to get across tone.' The ombudsman sighed. 'Perhaps you should have ended the letter with "LOL". That seems to be the modern answer to the conundrum.'

'What?' Audrey stared at him.

'You know, LOL, laugh out loud? Facebook? Texts? Simply finish every statement with the initials, LOL, and the world is reassured you're in a positive frame of mind.'

'You're talking complete nonsense.'

'Hmm, you're probably right. It's as likely to be poorly disguised passive aggression as good humour. There's no replacement for the good old-fashioned heart to heart. I'm with you there, Audrey.'

She snapped to attention at his words. 'Well, I didn't know that was an option. Come on then, pop me back and I can clear this up in a jiffy.'

The ombudsman pursed his lips. 'Good try, but it's not going to happen.' His head tipped to one side. 'Think about it, Audrey. How exactly would that work?'

'What do you mean?'

'Well, for a start, your remains are currently residing at the Peaceful Pastures Home of Rest. If you suddenly popped back into your body, I suspect it would make quite the scene. It might be more than just your granddaughter in need of therapy, that's for sure.'

Audrey huffed. 'I suppose you're right.'

'I generally am,' he reassured her. 'Listen, Daisy will get there in the end. She simply needs time and patience, and Finn seems to have plenty of the latter, even if you don't.'

'I don't have a lot of choice really, do I?'

A Reason To Be

'There is the other option, of course. Eternal rest?'
She narrowed her eyes. 'Come on. You're wasting time.'

CHAPTER 8

Daisy knew she was being unreasonable, but everything felt like such a big deal. She didn't really resent Finn being set up to keep an eye on her: she'd wondered why he was still hanging around, when his duty surely ended at the hospice, but his mentioning it made her uncomfortable. It made her feel like he might disappear the minute he felt he'd done his duty, and that he wasn't there because he wanted to be. In fact, what with her going off in a strop and all, he may well have made a run for it already, and who could blame him. In normal circumstances she wouldn't have behaved like such a diva, but these weren't normal circumstances, and she couldn't seem to help herself.

'Daisy?' There was a tap at the door. 'Daisy, are you alright?'

She buried her face in the pillow and felt something like relief wash through her. He was still there.

'I didn't mean to upset you. Can I... Can I get you anything?' There was a pause, but she didn't reply. 'Audrey didn't think you were a waste of space, you know? She was just concerned about you being on your own, what with your mum being away. If you... if you'd rather I went, I'll go. I don't want to be in the way.'

Daisy groaned into the soggy cotton of the pillowcase. She didn't want him to go, even if he was only there out of duty. Maybe in a few days, after everything had settled down, she'd feel able to cope without him, but right now she needed him around, something solid to hang on to. 'No, don't go,' she called, before reburying her face.

'Ok, I'll stay then.' There was a rustle outside the door, and she could picture him settling down on the carpet, leaning against the frame. 'Talking about your mum, have you let her know? About Audrey, I mean?'

She rolled over and sat up on the bed, wrapping her arms around her knees. Her voice was thick with emotion. 'No. Not yet. I don't know how to do it.'

'I know. It's horrible having to break bad news, especially over the phone.'

She sniffed. 'It's not that: Mum will deal with it ok, it's just… in my head I know Gran's gone, I've come to terms with it. But when I try to say it out loud, it makes it more real. Is that silly?'

'Nothing's silly about grief. It hits people in different ways, and each person gets through it in their own way.' There was a pause. 'I can ring her if you like.'

'Would you?' Daisy felt as if a weight she hadn't realised was there had been lifted from her shoulders.

'As long as you're sure you don't want to speak to her yourself.' He left a gap for her to change her mind, but she didn't. 'You'll need to give me her number.'

She got up and wandered across to the door, leaning her head against it as she spoke. 'It's on the pad by the phone, under Lizzy.'

'Ok.'

She heard him moving in the hallway. 'Finn?'

'Yes?' His voice was further away.

'If I come down in a few minutes, when you've finished the call, maybe we could look at Gran's instructions for the funeral?'

'That sounds like a plan. I'll put the kettle on.'

'Ok.'

His footsteps padded across the landing and halfway down the stairs. Daisy opened the door a crack. 'Finn?'

He stopped. 'Yes?'

'Thanks... for everything.'

'That's ok.'

Daisy closed the door and leaned back against it. She was actually going to have to do this, the planning, the funeral, sorting out Gran's things, all of it, and she couldn't think how she could possibly do it without help. Audrey was right, she didn't have the strength, but Finn did. Daisy wiped a tear from her cheek, looked up at nowhere in particular on the ceiling and whispered, 'Thanks, Gran.'

*

The ombudsman pulled out a large linen handkerchief from his pocket and handed it to Audrey. 'There you are. I told you we'd soon see progress. If I'm not sorely mistaken, Daisy is coming around to your way of thinking already. A little longer and she'll be back to her old self, still missing you, I'm sure, but not so doubtful of her own purpose in life.'

Audrey dabbed at her eyes. 'Maybe, maybe not.'

'I was expecting a more positive response than that. Only a few minutes ago we had "Gran thought I was a waste of space", and now we've got a touching show of gratitude. Surely the signs are encouraging?'

She raised one eyebrow. 'You don't have much experience of young women, do you?'

'More than you might expect.' He turned back to the scene which continued to play out in front of them. 'You're not convinced then?'

'Stubborn as a mule is my Daisy.' Audrey shrugged. 'Just like her mother.'

'Speaking of which, let's see how Finn's getting on with that call.'

'Knowing Lizzy, she won't even pick up his message until after the funeral.'

The ombudsman studied the scene, lips pursed. 'You may know Daisy, but perhaps you're not quite as well acquainted with your daughter as you think.'

CHAPTER 9

When Daisy heard Finn's conversation end, she made her way downstairs. It hadn't seemed right to eavesdrop on a conversation she ought to have been having, but communication between her and her mother was all but non-existent and now, more than ever before, she couldn't pretend a relationship which wasn't really there.

Finn's smile didn't reach his eyes. 'I've told her. I said I'll let her know the funeral arrangements.'

'She's not likely to find time in her busy schedule to fly across the Atlantic for a funeral. There's bound to be a vital convention or something. There usually is.' Her tone was sulky.

'Perhaps you should give her the benefit of the doubt. It is quite a big deal, after all, your own mum's funeral.'

'Did she say she would come?'

'Not exactly…'

'I rest my case.' Somehow being angry was a welcome relief from the constant sadness. 'What did she say?'

'Not much, actually, she was too busy crying. I said I'd call again when she's had time to take it in. It came as quite a shock. She didn't even know Audrey was ill.'

Despite her anger, Daisy felt guilty for not keeping her mother informed. It made her tone clipped. 'Perhaps if she kept in touch more often, she would have. Besides, it's not like she could have done anything.'

'Hey, I'm not judging. I'm just telling you how it went.' Finn's brow was furrowed, but he forced an unconvincing smile. 'Anyway, what about I make that cup of tea, and you find some paper and and a pen so we can make a list of what needs to be done.' Without waiting for a reply, he disappeared into the kitchen.

When he returned, Daisy was seated at the table, a huge file in front of her. 'We won't need a list,' she said. 'Gran's got it covered.' She opened the folder and removed piles of paper. 'The type of casket she wants; the flowers; the contact details of a nice vicar she met at last year's fete. Her preferred venue; the hymns she wants; the readings. Oh, and a poem she found in Readers' Digest, though I think we might be hard pushed to get Alan Titchmarsh to read it, which was also on her wish list. But apparently Mr Winterbourne from the corner shop is a close second.'

Finn's eyes widened at the wealth of information. 'Audrey did all that?'

'It was all I could do to talk her out of making a mood board – they had a WI session on them apparently, but hardly appropriate for a funeral.'

'She was one of a kind your gran, wasn't she?' He bit his lips to stop a laugh escaping.

Daisy spotted his struggle for composure and couldn't help but join in with a chuckle. 'Wait until you see the dress code.'

'Really?' He frowned as he tried to imagine what that could possible entail. 'Shall we get started?'

'I guess so. Are you finding Alan Titchmarsh's number, or am I?'

The ombudsman stared at Audrey, straight-faced. 'Alan Titchmarsh? Really?'

'Why not?' She declared. 'The mature woman's totty, he is.'

'If you say so.' He tipped his head at the screen. 'I'm wondering if we should move it on a tad, see what's afoot once Finn has helped Daisy over this understandably sticky patch. I think we'll only see the real Daisy re-emerge after the funeral. I suspect then we can put this whole business behind us and get back on schedule. What do you say?'

'Hmm.'

'Well? Yes? No? You obviously have something on your mind.'

She glanced sideways at him. 'I don't suppose…'

He waited, but she couldn't find the words. 'Whatever it is, I'm sure I've heard it before. Spit it out.'

'I'm quite happy to move on, there's nothing I want more than to see Daisy back to her old self, but, well… I don't suppose I could drop in on the funeral, could I? I'd love to see what people have to say about me. I've always wondered if old Mrs Scunthorpe was as nice behind my back as she was to my face. I doubt it, if truth's told.'

'Audrey, really? I can't see how it could possibly be helpful.'

'Have you ever actually died yourself, by any chance?'

'Well, no, I haven't.'

'Then take it from me, when you do, if the opportunity presents itself, you'll be champing at the bit. Go on. Wind it on.'

CHAPTER 10

Almost every seat in the crematorium was occupied, and there wasn't a peek of black to be seen. Daisy surveyed the room and smiled. This was exactly what her grandmother wanted - garish colours and funny hats – and the message had obviously been received, loud and clear. Morag had spread the word, no doubt. She'd proved herself extremely useful in recent days and was now installed on one side of Daisy in the front pew, with Finn on the other. Both seemed determined to stick to her like glue.

The music changed from Edith Piaf's Non, Je Ne Regrette Rien to the Bridal March, and Daisy's stomach clenched. It meant the coffin was about to be carried in, and she had no idea how she was going to get through the next half an hour. Morag's hand gripped Daisy's elbow even tighter.

Daisy sensed a ripple in the congregation and glanced back. She inhaled sharply when she saw her mother, incongruous in full make-up and one of her sexy work black trouser suits, shuffling past the bearers, who had paused to allow her through. Lizzy looked panicked as she tried to find a space to sit, aware of the attention she was drawing. Daisy tutted. Trust her mother to make this about her, arriving late, not adhering to the dress code and hovering in the aisle, to ensure everyone witnessed her smudged mascara and reddened eyes. Finn waved Lizzy forward and moved to let her in between himself and Daisy, but Daisy had other ideas. She grabbed his arm, so Lizzy had to perch on the other side of him, next to the aisle, instead.

The bearers placed the coffin on the platform at the front and the vicar turned to face the congregation, pausing until the bearers had settled into seats at the rear. He wore a fetching turquoise clerical shirt and, on his head, sat a tartan tam o'shanter, complete with a ginger wig. He cast his eyes around the room, smiling warmly.

'I thought I might have to explain this get up.' He waved his hand from his hat down to his lime green trainers, 'but clearly everyone got Audrey's memo. And you know, I did think about the solemnity of the occasion, after all, funerals are sad and serious affairs, and I wouldn't want to appear disrespectful. Should I really go all out with the wardrobe? Or perhaps just a nod to the theme would do? A stripy scarf perhaps, or leopard skin socks.' He tipped his head momentarily. 'For the record, I do own a pair.'

The congregation tittered.

'But then I thought, "no". This is what Audrey wanted - bright colours and patterns in all their clashing glory, and so that is what she should have. Today is not about us or convention: it's all about Audrey and a celebration of the amazing and individual woman she was.' He paused as everyone nodded at his statement. 'And as for the funny hat...' He paused again. 'Certain other clergymen get to wear one, so why shouldn't I?'

Another ripple of laughter spread around the room.

'Now, then, where's Mr Winterborne? I believe he's going to read a poem. Come on up, Mr W.'

A rotund, middle-aged man ambled to the front, eye-catching in tartan trousers and Hawaiian shirt, Toucans peering through jungle foliage with beady eyes. He positioned a page of notes on the lectern, tapping the side of the microphone before speaking.

'Woodland Burial by the wonderful Pam Ayres.' He cleared his throat. 'Don't lay me in some gloomy churchyard shaded by a wall, Where the dust of ancient bones has spread a dryness over all...'

Sharon Francis

The poem was read, followed by a eulogy, made up of anecdotes from people who'd been close to Audrey at various times in her life, broken up by carefully selected songs. A childhood friend told of pranks they'd got up to in the classroom, followed by a rendition of "Enjoy Yourself, It's Later Than You Think". A colleague from Audrey's working years remembered rushing through their workload to get away early for the Friday night dance, followed by an Elvis hit. Mrs Scunthorpe spoke in warm terms of memorable WI functions thanks to Audrey's interventions. Her tone sharpened with disapproval as she introduced a tune specially chosen for the WI and Knit and Natter ladies and "Ding, Dong, The Witch Is Dead" filled the room.

Finally, the vicar returned to his spot, gave a prayer of thanks rather than sadness, and pulled the curtains in front of the coffin. "Fly Me To The Moon" could not distract from the knowledge that Audrey was making her last momentous journey and, inevitably, tears fell but, as the singing faded, the vicar raised his voice above the music.

'Thank you for coming everyone. Audrey's family have asked me to remind you you're all welcome to a continuing celebration of her life at the function room at The Drunken Old Goat Inn. I'm sure you could all do with a cup of tea.'

Morag wiped her eyes. 'Does the Pope wear a funny hat?' she shouted.

All those who truly knew Audrey chuckled as they filtered outside.

Daisy's row remained seated, until the room was empty and quiet, except for Lizzy's sniffing.

'Do you have to do that?' Daisy tutted.

'Sorry...' Lizzy dabbed at her face.

Daisy looked anywhere except at her mother. 'This is exactly what she didn't want. Look at you. She didn't want weeping and wailing and mourning clothes. She wanted a celebration of her life.'

'I didn't know...'

'Perhaps if you visited more often, or listened once in a while, you would have.'

'I didn't even know she was ill. It's all such a shock.'

'And I refer you to my previous comment...'

Morag intervened, getting to her feet. 'Well, there's one thing I'd bet my boots on and that's Audrey wouldn't want her two best wee lassies at each other's throats at her dispatching. Come on, now. There are glasses on the bar waiting to be raised to Audrey's memory, and I suggest we go and do her proud.' She prodded Finn to urge him to action. 'Come on, young man. You escort Lizzy. I've got a firm hand on Daisy here. We'll be steady as a rock together.'

*

The ombudsman frowned at Audrey as the footage continued. 'The Bridal March? At a funeral?'

Audrey stuck out her chin. 'I was never lucky enough to find Mr Right, so this was my one and only chance to make the grand entrance. I couldn't turn that down.'

'I see.' He briefly raised his eyebrows.

Audrey sighed. 'Now, did you see Cyril Winterborne? If only I'd met him a few years earlier. Then I might have been able to put The Bridal March to better purpose. Voice like honey.' She shivered.

'If you say so. It was worth watching then?'

'Absolutely. And I owe Ida Scunthorpe an apology. She did shed a tear or two, come the end, though she's no sense of humour. I thought she was going to go apoplectic when she introduced that song.' Audrey giggled, holding her sides as she rocked on her stool.

'Well, 'the ombudsman intervened. 'It was rather unconventional.'

'Ha! Who wants to be conventional? There's enough sheep in this world without another one. My mother always said I was one to stand out in a crowd, and I wouldn't want to disappoint the old bat.' A thought occurred to her. 'I don't suppose she's here, is she? She passed a good few years ago now, but it would have been just like her to cause trouble and outstay her welcome.'

'Runs in the family, does it?' He rolled his eyes before checking his tablet. 'No, no sign of another generation of MacGills here. Perhaps you'll come across her further along on your journey.'

'Maybe.' Audrey tutted. 'But not if I see her first. Anyway, let's see how my Daisy's faring. Bless her. She's been holding up well under the pressure, and there's been no more of that "what's the point" nonsense. A great deal thanks to old Morag. She's a good friend.'

'A friend indeed.'

'Not too good to have a kiss and cuddle with Mr W at my wake though, I'll wager. The little minx.'

The ombudsman grimaced. 'I don't know if I want to watch anymore.'

'Don't then. I'll do the watching. You make another cup of tea.'

CHAPTER 11

A blackboard announcing *Private Function - Audrey Macgill - Wake* stood outside the pub, directing them away from the front entrance to a side door. A single gull circled above them, calling intermittently. The stark reality of the words hit Daisy anew, and a choking sound erupted from her throat as she suppressed a sob.

'Come on, now. The worst is over.' Morag slipped her arm around Daisy's shoulder and squeezed her tight. She and Daisy had separated from Finn and Lizzy, and hurried ahead of the other mourners, in order to welcome them when they arrived. 'And let me just say before we're inundated, you've done your grandma proud. Now…' They pushed through the door into the function room, past trestle tables laid with cups and saucers and sandwiches. Morag strode to the closed bar and leaned over, winking at the woman polishing glasses behind it. 'This looks bonnie, young lady.' She was at least fifty, if she was a day. 'But something a little stronger for the lassie. A wee something to bolster the nerves, if you don't mind. We'll settle the tab later.'

The barmaid took in Daisy's demeanour and her face softened. Putting down the cloth, she poured a couple of shots and tapped them on the bar top. 'Here. I'd say the pair of you could do with a quick snifter, all things considered. On the house.'

Daisy stared at the glasses, then at Morag.

'Would be rude not to, eh?' Morag nudged Daisy with an elbow. 'Come on, now. Down in one, before the tea and sympathy brigade arrive. It'll be our secret.'

Daisy did as she was told, swallowing deep, and coughing as a result. The empty glasses were swiftly removed from sight and the two women turned to face whatever lay before them, as the door opened and the first of the well-wishers arrived.

The majority of the mourners stayed for a cup of tea, a slice of cake and an exchange of stories about Audrey. Old photographs of her, stuck up around the room, had fuelled the memories, both recent and old, and Daisy laughed to hear some of her grandmother's antics. Gradually, the numbers dwindled, leaving a core of those who'd been closest to the old lady and, as if by magic, as soon as the vicar left, Morag leaned over the bar and retrieved a bottle of something much stronger than Earl Grey and a tray of glasses.

'Now then, folks. Let's do this properly.' Morag filled the glasses and handed them around to those remaining.

Daisy was bemused. She'd attended few funerals in her lifetime and had certainly never witnessed anything like this. Among the dozen or so in the room, Daisy spotted her mother with Mr Winterborne, his arm around her shoulders. Lizzy was still wearing the black trouser suit, but no longer stood out in the crowd, in an ill-fitting rainbow coloured cardigan, buttoned all the way up to stop it falling off. Something about the comforting nature of Mr Winterborne's stance irritated Daisy and she found a familiar anger, which she'd thrown off since leaving the crematorium. She felt a tap on her shoulder and, turning, a glass of whisky was thrust into hand.

'Has everyone got one?' Morag was on her toes, trying to see everyone in the room. Satisfied, she lifted her own glass into the air. 'To Audrey. The best friend a person could ever have.'

A ripple of 'To Audrey' travelled around the room, before settling.

Mr Winterborne stepped forward. 'To Audrey. A magnificent specimen of a woman, if ever there was one.'

A Reason To Be

Again, the toast was taken up by the group. The barmaid appeared from somewhere and passed from person to person, topping up glasses.

A grey-haired old lady, dressed in cerise culottes and a blouse covered in peculiarly bright depictions of tropical fruit, was next. Daisy recognised her from the Knit and Natter crowd, a quiet soul whose attention always seemed to be on her crochet, while the others fulfilled the natter requirement. The woman's voice was slow, as she enunciated each word with care. 'Nobody, and I mean nobody, could tell a dirty joke like our Aud.' Her head twisted slightly as she winked at the group. 'To Audrey.' Then she threw the contents down her throat as if it was something she did on a regular basis.

Daisy felt a giggle rise up inside her as she swallowed in time with everyone else. The grandmother who'd always seemed offended if Daisy so much as hinted at anything slightly rude, telling dirty jokes? It seemed impossible, and yet so had many of the stories she'd heard over the day.

A short man in blue jeans with a crease firmly ironed into them, an apricot shirt and a bottle green jacket, coughed to draw everyone's attention. 'She broke my heart years ago, and I'd have let her break it again, given half a chance, but she was always too good for the likes of me. She was...' He shook his head as if he couldn't find the words. 'She was a Goddess, was Audrey. A vision...'

A voice shouted from the back. 'Give over, Norman.'

The man stopped mid-speech, holding the backs of the fingers of one hand against his lips, as if he wanted to say more and was physically restraining himself. He let them drop and nodded sagely. 'To Audrey.'

Someone nudged Daisy forward and everyone looked at her, and she gathered it was her turn. A lump formed in her throat, and she felt someone sidle up close to her, holding her elbow. Glancing around, she realised it was Finn. He smiled at her and she swallowed the lump down. She could do this.

'To Gran. I don't know where I'd be now if it wasn't for her. She was my hero.' Daisy's voice cracked.

'She'll always be your hero, lassie.' Morag finished the toast for her. 'To Audrey.'

The bottle kept going round, the toasts kept coming, though they gradually became more and more garbled, and the faces on the mourners became more and more blurred to Daisy. When Lizzy stepped forward, Daisy had to narrow her eyes and stare to make out her mother on the other side of what had become a ragged circle.

Lizzy took an age to find something to say, anticipation growing as the silence stretched, that this was going to be something momentous and profound. Finally, she raised her glass, shrugged, and smiled a half smile. 'To Audrey. Who was always good in a crisis.'

The toast satisfied most of those in the room, but it riled Daisy. How dare she? How dare that woman refer to Audrey as Audrey and not as Mum? How dare she say something as devoid of feeling as "being good in a crisis"? What was that even supposed to mean? Daisy tried to slam her glass onto the bar rather than drink to such an inappropriate toast, but missed, and would have slipped down it to the floor had Finn not grabbed her.

'Oh, hey. Come on. Let's get you some air.' He pulled her upright, took the drink from her and led her outside to the beer garden.

The sharp early evening air was a slap in Daisy's face, but she'd imbibed too much to suddenly sober up. She shook her head to try and regain focus, and had to grab the edge of a wooden table to retain balance and sat down hard.

Finn sat on the same bench, one hand on either of Daisy's upper arms, waiting for her to achieve some level of stability before letting go.

'Did you hear that?' She stared at him, waiting for a reaction, but when none came continued. 'I mean where in the hell does that woman get off? Good in a crisis? What sort of a to...toast is that?'

A Reason To Be

Throwing her arms out in a dramatic shrug destabilised her and she almost slipped under the table.

Finn grabbed her again, but she shrugged him off. 'I don't know,' he said. 'I mean, I imagine it was true. Audrey was a capable lady. I bet she was good in a crisis.'

Daisy poked him hard in one shoulder. 'Well, duh! Of course she was, but like, is that all she could say? About her own mother? That's the sort of thing you say about... I don't know, about a teacher, or, or, or...' She flung her head around as she searched for inspiration. 'Or a politician, or anybody really. Except somebody who's not good in a crisis, somebody who's a complete moron in a crisis. But not your own mother. It's just, just, just...' She sighed deeply. 'Just so disappointing.'

'Perhaps she didn't know what to say? It was a spur of the moment thing, maybe.'

Before Finn could make further excuses on Lizzy's behalf, the door swung open, and the offender herself strode into the beer garden. 'Is everything ok? Daisy? Are you alright?'

'Am I alright?' Daisy frowned as if confused by the question.

'I saw you going outside, and I was worried.'

'Ha!' Daisy forced a laugh. 'Yes, I'm ok, though I guess I'm just not great in a crisis.'

Lizzy glanced from Daisy to Finn and back. 'You didn't like my toast?'

Daisy sighed. 'No. Your toast was rubbish.' She leaned forward to put emphasis on the last word, and Finn stretched out an arm to stop her rolling off the bench. She pushed him away. 'Gran was so much. She was so, so special. Was that the best you could do?'

'I'm sorry...'

'Oh, you're always sorry.' Daisy waved the excuse away.

Lizzy stood before Daisy, rubbing her hands together anxiously. 'You know how things were. I...I didn't have the sort of relationship with her that you did. I wish I did, but I didn't and I...I didn't know what to say.'

Daisy turned her head away and stared out over the beer garden, lips pursed as she considered Lizzy's words. Then she turned back and made as steady eye contact as she could manage. 'That's alright. I understand. I wouldn't have known what to say if it was you being buried either.'

Lizzy inhaled sharply. Daisy turned her face away again.

'I think it's time for me to go.'

Daisy's lip curled, but she still didn't look at her mother. 'Yeah, crawl back to wherever it was you crawled out from.'

Lizzy looked at Finn. 'You'll make sure she gets home safe?'

He nodded. 'Of course.'

Lizzy made to leave, then turned back, unbuttoned her cardigan, and tossed it to Finn. 'Can you see that gets back to whoever was kind enough to let me borrow it? Morag will know who it was.'

He nodded again, and Lizzy walked away.

It was quiet for many seconds before Daisy spoke. 'Has she gone?'

'She's gone.'

'Huh! I knew she wouldn't stick around. I guess we should have been grateful she fitted us into her schedule at all. It makes a change.'

Finn sighed. 'Well, you did tell her to go.'

'Don't stick up for her.'

He held his hands up, palms facing her. 'Hey. It's not up to me to defend her or otherwise. I barely know the woman.'

Daisy harrumphed. 'No, me neither.'

The pair fell into an awkward silence, broken eventually by a small group as they bundled out of the pub. They held each other up as they manoeuvred through the doorway, pausing only to wave at Daisy and Finn before staggering down the path.

'Finn, what am I supposed to do now?'

He thought for a moment. 'If people are starting to leave, perhaps you should go in and say your farewells.'

A Reason To Be

'I don't mean "now" now, you idiot. I mean now that Gran's gone. She's been my whole life for months and now there's nothing left. The best part of my life is over.' She leaned forward until her face was supported by her hands, elbows on the table. 'No offence. You're not really a ... nidiot.'

'None taken.'

Turning to look at him, she shrugged, arms wide. 'I have no goals, no ambitions, no direction. What is the point of me, Finn?'

'Oh, Daisy. Don't say that...'

'But it's true. I told you. I know you can't understand because you don't know what I did, but you've got to trust me, it was the best thing I could possibly ever do. I've reached by peak. It's all downhill from here.'

'I can't believe that no matter what you say. This all stems because you feel lost without your Gran, that's all. You've got your whole life in front of you...'

'Nah...' She tried to turn her back on him, but he prevented her with a hand on her shoulder.

'Listen to me. I am going to prove to you that you're wrong.' Daisy made to interrupt, but he continued his speech carefully and precisely. 'I am going to prove that you've still got so much to offer the world, and so much to look forward to. Me and you are going to get together and come up with a plan.'

She studied his face. 'Are we?'

'Yes, we are.' He shuffled backwards to untangle his long legs from the bench and stood up. 'But first, we've got to get you home so you can sleep this off.' Passing around the back of her, he kept one hand on her shoulder so she wouldn't tip sideways. 'Because right now, you couldn't come up with a plan to boil an egg.'

As Finn attempted to support Daisy to her feet, Mr Winterborne strolled out of the pub and stepped forward to offer assistance. With one either side, they half walked, half carried her down the path.

Daisy looked from one to the other. 'Actually.' she said. 'I don't really want a boiled egg, thank you.'

*

'Have you seen enough?' The ombudsman asked, as they watched Daisy manhandled into the back of a taxi.

Audrey held her face in her hands. 'Lord, this doesn't get any better, does it?'

'I thought you wanted to see your send off. They all had warm words to say about you: rather complimentary, in my opinion.'

She batted away his comment with her hands, before letting them drop into her lap. 'Oh, them. Get enough of the good stuff in 'em, they'll say nice things about anyone, especially that Norman. He'd have you believe his heart's been broken by half the women this side of the Atlantic. Drama queen.' She shook the thought from her head. 'No, I'm more concerned about Daisy. That didn't look like progress to me. She looks just as hopeless as the day I passed.'

'It is a particularly difficult event for her to deal with. Now the funeral's over, I'm sure she'll come on in leaps and bounds. It's a period of adjustment for her, and you heard Finn, he's going to help her find her feet once she's sobered up.'

'I suppose.' Audrey watched her granddaughter. Daisy's face was pressed against the window as she snored in the back seat of the car. Finn was resting his forehead on the opposite window, staring out into the dusk. 'I hope that boy doesn't let me down. I had a good feeling about him when I was in the hospice but, if truth's told, I don't really know him at all.'

'He seems a good enough sort.' The ombudsman observed Audrey's downcast face and smiled. 'Another cup of tea?'

Audrey's features rearranged themselves into an appreciative smile. 'Does ...'

'The Pope wear a funny hat?' He rolled his eyes. 'I don't know what your obsession with the Pope's headgear is all about, I really don't.'

'Actually, I was going to say, does a bear poo in the woods? Mr Clever-clogs. Did no one ever tell you it was rude to interrupt?'

A Reason To Be

'My apologies. I would hate to be rude.' He sighed, muttering under his breath. 'Whereas, discussing bears' toilet habits is the height of good manners, apparently.'

CHAPTER 12

Daisy's days had felt empty since the funeral. Despite all the admin she'd had to work through and phone calls she'd had to make, there was a void, and it wasn't just her gran. She'd seen nothing of Finn since the wake and, although their acquaintance had been short, she missed his presence. Not that she should have been surprised by his absence. After all, he'd only been hanging around because he'd promised Audrey he would and Daisy guessed he now felt he'd done his duty. On top of which, there'd been that palaver at the pub. She couldn't remember everything that happened, thanks to the generous toasting to Audrey's memory, but she was pretty sure she'd made a scene, and probably embarrassed Finn in the process.

When the doorbell sounded, Daisy groaned – Morag had whipped up Audrey's old crowd into a frenzy of support, and they kept turning up with Dundee cakes and elderflower cordial (and sausage rolls for some reason). It was nice, but it meant she had to make an effort, muster a smile and put the kettle on for yet more tea. Was she even fit to be seen? She looked down at her outfit. Yes, she'd pulled on jogging bottoms and a sweatshirt this morning, although for some unknown reason she also still had her pyjamas on underneath.

There was a tap at the window, and she glanced up, expecting to see Morag, but instead she saw Finn's nose pressed against the glass. As their eyes met, he allowed his own to cross and he stuck out his tongue at a jaunty angle. Despite herself, she laughed. He straightened up and tipped his head at the door. 'Come on, let me in.'

She walked across to release the latch.

'Your reflexes must be failing. I thought you'd have dived behind the sofa a full five seconds ago. You'll have to move quicker than that if you want to escape Morag's attentions.'

Daisy shrugged. 'If I don't let her in, she comes back every half an hour until I do, so what's the point? I suppose you want a cup of tea.'

'Ooh, yes please.' He chuckled. 'Good old Morag. She's something special, she really is.'

Daisy muttered under her breath as she stomped around the kitchen. 'You're not wrong.'

By the time she returned to the lounge and plonked his cup onto the coffee table, he was pulling a notepad and pen out of the pocket of his jacket. She collected her own cup and half a packet of Jammy Dodgers and sat opposite him, sliding the packet across the coffee table, eyeing him suspiciously. 'What are you doing?'

He'd helped himself to a biscuit, and put it in his mouth whole. After a couple of chews, he pushed the remains into his cheek to reply, waving the notepad at her. 'Coming up with a plan.'

'What sort of plan?'

He rolled his eyes and quickly chomped, wincing as he swallowed what was left. 'A plan to bring meaning back to the rest of your life, of course.'

She was a little annoyed at his presumption. 'I don't mean to be rude, but I haven't heard from you for three days and now, here you are, wanting to organise my life?'

He pursed his lips and breathed deeply. 'You don't remember, do you?'

'Remember what?'

'The last conversation we had after the wake?' He paused to allow her to think, but with no sign of recognition, he continued. 'I quote,

"Finn, what is the point of me? I have no purpose," and I said not to worry, I'd help you find your purpose, but first I had three long shifts at the hospice, and I would be here today at eleven. And here I am, as agreed.'

'Aaah.'

'You had forgotten.'

'Maybe.' She huffed. 'But what exactly do you think you can do anyway? The fact remains that I hit my high point years ago and now I'm just treading water. I don't see how you're going to change that.'

His voice was calm. 'And I told you, I can't believe that one single event could be so momentous it makes the rest of your days pointless. This lack of purpose comes from losing your gran and suddenly having a huge void in your life.'

'I'm like one of those child film stars, whose career is over when they stop being cute.' A look of horror crossed her face. 'Oh no! I'm that kid from Home Alone.'

He sighed. 'And I'm guessing you're still not going to tell me what this momentous event was?'

She shook her head. 'I promised I wouldn't'

'Ok.' Finn was not to be deterred. 'But I'm not buying it. Inventors don't invent one great invention and then give up. Doctors don't treat one patient and then stop because they've done their bit. You could still be doing loads of worthwhile stuff. You just can't see that right now, because of everything that's been going on, so I am going to help you, one way or another.'

Daisy accepted his point and, over the days since her gran's passing had recognised how she'd overreacted to the letter in the heightened emotions of the night, but it occurred to her that if she said so, Finn might give up on her and go away and, annoying though he may be, like the big brother she never had, she supposed, it was better than being alone. 'If you want to waste your time, who am I to stop you?'

A Reason To Be

'All I ask is you give my ideas a try. It might mean doing something new, outside of your comfort zone, maybe. Will you give it a go?'

'Within reason... I suppose.'

'Good.' He straightened up, balanced the notepad on the arm of the chair and positioned his pen ready to write. 'Then let's start. Tell me about yourself.'

She sipped her tea. 'What do you mean?'

'Well, I hardly know you, apart from what Audrey told me and she had other things on her mind those last few days than giving me your CV. All I know is you're an only child, brought up by your grandmother and you've got a dodgy relationship with your mother. That doesn't give me much to go on. Do you have a job? What are your hobbies? Tell me about Daisy.'

Her mind went blank. She didn't know where to start. Somehow, recently, she seemed to have lost herself. 'Umm, well, I'm twenty-one and I'm a student, or at least I was a student. I dropped out.'

'Dropped out? Weren't you enjoying the course?'

She shrugged. 'Yes and no. It was alright, but it wasn't what I thought it was going to be. Anyway, Gran was ill and she needed me. I didn't have time for all the course work and caring for her, and now it's too late.'

'What, and they wouldn't make allowances, under the circumstances?'

'I didn't ask. I just stopped going in.' Daisy shook her head. 'I couldn't face it anyway. Seeing Gran going through all that was... it was too much, you know?'

'I know.' He nodded. 'So, what were you studying?'

There was a long pause. 'Art appreciation.' She rolled her eyes. 'I know, not really useful to anyone. There, I said it before you had the chance to.'

'I'm saying nothing.'

'You don't need to. I've heard it all before.' She shuffled in her seat. 'Basically, I wanted to study art, but it turns out I'm not very good, so I switched course part way through. It's not what I had in mind, but hey, you've got to follow your skill set.'

'And you're good at appreciating art, I take it.'

'Are you taking the mickey?'

'Wouldn't dream of it.' Finn held his hands up, palms towards her, but there was a poorly disguised grin on his face. 'What does art appreciation consist of? Do you walk around galleries saying "Ooh, I love that painting"?'

'Philistine.' Daisy scowled. 'We're not all born carers, you know.'

'Hey, my career isn't exactly what I had in mind either, but sometimes life throws you a curveball.' He made a note on the pad. 'What about hobbies?'

She shrugged again. 'Not really. I still draw and paint now and then, but once my tutor told me I wasn't going to get anywhere with it, I pretty much gave up.'

He frowned. 'Nice tutor. Will you show me?'

'What?'

'Show me some of your pictures. Please? I'd like to see them. No need to be shy, I can't draw for toffee.'

Daisy took the stairs two at a time as she went to retrieve her sketch pads from her room. She couldn't actually remember when she last put charcoal to paper, but as she opened the books and flicked through the pages, a sense of pride trickled back. For all her tutor's negativity, Daisy was pleased with what she'd created. She tucked one under her arm, carried it back down to the lounge and handed it to Finn.

He opened it up to the first page, then flicked to the next, and the next, then looked at her. 'These are good. What the heck was your tutor talking about?'

Heat rose to her cheeks. 'The thing is, at degree level, everyone has an ability. Apparently, I just don't have anything "special".'

'That's complete and utter crap,' he said. 'Anyone who can create something like this has something special.'

A Reason To Be

Her blush deepened. She wasn't used to compliments, except from Audrey, who'd always been quick to sing her granddaughter's praises.

'I've got an idea.'

Daisy raised her eyes to his face sharply. 'You have?'

'Yes, I have. What are you doing tomorrow evening?'

She paused for a beat. She had no idea what Finn had in mind for her, but his compliments had filled her with a warm, fuzzy feeling and she wanted more of it, which meant going along with his ideas. 'I don't know. What am I doing tomorrow evening?'

'The right answer.' He smiled. 'You're coming to a youth club I help out at. I bet a lot of the kids would love to do some art, so let's test the water with them tomorrow and see if we can set something up on a regular basis.'

'What? Me? Teaching?' The concept horrified her.

'They come to the club for fun, not lessons. Think of it more as sharing your passion. It'll be fantastic.'

'I'm not sure.'

'Well, I am, and I'll be right there with you. Honestly, it's the perfect place to start.'

Daisy doubted it very much, but there was only one way to find out.

*

'Didn't I tell you Finn was a good egg? He's clearly taken your request to help Daisy to heart.' The ombudsman's smile was a trifle smug.

Audrey nodded, but her forehead wore a frown. 'So far, he's done alright but ...'

'But what? You don't think the art lessons are a good idea?'

'Oh, the youth club thing is a lovely idea and someone with my Daisy's talent should have no problem inspiring a few scallywags, but...'

'Audrey, do spit it out. I have all manner of gadgetry at my disposal but so far reading minds is still beyond my capabilities. What are all the buts about?'

She sighed. 'Well, it's men, isn't it.'

'Is it?'

'Of course it is. In all my life I never came across one that didn't let a girl down. I never knew my father. Lizzy's dad did a runner and who knows what happened to Daisy's.'

'I'm afraid you have had some rather bad experiences, but I assure you there are men in the world who can be trusted.'

'You would say that, being a man, wouldn't you?'

He tipped his head to one side briefly, in acknowledgement of her point. 'I speak from experience, not in defence of my own species. I could give you a whole list of good men if you'd like me to.'

'I'm sure you could, but it wouldn't serve to prove young Finn's character, would it?' Audrey pursed her lips as she studied the scene on the screen. 'There's something...' She shook her head. 'I could be wrong, but...

'We're back to the guesswork again, Audrey. Give me a clue.'

'I know my granddaughter and there's a certain glint in her eye. If I didn't know better, I'd say she's developing a soft spot for the lad. I just hope I haven't done the wrong thing encouraging him to stick around. The last thing I need on my conscience is setting Daisy up for a broken heart. Then I'd never be able to rest in peace...'

'Whoa, whoa, whoa. I can see where this is heading and there have to be limits. It's one thing to review a few weeks of a loved one's life to clear up a misunderstanding, but that's where it must end. If you think you're going to follow Daisy's life story into old age, you've got another think coming. Do you understand me?'

Audrey's eyebrows rose. 'Alright, stroppy chops. I was only saying.'

'As was I.'

'Well then. We'd better see how this youth club thing plays out, hadn't we?' She focused on the screen, but shot a quick glance sideways at him before continuing. 'And hope that all my questions are answered sooner rather than later, for both our sakes.'

The ombudsman glared at her, but her gaze stayed firmly on the moving image.

CHAPTER 13

Finn shook the heavy bags he was carrying in each hand. 'What is all this stuff?'

'I know you said the kids are all young teenagers, but I've no idea what they might be in to, so I brought everything I thought could be used for an art session. To be honest, Finn, I'm not sure I'm prepared for this.'

'Trust me, when it comes to a room full of hormonal teens, no one's prepared, and if they think they are, they're deluding themselves.'

She was falling behind, and he paused for her to catch up.

'All I can say, Daisy, is they can be rude, cheeky, sulky or just ignore you completely, but in general they're good kids. It's hard growing up these days. On one hand the world expects so much of them, and on the other, it's constantly putting them down.'

'You're not filling me with confidence.'

Finn turned into a gateway and a path, leading across a wide patch of grass to a squat, scruffy single storey building. 'I'll be right there with you.'

Mounting a single low step, he pushed a door and held it open with his back as she passed through into a cavernous space, with unpolished wooden floors. It had a raised stage at one end, and at the other, an arc of battered old sofas surrounded a hatchway, with a light, bright kitchen beyond.

'What is this place?'

'It's been all sorts over the years, but most recently it was a meeting hall for a bowling club. There's a green out the other side, though it's covered in mole hills now. We use it now and again for rounders and stuff, but not often.' He moved and the door swung shut behind him. 'Come and meet the others, before it all kicks off.'

Finn pointed to a figure attaching a table tennis net to a table on the stage. 'That's Chris. He's the main man around here.'

The man looked up on hearing his name, jumped off the stage and strode toward them, hand extended in readiness for shaking. 'Aah! Is this the new victim you promised, Finn?'

Daisy put her bag on the floor to accept his greeting.

'Yes, Chris, this is my friend Daisy. An artist.'

'Great!' Chris smiled at her. 'Just what we need, a Daisy Da Vinci, to inspire the youth of today. Right, let's create a quiet corner for you, away from the main to-ings and fro-ings. Maybe we could pull the sofas around and tuck you away in a space bottom left. You'll need tables laid out?' He turned back to Finn. 'Can I leave you to sort the stage area, while Daisy and I come up with a plan?'

Finn nodded and set about business, while a nervous Daisy trailed Chris to the end of the hall.

'So, Daisy, what did you have in mind?'

She took a deep breath, feeling out of her depth. 'Umm, I guess some tables and chairs. I've brought a load of supplies - paint, glue, stencils and stuff to stick, like beads and decoupage papers.'

'We've got supplies in the odds and ends cupboard in the kitchen you're welcome to pilfer from too, but if you decide to repeat the experience after today, I can sort you out a small kitty. We won't expect you to fund it yourself.' He moved across the room to a pile of tables and lifted one down, carrying it back to where Daisy was standing. 'What do you think, half a dozen?'

'I guess. Here, let me help you.'

'Thanks. If we split the kids up, so you only have a few at a time, that should keep it manageable. Otherwise, it could be carnage.'

A mousey haired woman appeared from the kitchen and Chris immediately switched his attention. 'Ah. Here she is. Joanna, this is Daisy. Daisy this is my better half, Joanna. Nothing would get done around here without her.'

'Don't believe a word of it. He's just trying to earn brownie points because he wants to go on a camping trip with the boys next month.' The woman threw a tea towel over her shoulder and stepped forward to shake Daisy's hand. 'Hi, Daisy. Is he looking after you properly?'

'Yes, very well, thank you.'

'So, he's shown you the fire exits and where the loos are and vital stuff like that?'

'Umm, no.'

'Thought not.' Joanna elbowed her husband in the chest. 'What are you like? You finish putting the tables out and I'll give Daisy the tour.'

'Whatever you say, my love. Whatever you say.' He winked at Daisy and walked away to fetch another table.

'Let me show you what's what.'

Daisy trailed Joanna around the building, listening to a running commentary.

'This is the kitchen, obviously. Otherwise known as the escape room, for two reasons. Firstly, once you're in here, you'll be lucky to get out before we close because there's a constant demand for squash and biscuits. No alcohol, cigarettes, vapes or energy drinks allowed on the premises, by the way. We've got our work cut out keeping them all in order without extra stimuli. And secondly, if you really need to get away for a minute you can close the door and pull down the hatch until you locate all your marbles.' She smiled. 'I jest, but there have been moments, believe me.'

Daisy looked around at the compact but well-equipped room.

'Oh, and this is the supply cupboard I heard Chris mention to you.' She opened the door for Daisy to look at the contents, then moved back into the main hall. 'That's a cloakroom, but nobody uses it. The kids wouldn't wear coats if their lives depended on it. There is a pile of old shirts in there for them to use though, when we're doing anything messy, so encourage them to put them on before you let them loose with paint or we'll have a posse of disgruntled parents come the end of the evening.'

'Old shirts. Right.'

She pointed at more doors as they passed. 'Ladies, gents, fire door to the rear playing field, office-come-dumping ground for staff use only. Put your bags in there, so you don't leave minus your phone or wallet. No kids allowed, ever. They're only allowed in the main area and the loos, for their safety and yours.'

'Ok. Got it.'

Joanna stopped. 'Listen, I don't want you to get the impression they're bad kids. They're not. Some do come from challenging backgrounds though, and we don't want to put temptation in their way. We're here to provide a service, give them an outlet for their energy and an alternative to the streets, the pier or social media.'

'How many are you expecting?'

Joanna tipped her head to one side. 'About twenty-five, maybe. It varies week to week. Depends what's on TV, what's on at school, which parents are applying pressure for them to come. A few parents are very supportive, and we usually rope a couple in each week to stay for the session, though their kids hate it. It seriously cramps their style.'

The main door to the building banged open and a couple of teenagers fell through it laughing hysterically in a heap on the floor.

'And we're off.' Joanna's eyebrows rose briefly. 'Right, stow your bag and I'll get you started.'

The arrival of actual children filled Daisy with fear, and she quickly ran to grab her things as instructed.

As she re-emerged, Finn passed in the opposite direction. 'Ready for the off?' He asked.

'I'm beginning to wonder what I've let myself in for.'

'You'll be fine. Anyway, if you survive the evening, I'll treat you to chips on the way home.'

'If that's supposed to make me feel better, you've failed.' She smiled wryly.

He laughed. 'I'm refereeing the table tennis, so I'll see you later.'

It was a slow start. Daisy felt like a spare part, as what seemed to be only partially organised bedlam carried on around her. Having made slightly awkward eye contact with one or two teens, who kept looking over at her but hadn't yet reached a sufficient level of curiosity to approach, she began to make use of the equipment, daubing paint on twisted pieces of pasta. A small group of girls were talking to Joanna, who was leaning against the doorjamb of the kitchen, and Daisy suddenly became aware they were discussing her.

'I promise she won't bite.' Joanna was chuckling.

Daisy stood tall. It was time for her to step up. 'Do you want to come and try it, girls?'

The group edged towards her, eyeing what she was doing from the other side of the sofa. The tallest spoke up. 'Not really, miss. We did pasta painting at primary school, when we were about seven.'

The others giggled at their friend's bravery.

Daisy didn't intend to fall at the first hurdle. 'Don't worry, I'm not suggesting you make your mums macaroni necklaces. You can do some really creative stuff with it.'

The girl's face fell. 'I haven't got a mum.'

Daisy's stomach clenched. How stupid. She should have known from her own complicated life history not to make assumptions. Her mouth opened and closed as she tried to think of something to say.

After a brief period of silence, Joanna butted in. 'I'll tell your mum that when she picks you up later, shall I, Harley?'

The girl giggled. 'Only joking, miss. But I had you, didn't I?' She climbed over the sofa and sat in the seat opposite Daisy. 'So, what are we doing?'

A Reason To Be

Daisy pursed her lips but said nothing. As the other two girls took the more conventional route to join them, Joanna caught Daisy's gaze and rolled her eyes, before returning to the hatch, to serve biscuits to a queue forming there.

'I'm painting these pasta shapes a base colour so that when they've dried, I can decorate them with metallic pens and little sparkles. They look lovely in a dish or a vase, as an alternative to those little coloured glass pebbles you can buy.'

The girls looked completely unimpressed.

'It's really good practice if you like doing your nails.' Daisy waved her fingers at them, showing off her intricately decorated digits.

'Wow! Did you do them?' Harley gaped.

Daisy nodded.

'What, they're not like bought ones you stuck on?' One of the other girls stared.

'Nope. All done by hand.'

'Right, where do we start?' Three sets of hands grabbed at the open bag of pasta in the centre of the table.

An hour and a half later, the last stragglers having wandered away, Daisy stared at a table covered in paint-daubed newspaper, paintbrushes and pots, and random bits of multi-coloured carbohydrates littering the floor.

'That went well.'

It was the first time she'd seen Finn all evening. 'You think?'

'There were no punch ups, no slanging matches, and no injuries. To my mind, that's a good result.' He chuckled. 'You kept them entertained. Did you spot any budding artists?'

She stood an old mug upright and collected up brushes in it. 'I have no idea. I was too busy trying not to make a complete idiot of myself. I'm twenty-one for goodness' sake. When did I completely lose touch with modern culture? I felt like an old granny.'

74

'You only wish you had Audrey's level of cool.' He began to help tidy. 'Besides, you can't have been that bad or you'd have been Billy-no-mates all night.'

'I guess. The girls seemed interested, the boys not so much.'

'They take a bit longer to come round.'

'Thank you. Thank you. Thank you, Daisy. You're an absolute star.' Chris arrived wielding a black rubbish sack and stuffed it with debris from the table and floor. He paused and looked at the pair. 'Listen. You two see to salvaging your equipment and leave the rest to me. I'm very grateful for your time tonight.'

'I don't mind helping.' Daisy jumped to her feet.

'No, I insist. Now, make the most of it and get off. It's not an offer I make very often.'

'Take it from me, he doesn't.' Joanna emerged from the kitchen. 'But assuming you're coming back again for next Tuesday night's session, if you're happy to leave your brushes and stuff here, I'll clean them for you. And that's not an offer I'll make very often either, but you've done a brilliant job tonight.'

Daisy blushed, not knowing what to say.

Finn stepped in. 'Course she's coming along again on Tuesday. Aren't you, Daisy?'

'Yes. Yes, I guess I am.' She agreed, shrugging.

The pair collected their belongings from the staff room and headed out into the dark, walking silently until they rounded the first corner.

'Hang on.' Daisy stopped abruptly. 'Didn't you say something about fish and chips?'

Finn kept walking. 'No, I don't think so.'

'Finn, you fibber.' She trotted to catch up with him.

'Oh, alright. You've twisted my arm.'

'Good, I'm famished. I haven't eaten since lunchtime and it's almost...' She reached for her phone to check the time, then groaned.

'What is it?'

'Four missed calls from Mum.' Daisy tutted and shoved the phone back into her pocket. 'What does she want?'

A Reason To Be

'Has she left a message?'

'No. She knows I never listen to them.'

'Perhaps you should ring her back.'

Daisy paused and looked at him. 'I definitely can't face that on an empty stomach.'

Finn halted too. 'It might be a good idea to get it done? Then you wouldn't have to waste time fretting about it.'

She raised her eyebrows, staring at him, and pointed over his shoulder.

He glanced around and realised they were outside the chip shop and, as the door opened allowing a customer to leave, the aroma of salt and vinegar wafted past them.

'It'll wait until tomorrow, and anyway, I'm too hungry to fret.'

He huffed. 'Alright, I'm going.'

Finn returned with two packages of steaming food. 'I got them open. I didn't think you'd want to wait until you got home.'

'Too right.' She dived straight in, and the pair idled along towards her house.

'So, be honest. What did you think about your first outing at the youth club?'

'It was alright, I suppose. I think I could have done better, been a bit more innovative. Maybe then I'd have got some boys to join in too.'

'I told you. Give it time.' He blew on a hot chip. 'I think you were brilliant.'

'Oh, please.' She rolled her eyes. 'You can stop with the flattery; I've already said I'll come again next week.'

'What? I sincerely think you did a good job. You shouldn't underestimate the impact it has on a kid when you take the trouble to spend time with them, get them involved in something new and, in the right circumstances, listen to what they want to get off their chests. It's priceless.'

She held a hand up to deflect his praise. 'Alright, alright! Message received, but let's be honest, it's something pretty much anyone could do. It's not like my special mission in life or anything, to get troubled kids to turn their lives around and release their inner artist.'

'I'm not trying to say that but, you know, it could be important.'

Daisy stopped at the end of her path and stared past him at the house, a frown heavy on her brow.

'What...?' He glanced over his shoulder.

She grabbed his arm and pulled him behind a tree. 'There's someone in there.'

'What? How can you tell?'

'The spare room light's on. I definitely didn't leave it like that.' Her voice was a harsh whisper.

'Are you sure?' He leaned to peer out.

'Yes, I'm sure. I'm not stupid.'

'No, I know that.'

She pulled him back. 'What should I do? Shall I call the police? Oh, I wish Gran was here. She'd know what to do.'

'Right.' Finn stood up straight, taking control. 'Give me your key. I'll go and check it out. You get ready to call the police if I'm not back out in two minutes.'

'What? You can't go in there.'

'Listen, chances are if someone did break in, they've already left. Burglars don't hang around, they're in and out as quick as they can. It would be really unlucky for us to have interrupted a burglary as it happened.'

'I don't know.' It all sounded a bit dangerous to Daisy.

'Trust me. It'll be fine.'

Daisy couldn't tell if he was trying to persuade her or himself.

He put his hand on the gate. 'Ready?'

'Ok.' She watched him; eyes wide with suspense.

'Phone?' He urged.

'Oh, yes.' She scrabbled to find her mobile phone then held it in both hands.

'Right. Here goes.'

'Be careful.'

A Reason To Be

Finn marched up the path, pausing only to look back at her as he put the key in the lock' He pushed the door open, shouting. 'Ok. I'm coming in, so if there's anyone in there, you'd better make a run for it, now.'

Daisy heard no more, as the door swung closed with Finn inside. She held her breath as she waited, one eye on the door, the other on the time on her phone. The clock clicked to the next minute, but to Daisy it felt like an age. Surely, he shouldn't be taking this long. Her finger hovered over the keypad, ready to dial.

'Finn, where are you? Come on,' she muttered under her breath. Images of him at the mercies of an armed intruder sped through her mind. She should have gone with him. It was no good, she couldn't wait any longer, she was ringing the police.

'Daisy. It's alright. You can come in.'

Her arm dropped down by her side, and she breathed a deep sigh of relief. She hurried up the path towards him, adrenalin still pumping through her veins. 'Oh, Finn. Are you alright? What took you so long? Is it bad? Have they wrecked the place?'

She joined him at the door and tentatively entered behind him.

'No, no. There hasn't been a break in.'

'But the light…'

'It's alright, it's nothing to worry about. It's just…'

Daisy pushed into the lounge, to see a familiar figure standing at the bottom of the stairs. A different kind of tension gripped her body, and her face took on an angry glare.

'Your mum,' Finn finished.

'Yes. I can see that.' Daisy turned her attention to her mother. 'What are you doing here? And why the hell did you break in?'

'Hi, Daisy. Good to see you.' Lizzy moved forward to greet her daughter then, seeing Daisy's reaction, held back, rubbing her hands together as if she didn't know what else to do with them. 'I didn't break in, silly. I've got a key.'

Daisy didn't speak, but her breathing was ragged and tense. She stared at her mother with simmering fury.

'And, you know, strictly speaking, it is my house too.' Lizzy took half a step back, but then stopped, holding her ground. 'And, with that in mind, I've decided to move in.'

Anger morphed into shock and Daisy's mouth dropped open.

Lizzy took advantage of the lull. 'Nice to see you again, Finn. I'd better go and finish unpacking.' She ran up the stairs, leaving Daisy still trying to make sense of what was going on.

Finn took Daisy by the shoulders and pressed her into the armchair. 'I think maybe a sweet tea would be a good idea.'

*

Audrey's hand was clamped firmly across her mouth, eyes wide as she observed the scene. 'Do you know, if I hadn't already carked it, I think that might have finished me off.' She let her hand drop to her lap. 'I had visions of my lovely old house ransacked and my limited-edition china dolls whisked off to the pawn shop, never to be seen again. Oh, my days.'

'Do not fear, Audrey, your china dolls live to see another day.'

'I'm not so sure. Their days might be numbered if Daisy and Lizzy try living together. What can Lizzy be thinking? I would have thought she'd be back in America by now. She never stayed any longer than she had to.' Audrey's brow was furrowed. 'Mark my words. There's something going on, I just haven't worked out what it is yet.'

'I'm sure it's something quite simple. Perhaps she merely wants to spend time with her daughter, particularly considering recent events. Perhaps she feels Daisy needs her on hand.'

'She's never worried about that before.'

'You've never not been there before.' The ombudsman gave Audrey a moment to absorb this idea. 'When an important pillar of a family passes on, it changes the whole dynamic. Other members of the group have to step up to fill the void, as it were.'

Audrey's face softened into a smile. 'I like you better when you're like this, you know? Earlier it was all "missing links" and "Tasmanian devils". Now, all of a sudden, I'm "a pillar of the family" and a void that needs filling.' She winked at him. 'I'm growing on you, aren't I? Go on, admit it.'

He pursed his lips. 'I was talking in generalisations, not specifics.'

'Yeah, yeah. You like me.' She sniffed and turned back to the screen. 'One thing's for certain anyway.'

'Oh, yes? And what's that?'

'The next few days are going to make very interesting watching.'

CHAPTER 14

Despite her simmering anger, Daisy slept well. She woke early, not because of fractured dreams and a knotted stomach, but because someone was vacuuming the stairs. She sighed, and for one brief moment imagined it was her grandmother, who'd always had dubious timing where housework was concerned. When reality hit, and she remembered it couldn't possibly be Audrey, her heart ached with the renewal of loss.

Getting out of bed, she pulled a large sweater over her pyjamas. She pushed the sadness away and allowed anger to seep in and replace it, partly about being woken up prematurely and partly because it was Lizzy's actions which had dragged grief back to the surface.

Lizzy was on her knees in the doorway of the spare bedroom, now her bedroom, vigorously running the nozzle of the cleaner around the skirting board. She stopped and switched the machine off when she spotted her daughter. 'Sorry. Did I wake you?'

'What do you think?' Daisy kept walking, round her mother's feet and down the stairs.

Lizzy jumped up and followed her down. 'Sorry, but I had to get rid of the cobwebs. You know, where there's a web, there's a spider and I can't be sharing my space with spiders.' She shuddered. 'I was going to make a nice breakfast as it's my first day. Do you fancy it? Pancakes, maybe?'

Daisy heard the determined and forced optimism in her mother's tone, but could take no pity. 'Pancakes? You're not in America now, you know?'

'Well, anything then. Eggs? Bacon?'

Having set the kettle to boil and put together the makings of a cup of tea, Daisy reached into the cupboard for a bowl. 'I'll stick with cornflakes, thanks.'

'Oh, right. Ok.'

There was silence as Lizzy seemed lost for something to say. Daisy longed to ask her what she was doing there, how long she was hanging around for, but didn't want to give her mother the satisfaction of appearing interested.

'Do you have anything planned for today?'

The question sounded dangerously like a precursor to Daisy being involved in something she had no desire to get involved in. She spooned a mouthful of milky cereal into her mouth and spoke through it, knowing it had always driven her grandmother mad and hopefully would her mother too. 'Things to do.' A spurt of milk dribbled down her chin and she wiped it with a sleeve.

'Oh, right.'

She dumped her bowl next to the sink, finished making the tea and carried it back up to her bedroom, feeling her mother's gaze on her back all the way.

Daisy kept a low profile for a couple of hours: checking social media; going through her old art books and searching for inspiration for the next youth club session. She was getting quite involved, when the doorbell interrupted her concentration. Daisy pushed the books to one side and strained to hear the voices from the floor below. There were at least two, but she couldn't tell who they were. After a couple of minutes she decided she was in desperate need of a glass of water and headed downstairs, denying any possibility it was merely nosiness about who was in the house.

On the landing, she picked out her mother, going on about how unseasonably warm it was for England, but of course she was used to much hotter climes in the US. Daisy screwed up her eyes in concentration as she listened, pussyfooting to the top of the stairs, so if she didn't like the sound of them, she could nip back to the bedroom without them knowing. So focused was she on the sound, she completely overlooked the hose from the vacuum cleaner snaking across the floor, tripped over it and landed heavily on her feet at the top of the stairs, in full view of the living room.

'Here she is now.' Lizzy's tone was polite. 'Daisy, look who's here. Mrs Scunthorpe was a friend of Gran's from Knit and Natter. She's brought a Dundee Cake. Isn't that thoughtful?'

The woman smiled. 'As I said, well-wishers remember those who've lost loved ones at the start, when it's fresh, but once the funeral's done and dusted, suddenly they're forgotten. It's like the world moves on, but I know when I lost my Frank, I was left reeling for months and the funeral was only a step along the road. I wanted you to know that the offer of help and so forth didn't expire at the wake, it's available for as long as it might be needed. And there's nothing like a slice of fruit cake with a cup of tea to fortify a soul when most in need.'

Daisy had heard many stories from Audrey about Mrs Scunthorpe and was sceptical to say the least.

The silence stretched, until Lizzy was compelled to fill it. 'Of course, yes, a cup of tea. Would you like one, Mrs Scunthorpe? And perhaps I could make a start on the Dundee cake right now? Will you join us for a slice?'

Daisy studied the elderly woman, trying to work out her motive for the visit, as her mother continued the conversation, first from the doorway and then the kitchen, popping in and out at intervals in the tea making process. Perhaps the prim and proper old lady had purely come along to offer support, but that didn't sound like Audrey's Mrs

Scunthorpe. Audrey's Mrs Scunthorpe would be there for some self-serving reason, like taking the opportunity to share a morsel of juicy gossip, though she was unlikely to have anything to impart that this particular household would be interested in, or...

'It's so nice that you've come back to England for a little while. I'm sure Audrey would have been so pleased, her daughter and granddaughter reunited at a time like this. Are you staying long? I suppose the house is yours now, so you'll have lots of awful paperwork to do before you go back. It's such a trial all that paperwork, especially if you decide to sell...'

Or, being the first to find out a titbit of news to pass on. Daisy could imagine how it would go. "Oh, yes. Audrey's house is on the market, don't you know. Her daughter and granddaughter are fighting hammer and tongs, don't you know. It's such a shame to see a family fall apart like that." Ooh, the old biddy would enjoy every minute. Daisy would make sure no fuel was provided to this particular gossip machine, but on the other hand, she wanted to know what her mother's plans were too. She bit her lip and slipped into a seat, one ear on her mother's responses, one eye on the scurrilous old woman. For now, she would watch and wait.

'Oh, we've no intention of selling at the moment, have we Daisy?'

'No, no intention.' It hadn't occurred to Daisy that selling was even a possibility and Lizzy's speedy response brought immediate relief to a stress that hadn't even existed until moments ago.

'It was Mum's home for years, has been Daisy's home too, and although I haven't lived here for some time there are still many memories. There's no rush for anything like that.'

'Aah. That's nice. So often these days the sale sign is in the front yard before the sausage rolls from the wake buffet have gone stale. Pound signs seem to be more important than memories to some, mentioning no names.' She tipped her head and winked as if she could say more if pushed. 'Anyway, good for you.'

All three sipped their tea, waiting for someone to move the conversation on.

'So, how's the corporation managing without you? Last I heard from Audrey, the place would fall apart if you weren't there to hold it together. She didn't know when you'd be able to come back to the UK. I said I was sure they could spare you for a week or two so you could come back and see your dear, dear mum, but no. Audrey was adamant you were far, far too important to the corporation.'

The implication was clear, Lizzy had prioritised work over her family. As much as Daisy was of the same opinion, she felt Mrs Scunthorpe had no business pointing it out. 'Gran had me. We were fine together, just the two of us.'

Lizzy produced a smile which reached no further than her lips and shrugged. 'You see, I was dispensable, here anyway.'

Daisy had meant her words to act in her mother's defence, but it seemed they were unintentionally double edged. Not that she felt guilty about it, Lizzy deserved everything she got.

Mrs Scunthorpe's radar was tuned to detect even the slightest blip. 'Just because they could manage without you, which of course they could - Audrey was a very capable woman - I'm sure they would have liked to see more of you. Wouldn't you, Daisy?'

Daisy realised she'd been backed into a checkmate situation. If she said, no they wouldn't have wanted to see Lizzy more, it hinted at discord, but if she said, yes, they would have, it set Lizzy up as the bad guy. Either way, the knitting group had their juicy story. 'Um, well, um...'

A knock at the door interrupted her search for an answer and was swiftly followed by Morag's head appearing around the door. 'Morning, girlies. Look who I found on the pavement.' The rest of her body emerged into the room, with Finn following.

'Morning,' he said.

'Why, Stella, fancy seeing you here. Not helping out at the old folks' home today?'

Mrs Scunthorpe huffed. 'As you well know, Morag, I don't help out at the old folks' home, I visit my infirm sister. And for your

A Reason To Be

information, she has an appointment with the visiting chiropodist this morning so I'm going a little later than usual.'

'Is that right?' Morag eyed the mug in Lizzy's hand. 'I don't suppose the kettle's still warm, is it? I'm gasping.'

Lizzy's smile was suddenly warmer than it had been. 'Coming right up. Will you try a slice of Mrs Scunthorpe's Dundee cake, too?'

'Och, thank you, but no. I can't be partaking of anything so heavy at this time in the morning. I'll be snoozing all afternoon.' Morag settled into her seat, ignoring the consternation on Mrs Scunthorpe's face at the description of her cake. 'Actually, Stella, I was only thinking about you a wee bit earlier. I was coming back from the Post Office and saw your friend Enid with...what's his name, oh yes, Reggie Nubuck. I had no idea they were walking out together.'

Mrs Scunthorpe immediately downed the dregs of her tea, grabbed her bag and shuffled forward to her feet. 'Is that the time? I really ought to be getting off. The chiropodist should be done by now.' She shared an unconvincing smile with the whole room. 'Where was it you said you saw Enid, Morag?'

'Going through the big gates into Midway Park from the seafront. Probably going to admire the Spring flowers. They're so romantic at this time of year.'

Mrs Scunthorpe met Daisy's eye. 'Thank your mother for me, Daisy. I'll see myself out.' With that, she was gone.

As the door banged, Morag chuckled. 'Miserable old bat. I thought that would get her moving. She's had her eye on Reggie Nubuck since he helped out at the jumble sale at the scout hall. He had quite the sales patter and she's an eye for a charmer, has that one.'

Lizzy reappeared with a laden tray. 'Oh, has Mrs Scunthorpe gone?'

'Aye, she had places to be.' Morag scooped up a cup and saucer as it was offered to her and settled it on her lap. 'Now, Lizzy, I'm hoping you could dig me out of a hole.'

'Me?' Lizzy sat next to Daisy on the sofa. 'What could I possibly help you with?'

'Well, I've got myself in such a kerfuffle, what with the funeral and all. I had a to do list as long as your arm and a couple of things dropped off the bottom. I suppose I bit off more than I could chew, but you see I always had Audrey as back up before and now...'

'But what is it you need me to do?'

Morag rolled her eyes at her own forgetfulness. 'Well, the WI meeting's coming up. A man was supposed to be coming to talk about chimney sweeping through the ages. He was booked months ago but then he decided to take early retirement in March, so he cancelled. I was meant to book a replacement speaker. If I'd got onto it straight away, I'm sure there would have found someone on the speaker list, but I let it slip and now, nothing. Unless I go for a young man by the name of Carlos who does a talk entitled "My Journey into the World of Male Stripping". Apparently, it's an eye opener, especially the demo at the end, but I don't think it would sit well with the vicar's wife's angina. I'd hate to be responsible for setting her off.'

Lizzy looked from one face to another in confusion. 'I don't understand. Where do I fit in to all this?'

'I was hoping you could do a wee turn for us, of course. Could you see your way to cobbling together a few words about... mergers and acquisitions is it, you do?'

A look of horror spread across Lizzy's face and Daisy had to bite back a snigger.

'Oh, Morag, I don't think anybody at the WI would want to hear about the stuff I'm involved in.'

'Now, Lizzy, don't sell yourself short. I'm sure you could jazz it up a bit with stories of your time in America, and the WI love variety. The talk last month about medium term investments for the over seventies went down a storm.'

'Oh, no, I don't think... I wouldn't know what...'

As Lizzy's discomfort grew, so did Daisy's enjoyment.

A Reason To Be

'I've got a great idea.' Finn's voice drew everyone's attention. There was a drawn-out moment of silence before he continued. 'Daisy could do it.'

'What?' Daisy was pole axed. 'Finn, what are you talking about?'

Lizzy and Morag merely stared at him, waiting for clarification.

He shrugged. 'You did a fantastic job with the teenagers at the youth club, and I bet you could do an equally good job with the WI ladies.'

'What's this?' Morag perked up.

'Daisy's an artist, Morag.'

If looks could kill, Finn would have been in ICU at the very least after Daisy's warning glance.

'No, Daisy, you're too modest.' He batted away any arguments before she could make them. 'Honestly, Morag, she's very good. I'm sure she could combine a few minutes of talking perhaps with a demonstration, or perhaps get everyone involved.'

'Finn...'

Morag leaned forward and clasped Daisy's hand tight. 'Oh, Daisy, would you do it for me? I really am in such a pickle, you'd be an absolute lifesaver. I've been so worried what the panel would say when they found out I'd stuffed up, but really, an art session would be grand. In fact, I think it would probably be better even than chimney sweeping through the ages. Your granny would be so proud of you.'

The denial on the tip of Daisy's tongue dissolved at Morag's mention of Audrey. How could she say no, now? She gave Finn a long, hard stare before forcing a fake smile for Morag. 'I guess I can come up with something, or should I say we?'

Morag patted her hand in thanks, one eyebrow raised quizzically. 'We?'

'Oh, yes, Morag - we. Because Finn will be coming to help. Won't you, Finn!'

*

Audrey shook her head as she watched the interactions of her loved ones.

'What are you thinking, Audrey? Do you think Daisy's heading in the right direction? I'm finding it hard to read.'

'I don't know what to think. There's such a mishmash of emotions going on in that room. It's like one of Eileen Thomsett's stews, but with feelings instead of spice and lentils. I never noticed when I was in amongst it myself. I suppose I was too focused on my own situation, but now, from here, my goodness there's a lot going on.'

'Impressive analogy. I like it. A tasty casserole with a pinch of anger and a sprinkle of jealousy and a soupcon of encouragement.' He kissed his bunched together fingers and exploded them into the air like an exuberant French chef.

Audrey side-eyed him. 'You can take a thing too far, you know?'

'Sorry.'

'It's all a bit confusing. There's Lizzy for starters. I can't understand what's going on with her. Why's she here? Why isn't she on the phone twenty-four seven? Usually, it's surgically attached to her ear. Something's going on. And then...'

'Don't tell me, Daisy's the main course...'

'Stop that now.' She glared him into silence. 'One minute Daisy's annoyed with her mother, the next she's defending her. But at least I won't have to worry about her falling for Finn now. Him dropping her in it with the WI will be an end to any romantic feelings she may have been starting to have. She can't stand being the centre of attention. She'll hate it and he'll be in the doghouse.'

'And dessert?' His eyebrows raised in amused question.

'I said, stop it.'

'Spoil sport.'

Audrey seemed lost in thought for a few moments, tapping her fingers as she went over the last scene in her head once more. The ombudsman waited quietly.

'I tell you what,' she said.

'What?'

A Reason To Be

'That Stella Scunthorpe was most definitely the fish course - conniving old trout.'

CHAPTER 15

Daisy marched her anger up and down the living room, as Finn watched. Lizzy was washing the dishes in the kitchen, having waved Morag off at the door, happy now her WI conundrum was solved.

'Finn, what were you thinking? How am I supposed to entertain a hall full of OAPs? It's bonkers.'

'I don't think they're all OAPs, but you could do all sorts of things. You could talk about different styles of art, then tell them what your favourite is and show them some of your pictures. Or you could start with a practical. Maybe get them to sketch a bowl of fruit or something, explaining different techniques as you go. There are loads of options.'

'Then you do it!'

He spread his hands wide. 'I would, but I'm not an artist. You are. Besides, it's another thing to add to our list. You know, the trying things outside of your comfort zone to find meaning project. You've started with kids, what better than trying something with a more mature audience? If you have a few different irons in the fire, you're likely to find the answer sooner.'

'I can tell you right now that standing in front of a roomful of women, waffling on about something I know little about, is not my reason to be. Some things you don't need to experience to know you aren't going to like them.'

A Reason To Be

'What do you mean "something you know little about"? You've almost got a degree in the subject. You must know a bit about it. And, if it doesn't pan out, at least you'll have ticked it off the list and you can look for something else to try. Think of the project.'

'What project's this then?' Lizzy walked in, wiping her hands on a tea-towel. 'Anything I can help with?'

Daisy opened her eyes wide, silently warning Finn to say nothing. 'No. We were just talking about what I can do for the WI, that's all, now Finn's dropped me in it.'

'Oh.' Lizzy folded the cloth and set it down on the table. 'Why don't you set up a gallery of your final project work for your degree? You could talk them through each piece, the inspiration behind them, and why you chose to submit those in particular. In fact, I'd like to see them myself. I've not seen any of your artwork for such a long time. It would be good to see what you've been up to.'

Finn stared at Daisy. Clearly Lizzy didn't know Daisy had changed course, or that she hadn't actually finished her degree.

Daisy avoided his gaze. 'Yeah, well, it's difficult to see what I'm up to from several thousand miles away, isn't it?' She wiped a piece of imaginary fluff from her sleeve, knowing she'd delivered a low blow to her mother, and, on this occasion, it was a diversionary technique. Eventually she would have to tell her about university, but today was not the day. 'Right, Finn. Are we going for that walk, or aren't we?'

They'd walked for ten minutes without speaking, Finn with his shoulders hunched and hands in pockets, and Daisy giving far more attention than necessary to every crack in the pavement, anything rather than look at Finn.

'Are we going to talk about this?'

'Talk about what?' Daisy acted innocent.

He stopped and leaned against the sea wall, his feet crossed in front of him, his hands still in his pockets, and looked her straight in the eye. 'You haven't told her. She thinks you've finished an art degree, when in fact you swapped courses and then dropped out.'

'I had to look after Gran, didn't I.' She studied her shoes.

'But from what you've told me, you changed course not long after you started uni. That must be, like, two years ago and more.'

'And?'

'She doesn't know.'

'And?'

'Don't you think she should?'

'She wasn't here, and she wasn't interested.' Her chin jutted out in defiance.

'Didn't you talk at all?'

'Yes. She rings every couple of weeks, when she can fit us in. When she **could** fit us in.' Her voice faltered as she realised she was still including Audrey as part of the unit.

'So, are you telling me that in two years she never asked how uni was going or anything about your course?'

Daisy kicked at a weed growing between the kerbstone and the tarmac of the pavement.

'Well?'

'Well, Gran never told her about the cancer.'

'That's different.'

'I don't see why.'

'Don't you?' He stared at her, but she had nothing to say. 'Look, when you've got a terminal illness like Audrey had, it's complicated. You're getting your head round it yourself; you're dealing with the feelings of those closest to you, trying to prepare them but protect them at the same time; you're trying to find a way to cope with every day. There are so many considerations to be allowed for in every decision that sometimes a completely different sort of logic kicks in. A decision that's right in some ways, can be wrong in others. It's a balancing act.'

A Reason To Be

Although Daisy's attention appeared to be on the wayward flora on the path, she was listening and interpreting what Finn was saying. 'You mean, you think Gran was wrong not to tell Mum?'

'No. Yes. Maybe. I don't know, because I don't know what was in Audrey's calculation when she was making that decision. I never was any good at maths. But what I mean is that that decision was partly about keeping things on an even keel for Audrey, partly about protecting Lizzy and probably partly about you as well.' He paused, trying to work out if she understood. 'You not telling your mum about uni is all about you.'

Daisy nodded as she inwardly accepted his accusation.

'You need to tell her, for your sake, as well as hers. Secrets aren't a good thing in a comfortable, well-adjusted, tight-knit family, let alone one as delicate as yours.'

'I'm not even sure we are a family really. We share the same genes, but that's about all.' Her voice was quiet and serious. A future on her own, without Audrey, without anyone significant scared her.

Finn poked her hard on the shoulder. 'You're sharing a house at the moment, and if you play your cards right, you could share more. Your mum coming back could be a fresh start for the pair of you.'

'Until she goes away again.'

'Talk to her.' He put his arm around her shoulders and started to walk. He had said his piece.

'Hmm.' She huffed as she was pulled alongside him. 'Though I don't know why you think I'd listen to you after dropping me in it with Morag's WI group. You clearly haven't got a clue what you're talking about.'

He laughed aloud and let his arm drop back by his side. 'It'll be great. Trust me.'

*

'Why, that little minx. I didn't know she'd been keeping that from her mother.' Audrey was miffed. 'And fancy holding me up as an example. I had my reasons for not letting Lizzy know I was poorly.'

'I suspect Daisy would say she had her reasons for not telling Lizzy about the issues regarding her education.' The ombudsman shrugged.

'Oh, no. I'm not having that. I'm with Finn all the way on this one. It's a different situation, a different situation altogether.'

'Of course it is. Every situation is different, although similarities may be present, as of course, each person's view will also be different. To an outsider it's very difficult to draw the line as to when a course of action which would generally be viewed as unacceptable suddenly becomes acceptable. When you're seriously ill, boundaries do seem to waver more than at any other time, but even then, opinions vary.'

Audrey held up a hand. 'Alright, alright. Enough with the psychology lecture. Listen, I'm asking you, if I'd drawn Lizzy in when I was diagnosed, who would it have helped? Not Lizzy - it would have interfered with her career. She'd have come back to the UK against her will because she thought she ought to.' The word "ought" was drawn out like an insult. 'Not me, because I was having enough trouble keeping Daisy above water. I didn't need another set of feelings to pussy foot around.'

'Perhaps Lizzy could have helped Daisy,' he dared to suggest.

'Not if past experience was anything to go by. They'd been at each other's throats since Daisy was eleven years old. It would have just given me something more to worry about, people around me arguing and falling out. I had enough on my plate with the appointments and the treatments and being blooming ill. I didn't need that too.'

'Hmm.' He stirred his coffee slowly and silently.

Audrey waited.

He continued to stir.

She tutted. 'Oh, come on then. Let's hear it. You've got an opinion about most things and I'm sure this is no different. Let me have it.'

'Well, it occurs to me that you don't give either of the women in your life a lot of credit. I'm sure they've been, as you say, at loggerheads in the past, but there was one thing which might perhaps have brought them together in this instance that had never occurred before.'

'Oh, yes, smarty-pants. And what's that?'

'Losing you, Audrey.' His forehead was rumpled by a quizzical frown as he gauged her understanding. 'Losing you.'

CHAPTER 16

Daisy arrived at the Youth Club half an hour early, in an effort to be more ready for the onslaught than she had been first time round.

'You look like you're on a mission.' Finn was on kitchen duty and, with a checked tea-towel tied round his waist, looked the part.

'I'm trying something different, to get more of the kids involved, if I can.'

He adopted a deep, dramatic American voice. 'It's art class, the sequel. Bigger and better than any art class you've ever seen before.'

She raised an eyebrow at him. 'Whatever.'

He dropped the accent. 'Seriously, what are you doing?'

'Well.' She shuffled papers round on the table to show him. 'It's banners. You know, like stylised text and bold graphics. I've got some basic templates, but they can be adapted to suit whatever sports team or band they follow. '

'Interesting.'

She studied his face. 'Do you think so? Or are you just saying that?'

'No, it really is. I don't suppose I'll get much of a break from pouring squash for the rest of the evening, but if I get a chance, I might have a go.' He pushed a few pages around to look at those hidden beneath the pile. 'Anyway, better go open another dozen multipacks of crisps. See you later.'

Daisy felt a warm glow from his comments. Hopefully the children would be as positive.

Harley and her posse were first on the scene. 'Do you want to see my nails, miss?'

'Daisy.' Daisy reminded her. She felt ancient enough already next to these teenagers, without them treating her like a teacher. 'Yes, let's have a look then.'

The girls made fans of fingers for her to admire.

'Wow, those are some cool colours.'

The group smirked at each other. 'Yes, miss. Cool.'

Clearly the term was no longer in vogue. 'Would you like to try something different this week?' Daisy moved some of the printouts around to get their attention. 'Fancy making some banners?' Glancing up, she noticed their faces falling into a lip curl. 'Are you part of a sports team? No? Do you have a favourite band?'

Harley adopted a bored tone and pointed to the end of the hall where three snooker tables had been set up. 'There's a pool tournament tonight, sorry.'

'Oh. Ok.' Daisy was disappointed, but not discouraged. Not everybody would be playing pool all evening, surely.

Forty minutes of drawing a complete blank made Daisy realise that, yes, everybody could be playing pool or, if not playing it, watching it, or lining up for refreshments to keep them satisfied while watching.

Out of desperation, she walked the disorderly queue, determined her efforts should not be for nothing. A group of boys hovered together, chuckling as they listened to a central character relating a compelling tale to the others, while shuffling forward.

'Hi, boys. If you're not playing, do you want to try some art?'

There was a drawn out silence as they glared at her, seemingly shocked at her nerve for interrupting them.

'No? I just thought it might fill a gap while you weren't playing. Making banners for whatever sport you support or band you like?' She paused in case someone spoke up. 'Anyone interested?'

The central boy acted as spokesperson. 'We don't draw.'

She was not to be deterred. 'It's not all about drawing. It's graphic design, block colours, fancy writing?' She held some example sheets up for him to see. He was clearly the ring leader.

'Nah! Besides, I'm up again in the next round. I haven't got time for messing about. '

One of the others chipped in. 'You're going to win, aren't you, Lewis!'

The boy shrugged modestly.

Daisy's shoulders dropped. 'Ok, never mind.' She turned away and huffed. It looked very much like she'd wasted her time with all the preparation earlier in the day. She'd been shuffling forward with the boys and was almost at the door to the kitchen.

Finn poked his head out of the door. 'You alright? Not much going on?'

'No. I can't compete with the pool tonight, and I was really hoping to make some progress with the kids.'

He squeezed her shoulder. 'I know you'd put in a lot of effort too. Don't worry though, next time could be a completely different story.' The crowd waiting for refreshments were getting noisier, and Finn glanced back at them over his shoulder. 'I'd better get on, but if you really want to make progress, why don't you give Chris a hand with the tournament.' He shrugged. 'If you can't beat 'em, join em.'

She thought about it for a moment, an idea beginning to form. She turned back to the group of boys. 'Is it too late for me to join the tournament? Would I be allowed to play?'

The boy referred to as Lewis sniggered, and the others swiftly joined in. 'You'll have to be quick, round one is nearly finished.'

'What do I do? Do I have to sign up or something?'

'Just tell Chris. He'll set you up.' His head tipped to one side. 'There are a lot of good players here, you know? Are you sure you want to show yourself up?' More laughter.

'It's got to be better than sitting in the corner all night doing nothing, hasn't it?'

'If you make it past the first round. Otherwise, you'll still be in the corner doing nothing.' More laughter.

He was trying to wind her up, but she wasn't going to fall for it. She smiled at him sweetly. 'I tell you what, Lewis, is it? How about if I do make it past the first round, you come and do some art with me?'

'Not likely. It's no skin off my nose either way.'

'Alright, then. What about if I beat *you* in a match you come and do some art before the end of the session?'

His eyes narrowed but he didn't reply.

'Sorry. I didn't mean to scare you.'

This time there was laughter and catcalls from the other boys, but Lewis merely shook his head in derision. 'Ain't going to happen, but if you really want to show yourself up, miss, go ahead.'

Her smile stayed exactly where it was. It was a year or so since she last played, but surely the secret weapon of the University freshers pool team couldn't have lost all her skills already. 'I'll put my name down then. See you later, Lewis.'

At the end of the session, Finn was waiting for her, as she emerged from the staff room, pulling on her jacket. 'I think that's what you call a hustle. Where did you learn to play like that?'

She winked. 'I guess I must just be a natural.' She juggled a couple of bags of supplies. 'At least I got the boys involved on my art table at the end, even if it was only for a short while. No sign of any girls though.'

Finn relieved her of a bag and fell in beside her. 'I thought Lewis took his defeat well considering, and where Lewis goes, the pack tend to follow. Anyway, maybe that's the way it goes, lads some weeks and girls the other. It's all good in the end.'

'I guess so, but I can't help thinking there must be something that would get them all excited. I just haven't thought of it yet.' She grinned. 'I am chuffed though. Some actually asked to take their artwork away with them.'

He held the door open for her to walk through and, as she did so, she halted on the step. Ripped up papers lay all across the front yard, stuck in the hedge and blowing in the breeze. She inhaled sharply and Finn stepped past her, bending to pick one up. 'What the heck?' He flattened it out and they could both see it was one of the posters produced during the session. 'Oh, no.'

Daisy snatched it from him and screwed it back up. 'Well, that's great, isn't it?'

Finn sighed, patted her shoulder and turned back. 'I'd better go get a bin-bag or this lot'll be halfway down the High Street. We don't want to give the neighbours any more reasons to kick off.'

He returned inside and Daisy began to collect up the papers. That would teach her to feel smug.

Their walk home was subdued. Daisy was ruminating over the evening's failure and, though Finn tried to lift her spirits, she was beyond reach. When they got to the house, she entered but Finn hovered in the doorway.

'Are you coming in?'

'I've got an early start in the morning, so I should get off.'

'Alright.' She shrugged. 'I'll see you, then.'

He paused. 'Listen, don't let this evening put you off. Kids are just kids, you know? It doesn't mean anything.'

'It means I'm wasting my time.' She leaned against the door frame, her head resting against the wood. 'If you thought this youth club thing was going to be my reason to be, I'm afraid you're way off.'

He chucked her under the chin. 'Come on. Don't give up so easily. It's a knock back, that's all.'

'I don't really need any more knock backs right now.'

He stepped in closer and placed a hand on her upper arm. 'Look, don't make any rash decisions. Give it some thought and some time. I know Chris and Joanna have really appreciated your help, and I like you being there.'

'You do...?'

Lizzy's voice rang out from the lounge. 'Finn? Finn is that you?'

Daisy rolled her eyes at the intrusion into what had felt like a strangely intimate moment between her and Finn, a warm closeness she'd never felt with him before, but he smiled and leaned around her to speak to her mother. 'Yes, it's me. Are you ok?'

'Good, thanks.' Lizzy joined them at the door. 'I'm glad I've caught you. I was wondering if you'd like to come for dinner one night this week?'

Daisy sighed loudly. 'Oh, Mum, Finn's busy. Don't hassle him.'

'If by hassle you mean feed me a home-cooked meal, I don't mind being hassled.' He turned to Lizzy. 'I'm working the next couple of days, but I'm free on Friday.'

'Then Friday it is. See you then.' She disappeared back into the kitchen.

Daisy huffed. 'Sorry, I hope you don't mind.'

'Mind? Why would I mind?'

'Oh, you know what she's like. Always interfering.'

'Last week she couldn't be bothered, this week she's interfering.' He chuckled. 'If you'd rather I didn't come, I won't, but otherwise I'd love to. It'd be nice.'

She shrugged. Part of her welcomed an excuse to spend some more time with him, not surrounded by teenagers, but she didn't really want her mother to be part of the equation.

'Then I'll see you on Friday. We can talk about what you're going to do for the WI meeting.' He grinned.

'Thanks for reminding me.' She groaned.

'You're welcome. See you.' He gave her a cheeky wink, thrust his hands in his pockets and strode off down the path.

Daisy closed the door and marched into the kitchen. 'What's the idea? Why are you inviting Finn to dinner?'

'Why not? I thought I should get to know your young man a bit better, that's all.'

Daisy's eyes widened. 'He is not my young man.'

'Isn't he? Oh, I thought because he was here quite a bit that the two of you were...' Lizzy left the sentence open.

'It is possible for a male and female to be friends, you know. Just because they spend time together, it doesn't mean they're a couple.'

'Ok, well, in that case I've just invited your friend for dinner, which is completely normal.' Lizzy shrugged. 'I'd like to get to know him better anyway. I don't know anything about him.'

Daisy tutted, and strutted away to her room. When she thought about it though, despite spending so much time with him, she didn't really know anything about Finn either.

*

Audrey's palm was pressed against her chest, eyes wide with distress. 'Oh, my heart breaks for her. All that effort, and the little tykes ripped it to shreds. The youth of today! It wouldn't have happened in my day, I can tell you.'

'A career in education requires a stoic constitution, but the rewards can be immense, if you stick with it long enough to receive any,' the Ombudsman said.

'I'd give the lot of them a clip round the ear: teach'em a bit of respect.'

'I'm not sure violence is the answer, Audrey.'

'Maybe not, but at least I'd feel better.' She wriggled in her seat and then pointed at the screen. 'I can't work out what's going on there, you know. That daughter of mine is up to something, but I don't know what. And that Finn - there's more to him than meets the eye, you mark my words.'

The ombudsman pursed his lips. 'You're of a very suspicious nature, Audrey.'

'Perhaps, but it comes from experience.' She sighed. 'Oh, well. I'm sure it'll all come out in the wash. We'd better get on with it. I know you're in a hurry and I wouldn't want to hold you up unduly.'

He rolled his eyes. 'Thank you, Audrey. You're all consideration, you really are.'

CHAPTER 17

While Lizzy was cooking, Daisy laid the table. The last couple of days had given her the opportunity to think, and she'd realised the "family dinner" situation could work to her advantage in her quest to find out more about Finn. It felt a little late asking now, after they'd spent so much time together. She also wanted to know what Lizzy's plans were and, by having dinner with them both together, the chances were she might get answers without having to do the asking herself. She didn't want Finn to think she was nosey, and she didn't want to give her mother the satisfaction of thinking she was at all interested.

'That looks nice.' Lizzy stood in the doorway, wiping her hands on a tea-towel. 'And you're sure he likes pork? I'd hate to serve something he hates.'

Daisy shrugged. 'He's never said he doesn't like it.'

The doorbell sounded and Lizzy jumped. 'Ah, well, we're about to find out. Can you let him in while I prepare the jus?'

Daisy moved to the door, muttering. 'Why can't she call it gravy like normal people?'

Finn was standing on the step, bunch of flowers in hand. 'Alright?'

'Come in, honoured guest. Your banquet awaits.'

'Ok?' He raised his eyebrows, following her inside.

'Hi, Finn. It'll be about five minutes. Daisy will get you a drink.' Lizzy called from the kitchen.

'Thanks.' He handed Daisy the flowers. 'These are for your mum.'

Daisy took them from him, dumped them on a side table and pointed at a seat. 'Will sir have a glass of wine, or a juice d'orange or a water de tap?'

He frowned in puzzlement. 'I'll have a glass of wine, please. I've got a feeling I might need it.' He gave her a wry smile.

Lizzy leaned through the doorway. 'You do like pork, Finn, don't you? Tell me you like pork.'

'I love anything I haven't had to cook myself.'

'Phew. Thank goodness for that. Otherwise, you'd have been having a plateful of vegetables and nothing else. Oh, are those for me?' She indicated the flowers.

'Yes, they are. To thank you for dinner.'

'You are thoughtful.' She disappeared with the bouquet back to the kitchen, only to reappear moments later with a steaming platter of carved meat. 'Start helping yourself right away. The rest is on its way.'

There was a flurry of activity as Lizzy raced in and out with dishes, and Finn and Daisy filled their plates.

Finally, Lizzy settled into her seat and began to help herself. 'Go on, you two. Don't wait for me. Eat it while it's hot.'

'This looks lovely.' Finn took a first mouthful.

'Thank you. So, I take it you live alone, Finn? You said about doing all the cooking yourself.'

Daisy ears pricked up.

'Yes, it's only me.'

'And how long have you been at the hospice? That is where you two met, isn't it?' Lizzy drew Daisy into the conversation.

Daisy nodded.

'I've been working there a couple of years, though I did a bit of volunteering before that.'

'Interesting choice of work for a young person, challenging. Not something just anybody could do, I would have thought?'

'It has its moments.' He made appreciative noises. 'These potatoes are amazing. Where did you learn to cook?'

Daisy had been watching Finn carefully and suspected this was an intentional change of subject. He didn't seem to want to talk about his work, but having spent time with him in that environment, she could understand that. 'Yes, Mum. Where did you learn to produce food like this? It's better than what you used to dish up.'

Lizzy shrugged. 'I did a course. I've always wanted to cook, and had some spare time, so I thought, why not?'

'If this is the result, it was money well spent.' Finn took another mouthful. 'Perhaps I should have some lessons. I could serve myself up something more exciting than beans on toast once in a while, though America's a long way to go to learn to cook.'

'Oh, no. It wasn't in America...' It seemed as if Lizzy was about to say more, but changed her mind at the last moment.

Daisy absorbed her mother's response. Something was off, but she couldn't think what.

'Daisy, have you thought any more about what to do for Morag's WI group?' Finn moved on.

'No, not really.' Daisy wasn't ready to have the subject changed.

'I think she should show off her skills.' Lizzy said. 'I bet your final project work was fantastic. In fact, I'd like to see your portfolio. She always was very creative.' Lizzy turned from Finn to Daisy and back again.

Finn was looking wide-eyed at her, probably realising the direction the conversation was heading. This was the moment when Daisy should come clean, tell her mother about dropping out, but there were other things on her mind. 'Where did you learn to cook, Mum?'

'I told you, lessons.' Lizzy's eyes could not hold Daisy's gaze. 'Will you have seconds, Finn? There's plenty here.'

A Reason To Be

He had no opportunity to accept or refuse as Daisy rushed on. 'Yes, but where did you have your lessons. You said not in America.'

'No, I had them in the UK, in London.' She smiled a dead smile. 'So, when can I see your final project work?'

'You can't. What do you mean, you had them in London? When were you in London long enough to do cookery lessons?'

Lizzy waved her question away as unimportant, but couldn't meet her eye. 'Oh, you know, I was backward and forward quite a bit, and fitted them in here and there. Why can't I see your work? Have you seen it, Finn? I bet it's brilliant. You're too modest, Daisy.'

'No, I haven't.' Finn shuffled in his seat and glared at Daisy, having urged her to tell her mother about dropping out before now.

'When were you backward and forward quite a bit? I haven't seen you for two years.'

'Oh, you know. Last year sometime. Anyway, about this artwork…'

'There is no artwork.' Daisy roared. 'I quit the course. You were in the UK last year, long enough to do a cookery course, and you didn't come and see me and Gran?'

'You quit the course?' Lizzy matched her daughter's volume. 'When?'

Finn's mobile phone rang and both women turned to look at him. 'Excuse me. I'll take this outside.' He pushed back his chair and made a swift exit.

Lizzy and Daisy continued to fling accusations and questions at each other, at first in harsh whispers but gradually louder, until Finn sidestepped awkwardly back into the room. 'Sorry about that. It was Chris.' He looked at Daisy. 'The Youth Club's been vandalised. It's been left in a right mess and the neighbours are kicking up a stink. He's there now and I said I'd go down, see what needs to be done and if there's anything I can do to help. Is that ok?' He turned to Lizzy. 'I'm sorry. The food was lovely. Do you mind?'

Lizzy forced a smile. 'No. I think we're done here anyway.'

Daisy got up from the table and headed for the door. 'I'm coming with you.'

CHAPTER 18

The Youth Club building was daubed in lewd graffiti, a small windowpane smashed, and it looked as if a fire had been set at the base of the front door, resulting in a scorched blister patch blooming from the bottom edge up to the lower hinge. The grounds had not escaped attention either, with piles of rubbish scattered around, and a couple of paving slabs broken.

'Why would anyone do this?' Finn threw his arms wide, shaking his head at the mess.

Chris was standing, hand on hips, observing the scene, harshly illuminated by the rectangular flood lights dotted around the eaves of the building. 'There have been a few cases recently around the area, revellers, late at night, using an empty building as a place to carry on partying after they're thrown out from wherever. The police don't think it was personal.'

'It doesn't look like the result of any party I've been to.'

Joanna arrived with a shopping bag and rifled around in it. 'The drug paraphernalia lying around backs up the theory. Here, rubber gloves all round, but please be careful, there are sharps amongst the debris.' She handed a pair to Daisy. 'Thank you for this. You've got better things to be doing with your Friday evening, I'm sure.'

'Not really.' Daisy pulled the thick rubber over her hands and accepted a rubbish bag. 'How does it look inside?'

'They didn't make it past the heavy-duty door, thankfully. The damage is all external, but that's bad enough.' Chris seemed downtrodden. 'It's all we need. The locals have been putting pressure on the landlord to kick us out already and this will only add fuel to the fire. Speaking of which…'

A group of three men turned in at the gate. The eldest, a tall, thin man wearing wire-rimmed glasses, was clearly trying to placate the other two, patting the air with his palms. 'I don't see how you can hold the Youth Club responsible, when this obviously happened in the early hours of the morning, and had nothing to do with the children. It's the vandals at fault here, not the tenants, or the landlord, come to that.' He turned to Chris. 'My, this is a sorry state of affairs. How bad is it?'

'What you see, Mr Cahill. They didn't get inside, so it's mainly superficial…'

The taller of the men interrupted. 'It may be superficial to you, but this impacts on all the local businesses and homeowners. Who would want to live or shop next to this eyesore? It's a monstrosity.'

Not part of the discussion, Finn and Daisy had already begun to fill their rubbish sacks.

'My lovely helpers and I will have the bulk of it sorted in a couple of hours and we'll come up with a plan for the door and paintwork. Hopefully most of the graffiti will come off with a bit of elbow grease,' said Chris.

The third man was not to be left out. 'Elbow grease? Pah! That'll take more than a lick and a prayer. You're talking about a complete repaint and probably several coats at that, if the filthy language isn't going to show through. And how long is that going to take? In the meantime, we've got to live with it. My poor mother's in shock. She goes out for a paper first thing, only to be confronted by this profanity. It's simply not on.'

'I'm sure it was quite a shock and I do sympathise with your mother…' The landlord's attempt to calm the tone was cut off.

'Sympathy doesn't cut it. The poor woman's beside herself,' the shorter man continued. 'She's lived in this neighbourhood all her life, and it's not what we expect.'

Chris tried again. 'I promise you, I will do everything I can to put the building back to how it was, as quickly as I possibly can, and I'll try to do something about the graffiti straight away, even if I can't get rid of it completely.'

The taller man was not to be placated. 'Putting the building back to how it was isn't good enough, to be frank. It was an eyesore before, and this is simply the last straw. Mr Cahill, I have asked you before, and I will ask you again, will you please evict the Youth Club, and come to some sort of alternative usage which is acceptable to your neighbours? You have a duty to the locals.'

As the men were paying no heed to Chris's assurances, Chris also turned to the landlord. 'Mr Cahill, I would remind you what a valuable resource this is to the local young people. They have so few options and they're surely better off here than roaming the streets getting up to mischief.'

As voices became raised, and the argument flew back and forth, Daisy sidled up to Finn. 'This isn't good. Do you think they'll shut us down?'

'It's been on the cards for a while, and this might do it. Goodness knows where else we'd be able to get to hold the sessions, and even if we could find a venue, we probably couldn't afford anywhere else. Chris and Joanna have fought tooth and nail to try and keep it going.' He smiled. 'I like the fact you said "us" though.'

'Did I?' She smiled back, her cheeks turning pink at the connotation.

'You did. I'm glad you feel part of the team, even if it hasn't been plain sailing.' He sighed. 'Hopefully it won't take too long to find somewhere else, if it comes to that, and your art sessions can start to take off.'

Daisy nodded, but was distracted by the growing heat of the conversation going on behind her. She could tell Chris was losing ground, and not just because he was outnumbered.

'This was once a magnificent old pavilion but, if you ask me, the time has come for this ground to be developed, and I know you're not short of offers.' The tall man's tone changed, became wheedling. 'Come, Mr Cahill. You don't need this sort of stress at your time of life.'

'I certainly don't, but I promised my aunt I'd keep the pavilion as a resource for the local people if I inherited it, and I can't give up at the first sign of trouble.' Mr Cahill dabbed at his forehead with a handkerchief.

'If it was the first sign of trouble, that would be one thing, but it's been one thing after another. Look at it. It's an eyesore, with or without the graffiti, and a lick of paint isn't going to work a miracle. It'll soon be grubby and tatty again.'

Daisy had heard enough. 'Excuse me. Can I say something?'

The first annoyed neighbour faced her. 'And who are you?'

'I'm one of the helpers at the Youth Club, and I've got a suggestion.'

Everyone turned to look at her, but the second neighbour scowled. 'No offence, but I can't see what you can possibly have to say on the matter that could be useful.'

Mr Cahill frowned at the man. 'Any positive input would be welcome.'

'Well, I was thinking, what about a mural?' Daisy felt uncomfortable being centre of attention.

'A mural, pah!' The neighbour was unimpressed.

'No.' Mr Cahill held up a hand to stop the man interrupting. 'Tell me more, young lady.'

'The gentleman's right, even before the vandalism the place looked a bit tatty, and if you just paint the whole thing white again it will soon get dirty with the amount of footfall coming through and balls being kicked against it and stuff. But really, it's a lovely huge blank canvas.' She stood back from the wall and waved her arms as her imagination took over and she described a scene. 'Rather than one plain block of colour, you could have a complete scene. Perhaps a meadow at the bottom with grass and wild flowers, poppies and daisies and buttercups, or a field of corn, standing against a backdrop of blue sky and white clouds, maybe trees and birds. It could look fantastic and be more practical. The odd handprint or muddy ball print would hardly show up.'

There was several seconds of silence, then Chris interceded. 'That's a lovely idea, Daisy, but we'd be hard pressed to cover the cost of a few tubs of trade white paint, let alone all that.'

'Who'd paint it? Murals take huge amounts of man hours to complete, and you'd need an expert, and that would cost a pretty penny too. Seriously, Mr Cahill, be realistic.'

'I'd paint it.' Daisy said. 'And I'm sure the others would help out too, with the bits that needed less creative input.'

'But the paint...' The lines on Mr Cahill's brow deepened.

Finn stepped up. 'We could probably ask for donations from people's sheds, especially if we only need small amounts of most colours. It's the sort of thing communities likes to get behind. I'm sure Daisy could even come up with a design around whatever is donated. Couldn't you, Daisy?'

'Yes, the options are endless.'

Mr Cahill was staring from the blank wall to Daisy and back again. 'Do you really think you could do it?'

'Yes, I think so, but I guess the first step is to get the paint. We should ask around and see what's available.'

'She's a very good artist, Mr Cahill, and the Youth Club could run a project, to get hold of the paint and equipment. Couldn't we, Chris?' Finn lobbied for support.

Chris shrugged. 'Nothing ventured, nothing gained. We're always up for a challenge.'

'A challenge?' The first annoyed neighbour was shaking his head. 'It'll fall on its face before you even get started. In a month's time we'll be back here talking about whitewash again and no further forward.'

'Do you know what?' Mr Cahill faced the disgruntled man. 'It's a risk I'm willing to take. In fact, if there's no serious progress in a month's time, come and see me, and we'll talk again about the development ideas you have. How's that?'

'One month?' The man seemed to be considering it. 'It's a waste of four weeks, but you're on.'

'Good. That's sorted then.' The complainers left and Mr Cahill turned to the group. 'At least that'll get them off my back for a day or two. I hope you know what you're taking on here.'

'Don't worry, Mr Cahill,' Chris reassured. 'Leave it with us.'

'Oh, I will, but I'll be back in a month's time. What with one thing and another, the neighbours around here have been a headache since the day I inherited this place. If it isn't sorted by the time I come back, not only will I speak to the developers, I'll have no choice but to let them take it off my hands, for my sanity's sake.'

He marched away, leaving the group to slowly absorb the immensity of the task ahead of them.

*

'I have never been so proud.' Audrey's palm was pressed to her chest. 'Did you see my girl? Did you see her? Standing up to those bullies without batting an eyelid.

'Indeed I did, Audrey.' The ombudsman nodded in agreement. 'She certainly has some gumption.'

'She gets that from me, you know.'

'I daresay she does.' The ombudsman gave a wry smile. 'More to the point, perhaps this is just what she needs to feel some purpose in her life. This could be what we've been waiting for, Audrey.'

'I suppose it could,' Audrey conceded, somewhat unwillingly. She was enjoying this unexpected extended time with her granddaughter and didn't want to cut it short. 'But it's early days. We shouldn't jump the gun. We had better watch some more to see how she goes on, to be sure.'

'I had a funny feeling you might say that. Alright, let's see how this pans out.'

CHAPTER 19

After the landlord left, Joanna hugged Daisy tight. 'Well done, Daisy. I think you might have saved the day.'

Finn was smiling, but Chris was scratching his chin.

'Come on, Chris. We've at least bought ourselves some time. Cheer up.' Joanna squeezed her husband's arm.

'I do appreciate that. Thank you, Daisy.' He nodded at her. 'But do you realise how much work this is going to involve. It's a mammoth task. We'll need cleaning equipment, paint, in various colours, rollers, brushes, paint trays, ladders, safety equipment. Even getting hold of the materials will be a challenge, let alone the man hours needed to whitewash the walls to get rid of this graffiti and then actually finish the job. I'm not even sure where to start.'

There was silence all round as they considered his concerns. Finn was the first to surface. 'Lists!'

'Sorry?' Chris was still frowning.

'Lists. We need to make lists of everything we need for the job and where we can get it. Work out how much of it we can afford to buy, and think about who might be prepared to donate the rest. Maybe local shops would help out.'

Daisy wasn't to be left out. 'We can start a social media campaign for donations. People love a good cause, especially if they can donate something they no longer need rather than handing over money. We might even get a few volunteers to help with the donkey work.'

'But to do all this in a month…' Chris was still unconvinced.

Joanna rubbed his arm. 'One day at a time, Chris. But we've got to do something, and I for one can't think of another alternative. I think we've got to give it a try, even if we fail.'

'I suppose you're right.'

'Of course she's right.' Finn's enthusiasm was growing. 'And we won't fail anyway, with Daisy doing the artwork, eh, Daisy? It'll be brilliant. We really could do this.'

Daisy was staring at the wall, imagining all sorts of colourful images covering its expanse, a tree here, a bird there. She stepped to one side and skidded on half a ham sandwich which had been discarded there. 'Hmm,' she said. 'But before we start creating a work of art, we'd better finish clearing up this mess.'

By the time they'd cleared the decks and thrown together a number of lists, it was late, and Daisy was pleased to find that Lizzy was already in bed. She had no wish to resume their earlier conversation, despite wanting to know why her mother had been in the Country without telling her. At some point she was going to have to explain the situation about her degree course, but as it stood, it seemed neither of them had been particularly honest with each other and Daisy didn't feel she should have to explain herself under the circumstances. Lizzy deserved no explanation.

CHAPTER 20

The next few days were a whirlwind of activity. Daisy was up with the larks, rushing to the pavilion to continue preparations. The insurance company had coughed up for a new fire door, which was fitted urgently to protect the place, but everything else was down to them. Chris had conjured up some thin white paint from somewhere, to tone down the foul graffiti, though it would probably take a dozen coats. First, they had to scrub years of grime from the walls, before they could even think about anything creative.

By Tuesday night – the next scheduled youth club session - the exterior looked better, but the toll showed on the glum faces of the workers. The teenagers were taken aback as they arrived to see a hall laid out with rows of chairs, facing the stage, and not a snooker table in sight.

'What's all this, sir? Is youth club cancelled tonight, or what?' A boy called from a huddle of teens by the door. They clearly didn't want to commit to coming further in until they knew what was lined up for them.

Chris's smile was a weak one. 'It's alright, guys, come in. The session's not cancelled, but we do need to talk to you about stuff that's going on first.'

The young people glanced at each other, still unsure.

'It'll only be a few minutes, then we'll get the tuck shop open.'

A Reason To Be

That seemed to do the trick, as they all piled in and sat down.

Daisy watched from the sidelines, her foot tapping a staccato rhythm.

Finn nudged her with his shoulder. 'Don't worry. You'll be fine.'

'What if they're not interested?' She fretted. She'd been tasked with presenting her idea for the mural, to drum up help with collecting supplies, and with the artwork itself. The need to inspire these youngsters weighed heavy on her shoulders, as she'd quickly realised the project was far too much for her to handle alone. 'What if they don't care if the club's shut down?'

'I think you might be surprised.'

The hall gradually filled, facial expressions ranging from intrigued to highly suspicious. Many paused in the doorway, but were encouraged by friends already seated.

Chris checked his watch, then moved to centre stage. 'Right, time's getting on, so let's make a start. I don't want to take up too much of your evening. We can fill in any latecomers after.'

The door banged open and a trio of girls tumbled through, breathless and laughing, but stopped abruptly as they realised they were centre of attention. 'Sorry, sir,' one said.

'Hi, girls. Come on in. Find a chair. There are spaces down here on the left.' He waved his hand and continued to address the crowd, while the girls scuttled around the back of the room to the spare seats. 'So, you're probably wondering what this is all about.' He took a deep breath. 'For those of you who don't already know, the place was vandalised on Friday night. You might have noticed the state of the front of the building on your way in. We've carried out emergency repairs, but there's still a great deal to do.'

'It wasn't any of us, sir.' A voice called out from the rear.

Chris stretched up to see past the sea of heads to the origins of the voice. 'No, I'm sure it wasn't. Anyway, the police are dealing with that – we have other things to worry about. The landlord, who kindly allows us to use the hall, was already under pressure from the neighbours, to kick us out. They're not keen on having a youth club in their street, what with the footfall and noise that goes with it, and, although he's resisted until now, this has been almost the last straw. However, he's offered us one final chance - one month to get all the work done, including making the front less of an eyesore.'

'Can he do that?' A girl from the second row piped up.

'I'm afraid he can and, to be honest, he's treated us more than fairly in the past. Now, we have to be fair with him too and try to live up to our responsibilities.' He paused to allow his words to sink in. 'But we do have a plan. Daisy...' He glanced in Daisy's direction and held out a hand inviting her to join him. 'Most of you have met Daisy here over the last few weeks, I'm sure. But anyway, Daisy has a plan. It's a challenging one though, and not something the four of us alone can achieve. I'll let her explain.'

Daisy joined Chris centre stage and looked out at all the young faces staring up at her, and her stomach clenched. She wasn't much older than them, why would they listen to her? She opened her mouth to speak but nothing came out.

'Go on, Daisy. Tell them.' Finn's words were whispered, but they cut through the discouraging voices in her head.

She coughed and tried again. 'Well, one of the problems is how shabby the front looks. Obviously, right now it's even worse than usual with the graffiti. Even after three coats of whitewash the spray paint shows through, and the neighbours don't like it, and who can blame them?'

All eyes were on her. 'So, I've suggested a mural, something fun and colourful, that won't be spoilt if the odd muddy football hits it. That's where you guys come in.' A low rumble started, but she raised her voice above it. 'I can do the more complicated bits myself, but I'll need materials and I'll need help, because it's going to involve a lot of time, effort and hard work.'

'We've got school and homework and stuff. My mum won't be happy when I've got exams coming up.' A girl Daisy didn't know gazed intensely up at her

'Yeah. Besides, why should we?' Another sullen looking boy muttered to his friend, next to him.

This was not what she wanted to hear. Frustration kicked in, but she tried not to let it show. 'I know everyone's busy, and has stuff of their own to do. I'm just saying that if you want the club to continue and feel strongly enough to get involved, now's your chance. I'm prepared to do my bit, but I can't do it on my own – it's as simple as that. This is your opportunity to stick your hand up and get involved with something worthwhile. It's completely up to you.'

A long, drawn out silence allowed Daisy's disappointment to bubble up into something else – anger, that after all Chris and Joanna's hard work to keep the club going, to give the kids somewhere to go, this was their response, how they showed their gratitude.

'Do you know what? I expected a bit more than this. I've only been helping out at the club for a couple of weeks, but even in that short time, I've seen how valuable it is for you guys. Without it, where would you go on a Tuesday night? The streets?' Her speech was met with silence and her heart sunk as she scanned the faces in the crowd, some familiar, others not so much. Her gaze fell on one she knew was a leader of his particular pack. 'What about you, Lewis? Where will you practice your pool skills?'

She saw his eyes narrow in thought and felt she'd hit home. Perhaps that was it, she needed to make this personal. She searched for another face. 'And Harley? Where are you and your mates going to practice your dance moves for TikTok?'

There were a few moments of loaded silence before a lone female called out from the middle of the room. 'Alright, miss. No need to get your knickers in a twist.' It was Harley. 'Nobody said we weren't gonna help, they just asked why we should. Now we know, so what do you want us to do?' The girl grinned.

Daisy's mouth dropped open and she could find no words.

Finn chuckled beside her. 'That's great, Harley. That's really great. This is what we need...'

They split the taskforce into four groups - one to search out materials, one to help with the labouring, one to promote their story on social media, and one to do the artwork itself. The teens were allowed to choose which they joined, according to what they considered their strengths to be. Daisy headed, up the arty team and was pleased to find herself surrounded by a small, but enthusiastic bunch, including Harley. Each group formed a huddle to discuss what they needed to do and the hall buzzed with excited voices, sharing ideas and talking over each other.

As the noise rose, Chris jumped back onto the stage and shouted for hush. It took a few moments before he got everyone's attention. 'Thank you. Thank you, everyone.' They turned to listen. 'I know it'll take more work and fine tuning, but I think we've got the bones of a plan, and we might actually be able to do this. The materials team...' He looked at the group huddled around Finn. 'You've got a really important job upfront, because the Easter holidays start next week and the artists need to start painting then if they stand any chance of finishing on time. Without supplies they'll have nothing to paint with. My group, labourers, I'm going to be working here every spare minute I've got to do the remaining repairs and get the wall back to a blank canvas. There'll be other work to do throughout, but this week is going to be busy. Joanna and media buffs, we need you to drum up interest, so that supplies don't dry up, and maybe we can get a few extra volunteers along the way too, if you spread the word. We want the whole neighbourhood to see the hard work going in to the project, and how important the club is to you all. And creatives, you've got this week to come up with the design for the mural and work out how you'll make it a reality.'

As he addressed each group the mumbling began again until, when he finished, the room was a cacophony of sound. He laughed at the enthusiasm of the response, shaking his head as he looked around and observed the hive of activity, before hurrying down the steps, back to his own huddle. Passing Finn and Daisy along the way, he leaned in and shouted, laughing. 'I think we've created a monster. I only hope we can keep it under control.'

CHAPTER 21

The response to the Youth Club's call to action was steady. During the day, a slow trickle of strangers dropped by, carrying part used pots of paint and tatty, but functional, equipment. The club leaders took turns meeting and greeting and accepting donations, stowing them in a corner of the pavilion selected for the purpose. Outside school hours, footfall picked up, with teenagers arriving with family members, unloading materials they'd collected from friends, neighbours and relations, then pulling up their sleeves to help out.

Chris allocated suitable roles to whoever turned up, and Daisy tried to organise the growing pile of DIY accoutrements into manageable order. Her team of volunteers had proven enthusiastic and willing to get stuck in, and had an abundance of ideas as to what the final design should be, but Daisy was far from decided. In fact, as the weekend approached, and she realised she only had a short time left before the creative work was to begin, the whole thing overwhelmed her.

Finn found her hiding behind a mound of paint pots, hugging her knees and biting her nails to the quick. 'I wondered where you'd disappeared. What are you doing here?'

She gave her nails a break and chewed on the inside of her cheek instead. 'Nothing much. Just working out if there's a difference between classic crème and mystic white.'

'And?'

'I couldn't honestly tell you.' Frowning deeply, she turned her gaze from the paint to Finn. 'Oh, Finn, what am I going to do?'

'Maybe take the pots outside where the light's better.'

'No,' she hissed. 'Not about the colours.' She stretched up to check no one was listening before hugging her knees with renewed fervour. 'I mean about the mural. I have no idea where to start, or what to start. What was I thinking getting involved in this?'

He smiled. 'You were thinking you wanted to do a very good thing, and you are doing. I've heard the ideas floating around and they all sound fantastic, so what's the problem?'

'The problem is that having ideas is one thing, but converting them into reality is another. Plus, everybody on my team wants something different and I don't know how to choose. I can't please everyone. How do I decide which idea to go with? One wrong move and I'll have a riot on my hands.' Her eyes grew wider with panic with every word.

Finn circuited the paint pots and sat next to her, leaning back against the wall, his shoulder nestled against hers. 'I don't know. I guess there are practical things to take into account, like the colours available, and the level of detail and time required? Bearing in mind there's only three weeks from Monday to get it finished.'

'Finn, I know you're trying to help, but I didn't need reminding about that right now.'

'Fair point, what about the fact we have about fifteen shades of off-white but only small amounts of other colours?'

Daisy huffed. 'I suppose it does rule out Aiden's idea for a scene from outer space and Jessica's giant sunflower heads, but, oh, I don't know. I can't think.' She shook her head.

'What you need is time away from the problem, so you can come back to it with a clear head.' He squeezed her arm in reassurance. 'Perhaps it's a good thing you've got the WI talk tonight. It'll take your mind off of things. Have you decided what you're doing yet?'

A slow smile spread across her face. 'Oh, yes, I was going to talk to you about that. You're still up for helping, aren't you?'

'I said I would, didn't I?'

'Good.....'

Harley's face appeared above the paint pot parapet. 'Hey, love birds. Chris wants you outside.'

Daisy and Finn glanced at each other, in surprise at the description, and scrambled away from each other.

'Right, I'd better go and see what Chris wants.' Finn backed away. 'I'll see you later at yours, help you get your stuff to the WI hall, shall I?'

'You're sure you're definitely coming, then?' Daisy tried to hide her embarrassment, making herself busy, straightening piles of brushes.

'I promised, didn't I?'

She nodded. 'That would be great then, thanks.'

'Do I need to bring anything?'

'Oh, no.' A smile reappeared back on her face, as she recalled what she had in mind for the session. 'Just bring yourself. I've got everything organised.'

Finn looked at her quizzically but she said no more. 'Ok, then. See you later.'

CHAPTER 21

Daisy's skin tingled with fear as she faced the room of women, staring back expectantly from their rows. One of the WI committee had welcomed them all and talked through some important notices and reminders about future events, then handed over to her. Daisy fiddled with her notes to buy time, surreptitiously checking around for a friendly face, anything to calm the nerves.

Morag smiled and winked encouragement from the end of the second row, but somehow it didn't help. Daisy spotted Lizzy in the seat next to Morag and inwardly huffed, but at least being annoyed with her mother made her forget how nervous she was for a minute. What was Lizzy doing here? She wasn't a member of the WI. Daisy wasn't even sure there was a WI in America.

Somebody coughed from the back of the room and Daisy became aware of time ticking on. She cleared her throat. 'He...hello. My name's Daisy...'

A couple of voices said hello back, which completely threw her off her stride. 'Yes, hello, hello.' She smiled in the general direction of the voices. 'Today, I'm going to talk to you about art, umm, mostly about drawing, or sketching, and things to think about if you want to improve your drawing, if that's something you're interested in. If not, then it's just a bit of fun really.'

'I thought we were having a chimney sweep this week.' An elderly lady called from the back.

Morag stood up and shouted back. 'He couldn't make it, Phyllis.'

The woman cupped her ear.

'He couldn't make it.' Morag spoke slowly and loudly. 'He's retired.'

'He's too tired? That's no excuse.'

'No, he's retired. Stopped working, Phyllis.'

'I haven't got any chimneys, anyway.'

Morag sat down and attention returned to Daisy.

'Sorry, I don't know anything about chimneys.' She chuckled. 'Except how to draw them.' There was no response, so she continued, waving behind her at two tables, each widely circled by chairs. 'If you'd all like to sit at one of the areas there, we'll all have a go at creating our own work of art.'

No one moved, so Daisy went first, waving at them to do the same. 'Follow me. Find a seat. There's a pencil, paper and a few other bits and bobs you might need on each one.'

As a murmur spread around the room, she removed a table cloth from a mound of fruit in the centre of the first table. Soon she could hear people moving. 'That's right. There's space for everyone.'

Chatter had started up about who wanted to sit at which display.

'What's on this one, Daisy? Just a chair?' Morag asked.

For the first time since she stood in front of the group, Daisy released a genuine grin. True, an empty chair sat on the floor in the midst of the second circle of chairs, but it was about to be filled. She strode across to a door, which led to the toilets, and leaned out of it. 'We're ready for you.'

The ladies watched, bemused.

'I've got a real challenge for this group, but don't worry, you can all swap seats halfway through. Group two are going to try some life drawing. Come in, Finn.' She chuckled. Having dropped her in it with Morag to lead the class, Daisy had no qualms about getting her own back and manipulating Finn into being model for the evening. She leaned out into the hallway, whispering. 'Come on. You promised you'd help.'

'Yes, but this wasn't what I had in mind.'

'I thought you were all for trying things outside your comfort zone.'

Finn's eyes narrowed at having his words thrown back at him and sidestepped into the room, clutching an oversized bathrobe around him, a pair of hairy shins poking out the bottom. A murmur started up as he circuited the perimeter of the room to reach his post.

Daisy bit back a chuckle as she watched.

'Don't be shy, lad. Come on in.' The shout from an onlooker did nothing to encourage him, and his grip tightened on the front of the robe. Daisy moved to join him and manoeuvred him through a gap in the tables to the seat in the centre. 'There you are. That's better.'

She stepped away to a space where she'd set up a whiteboard, and started to draw a grid of lines. 'For those of you who've never tried drawing before, it can be really helpful to make a grid like this. Then, you look at the object you want to draw through the transparent grids I've supplied you with. It can help you work out what needs to be where on the page and to keep perspective.' She gave them a swift demonstration. 'You see? But, of course, if you just want to keep it simple, you can do it freehand. Has everyone got what they need? '

Some had and some hadn't, and Daisy raced around the room to supply anything that was missing. Chatter started up as the ladies followed her instructions and she wandered between them, giving tips and general encouragement. Finn caught her eye and she crossed to where he was perched on the chair.

'Hang on, Finn. That's not what we discussed, is it?'

'I'm fine like this,' he growled.

'No, no. The robe is too bulky, too vague. We need to see your arms and legs properly, so we've got clean lines to draw.' She met his eye, a smile playing on her lips and leaned in close so only he could hear. 'Come on, you agreed.'

He scowled. 'It's chilly in here.'

'No, it's quite warm, and, besides, it won't take long.'

After a brief pause, Finn stood up and slipped his arms out of the robe, pulling it around so he was holding it in front of him.

'Shall I take that for you?'

'It's alright, I can hold it.'

Morag called out from the onlookers. 'Come on, lad. Let's be having you.'

Finn huffed, then handed the robe to Daisy and perched back on his chair.

She took it and turned away to place it on her own seat, his discomfort highly amusing to her in this moment of sweet revenge, but as she turned back, a whole different feeling raced through her. In her head, she had pictured a vision of sharp angles, all elbows and knees, but it turned out that Finn, bare-chested in his running shorts looked anything but awkward.

'Now then, Phyllis.' Morag nudged the woman next to her. 'I'll be needing the grid to keep his six-pack in perspective. Isn't that right, Daisy?'

Daisy's face flushed as she struggled to draw her eyes away from the breadth of his muscled shoulders.

The vicar's wife spoke up. 'Do you think he should lose the shorts as well?'

Finn recoiled in fear. 'No!'

Daisy snapped back to the room. 'Absolutely not. I think we've got quite enough to work with as it is.'

*

The ombudsman shook his head. 'That poor boy – like a lamb to the slaughter.'

Audrey peered closely at the scene. 'He's more man than boy from what I can see.'' She paused. 'Can we zoom in?'

'No, we can't.' He glared at her. 'You're as bad as the rest of them.'

She chuckled. 'He'll come to no harm with a group of old ladies.'

'I'm not worried about physical harm. But an experience like that could scar him for life.'

'It'll teach him to think twice before dropping my Daisy in it again, though, won't it?'

'But you must remember, Audrey, he was only acting for Daisy's good: trying to help her find her purpose. That's what all of this is about at the end of the day, and once he's achieved it, we can all move on.'

'That maybe so.' She sniffed. 'But I don't think she's going to find it in a damp village hall on a Friday evening, surrounded by geriatrics. Do you?'

'You're probably right, Audrey.' He sighed. 'You're probably right.'

CHAPTER 22

Daisy had expected some fallout from the WI meeting – Finn had put up with a lot since she'd known him, but it would take someone pretty special to be strong armed into getting his kit off and modelling for a roomful of senior citizens and not feel a little bit miffed about it. After getting dressed, he'd disappeared into the night, leaving her to wander home with Lizzy and Morag. Daisy guessed this was partly because he was annoyed with her, and partly to avoid an enthusiastic bunch of elderly groupies, who'd hovered around, hoping for another glimpse.

When she'd arrived at the pavilion the next day, Finn was already up a ladder, and managed only a grunt in greeting. By mid-morning, he was still keeping a wide-berth and, as much as she felt she'd been entitled to her moment of revenge, Daisy was beginning to feel bad about it. After all, he'd sat there, semi-naked, for an hour, as all those women ogled the breadth of his shoulders and his bare chest and those strong, rugged thighs. Daisy had been tempted to join in and sketch him herself.

'You alright, miss?' Harley interrupted Daisy's thoughts.

Daisy coughed as she realised the direction her imagination had taken her, and that she'd been staring, watching Finn work, and not doing anything herself. 'I'm fine, Harley. I was trying to picture the mural ideas up on the wall and wondering how best to do it.'

'That'll be why you're all red in the face and breathless then, miss.'

'Sorry, what?'

Harley grinned. 'Too much thinking. It's not good for you.'

'Right.' Daisy hid her embarrassment at the girl's comments by brushing herself down. 'I'm going inside for a drink. I'll only be a minute.'

'I'm thirsty too. I'll come with you.'

There was no getting away from her.

Daisy walked into the kitchen but Harley, knowing the drill, stayed on the other side of the hatch, leaning on her elbows as she watched Daisy through it.

'Orange squash?' Daisy asked.

'Please.'

'It's thirsty work all this DIY lark, isn't it?' Daisy figured if she wasn't going to escape the girl, she could at least change the subject.

'Yeah.' Harley agreed, accepting a tumbler from Daisy.

'Do you get roped in at home with this sort of thing?'

She shrugged. 'Nah. Mum's feller gets someone in if anything needs doing. He's loaded.'

Daisy chuckled at the girl's openness. 'Oh, right.'

'He always knows somebody who knows somebody, if you know what I mean. Mum says he's "well connected".' She sipped her drink. 'It's just as well, 'cos they'd fall out if they tried doing it themselves, like you and Finn.'

The first thing Daisy noticed was that Finn was honoured with the use of his first name, whereas she was still a formal "miss", despite having requested the use of her actual name on numerous occasions. The second thing was that Harley was referring to Daisy and Finn as a couple. Daisy wasn't sure how to address this but knew it had to be done, before the idea spread, if it hadn't already. 'I haven't fallen out with Finn.'

'No? Well, he's fallen out with you. He's been looking daggers at you all morning.'

Daisy batted it away. 'No, he hasn't. He probably got out the wrong side of the bed, that's all.'

'You should know.' Harley laughed.

Daisy gasped. 'Harley! It's not like that. We're just friends, you know.'

'Right, miss. If you say so.' Harley made a big show of winking at her, like it was a shared secret.

'No. Seriously, that's all.'

The girl shrugged. 'Maybe Lewis was right then, after all.'

'Lewis? What's Lewis been saying?'

'Lewis found a wallet on the path the other day and, when he looked inside, there was a picture of a hot girl with red hair. Then Finn came along and said it was his wallet. Thanked him for finding it. Lewis reckoned it was Finn's girlfriend, but I said no, because of you.'

Daisy's heart did a flip. Finn had a picture of a pretty red-head in his wallet? She realised she needed to say something to avoid appearing suspicious. 'What was Lewis doing going through the wallet?'

'To see who it belonged to, of course. Anyway, I reckon it was probably a picture of his Mum, so don't worry about it.' She replaced her empty tumbler in the hatch and went back outside.

Daisy watched her go, mulling over what Harley had said, until Chris called to her from the pile of donated materials.

'Daisy, can I get your take on this, please?'

Daisy strolled across the hall to him, half her attention still on Harley. 'What's up?'

Chris swept an arm around him indicating the paint supplies. 'This isn't working, is it? I mean, we have lots of paint, but it's all whites, creams and magnolias. I'm no expert but, can you create much with that?'

'I can give the pavilion a freshen up, but I haven't got the makings of a bright, colourful mural, no. There are small amounts of coloured paint but not enough. I haven't been able to choose a design yet because of the lack of colour. We've still got a couple days before I need to start though.' She shrugged.

Chris scratched his head. 'I love your optimism, but I'm worried. These odds and ends aren't going to be enough. We're going to need large quantities, maybe even a trade donation, which in the current financial climate is unlikely. Perhaps I should call the landlord and admit defeat, or at least beg for more time. He's a decent chap, he might come round.'

'Do you think it's that desperate? All we need is an extra flurry of donations.' She hated to consider failure, and the possible closure of the youth club.

'We need more of a tidal wave than a flurry. I can't see what else we can do? Who we could turn to?'

Daisy thought for a moment, and the conversation she'd had with Harley sprang to mind. 'What we need is somebody who is well connected, who could put us in touch with the right sort of people who could help.'

'Well, that goes without saying.'

A smile lit up Daisy's face. 'I've got an idea. I'll get back to you.' She marched away and out of the door to where Harley was sanding a wooden window frame with one hand while scrolling on her phone with the other. 'Harley, you know you said your mum's partner has connections?'

'Yeah? We can't leave the house without somebody stopping him to chat.' She rolled her eyes.

'I don't suppose he knows anyone in the DIY trade who might donate some paint – that isn't off-white?'

'I don't know.' Harley shrugged.

Daisy's shoulders slumped.

'I could call him, if you like?'

Daisy perked up again. 'Would you?'

'Sure.' She laid the sandpaper down, selected a contact from her phone, and put it to her ear. 'Especially seeing as you're having such a bad day, what with falling out with Finn and all.' She grinned and backed away as the phone was answered, denying Daisy the chance to set her straight about the Finn situation.

It seemed like an age, before Harley finished her call and turned back to Daisy.

'Well? Did he have any ideas?'

Harley picked up her sandpaper and returned her attention to the window frame. 'He's gonna make some calls and get back to me.'

'That's great.'

'Yeah. He's picking me up later for a "nice family meal, where I don't give my mum any of my usual cheek".' She shook her head, sanding with renewed vigour. 'Whatever that's supposed to mean.'

Daisy smiled. 'I can't imagine.'

Daisy waited on tenterhooks for Harley's mother and her "feller" to arrive, every finger and toe crossed that he would bring good news. Chris passed by as the well-dressed couple strolled up the path, and greeted them, not knowing Daisy was pinning her hope on the man, and a conversation was had. Daisy strained to hear, but couldn't catch what was being said. Instead, she had to rely on body language and facial expressions from Chris, the only one of the group in her line of sight.

He began passive but welcoming, then slightly surprised, and she guessed he was being told about the call for help. His shoulders lifted as if a weight had been removed and she felt sure positive news had been imparted, but then, the same shoulders slumped and Daisy's hope was dashed. But it wasn't over – Chris's head tipped to one side, listening carefully. Finn, who'd been up a ladder behind the couple, climbed down, and was called in to the discussion. He rubbed his chin, nodding. How she wished she could hear what was being said.

Chris leaned back and looked in her direction. Louder. 'Daisy?' He beckoned to her. 'Can we borrow you a minute?'

Was she in trouble for asking the parents for help? She put down her utensils and joined the group. 'Hi. What's up?'

A Reason To Be

'Apparently, Harley asked Joel here for some help finding supplies or suppliers, and I understand that was down to you?'

'Well, Harley was saying how well connected he... you were.' She wasn't sure who to direct the response to, but eventually settled on the man identified as Joel. 'I'm sorry if that's not ok. I didn't mean to cause stress to anyone or...'

Christ interrupted her apology. 'No. Joel isn't here to complain. But he doesn't have any contacts in the DIY trade unfortunately.'

Daisy was disappointed but rushed to play it down, already feeling awkward about drawing the man into their problems. 'Oh, well. Never mind. It was worth a shot.'

Chris gripped her shoulder to stop her talking. 'But he does have are contacts on the local news program.'

'Oh!'

'And he's got us a slot on Sunday's teatime show. They want someone from the project to go and explain what's happening and make an appeal. We think you'd be the best person for the job.'

'What? Me? But you guys run the youth club. Shouldn't you be the faces of the project?'

'Umm.' Chris considered this. Joanna elbowed him. 'Ah. Yes. No, we can't. We've got to visit Joanna's parents up north. It's her mother's birthday and we've been promising to go for weeks. It's an all day job, I'm afraid. No way we could be back by teatime. But how about you and Finn go? Finn knows the history of the youth club and you know what's needed for the mural. Ideal.'

Joel held his arms out, palms up, like it was the perfect answer. 'Nothing makes better telly than a good looking couple with a sob story. My mate'll be over the moon.'

'We're not a couple.' Both Daisy and Finn replied at once, then stared at each other, taken back by the coincidence.

Joel raised his eyebrows to Chris and pointed from Daisy to Finn and back again. 'I'll Whatsapp the details to you, mate, but you'll need to sort this pair out, make sure they're on the same page.

Remember guys, teamwork makes the dream work.' He slipped his arm around Harley's mum and walked away, Harley trailing behind.

A serious Chris turned to Daisy and Finn. 'Is everything alright? Are you ok with this?'

The pair looked at each other and Daisy saw Finn's shoulders relax. 'Of course we are,' he said.

'Good,' said Chris. 'Because this could be our only chance of making the project work.'

*

'Daisy seems to be finding her feet, doesn't she? Dealing with problems, coming up with solutions?' The ombudsman checked his watch, then side-eyed Audrey, trying to read her response. 'Are you starting to feel more confident about her future? She certainly seems to have found a new sense of purpose.'

Audrey glared at him. 'I know your game. You want to move me on. You're like one of those traffic wardens hovering around when my ticket's about to run out. Well, I'll have you know, I'm going nowhere. That girl's not dealing with anything. She's a headless chicken that's been lucky enough to run in a straight line for a minute or two, that's all. She's no direction and no plan, and if this mural idea falls flat, so will my Daisy. And I dread to think how she'll cope if that Finn let's her down. So, no, I'm no more confident about her future than the first moment I arrived here.' She punctuated her speech with an emphatic nod. 'Put that in your pipe and smoke it!'

The ombudsman stared at Audrey, waiting to be sure she'd finished, then gulped in relief when he realised she had. 'I'm sorry I asked.' He nodded at the screen. 'Back to it then, yes?'

'I think that's a very good idea,' Audrey's tone was firm. 'Don't you?'

He didn't dare disagree. 'I wouldn't have it any other way.'

CHAPTER 23

As the evening drew in, the helpers gradually drifted away, until only a few stalwarts remained. The atmosphere between Daisy and Finn still hadn't cleared and, considering the task set before them, to represent the youth club together on television, Daisy felt she must put things right, sooner rather than later.

She hovered around, waiting for a good moment to catch him on his own. At last, Chris and Joanna went inside to pack away, and Daisy saw her chance. 'Finn, can I talk to you, please?'

He was up a ladder, fixing a loose piece of guttering in place, and didn't even look at her. 'I'm in the middle of something, right now.'

'Ok, I'll wait.' She figured he couldn't stay up there much longer – it was getting dark, but, after a couple of minutes of silence, she began to fear the others would reappear before she had a chance to say what she needed to say. 'It's quite important,' she urged.

'So's this.' His tone was brusque.

She tutted. 'Am I going to have to come up there?' As the words left her mouth, she recognised them as something her gran had uttered on many an occasion, when Daisy refused to come out of her room to face the music for some misdemeanour or other, and her heart clenched at the memory.

He stopped what he was doing to scowl at her. 'You would too.' He begrudgingly stepped down to her level. 'What's so urgent it can't wait five minutes?'

'Humble pie,' she said, with a grimace.

'What?'

'Humble pie. Gran used to say it tasted vile in the eating but left a much more pleasant aftertaste.'

He shook his head. 'I don't know what you're on about.'

She bit her bottom lip. 'I don't find apologies easy, but I owe you one after last night and I'm sorry. Making you pose for the WI started as a joke, you know, payback for dropping me in it with them, but it went too far.'

'You're telling *me*.' He rolled his eyes.

'I know, and I'm sorry if you were embarrassed…'

'Embarrassed? I was lucky to get out of there in one piece. A couple of those old ladies were scary.'

'I know, especially the vicar's wife. Who would have thought?' She bit her lips together to stop a smile at the memory, not sure he was ready to see the funny side. 'Anyway, I mean it. I'm really sorry and I promise never to do anything like it again.'

'Hmm.' His frown held firm. 'You know I only volunteered you for the WI thing with good intentions. I thought it would help you with the whole sense of purpose thing, you know?'

'I know, though I don't know where you thought I was going to find a sense of purpose in a room full of rampant geriatrics.'

'They weren't all geriatrics.'

'But they definitely were rampant.' She paused. 'Come on, Finn. You've been so good to me since Gran died, a really great friend and I'd hate to think I'd stuffed that up.' Her smile evaporated and the heartfelt words brought a tell-tale glisten to her eyes.

He sighed. 'Now, stop that. That's not fair. I'm justifiably cross. You're not allowed to make me feel bad about it by crying.'

'What? I'm not crying. What are you talking about?' She shook her head and slyly wiped a stray tear away. 'But can we clear the air? I hate that I've upset you. Say you'll forgive me.'

'Alright. I forgive you. There's no need to make a big thing about it.'

'Thank you!' She threw her arms around him and hugged him, then hurriedly backed off when she realised what she'd done, trying to ignore the surprised look on his face. 'I hate atmospheres, that's all.'

He laughed out loud.

'What?'

'You? Hate atmospheres?' His eyebrows were raised in amazement. 'You're usually the one who creates them. Look at you and your Mum.'

'That's completely different.'

'No, it isn't.' He turned away and started to fold up the ladders, proving that the important work he'd been doing previously wasn't as urgent as he'd made out. 'If you expect me to forgive you for… for… throwing me to the wolves last night, then I think you should take a leaf out of your own book. Go home and sort things out with Lizzy.'

She followed him as he carried everything inside, scooping up a dust sheet to make herself useful. 'Ok. Well, I'll think about it, at least. Do you want to go get some chips? My treat this time.'

He retrieved his jacket from the cupboard and pulled it on then paused to look her straight in the eye, letting her know she was not getting off the hook that easily. 'No, thanks. I'm going home for a bath and an early night, as I've a shift tomorrow. Let me know how you get on with Lizzy.' He smiled. 'You can tell me all about it on Sunday on the way to the studio.'

'But…' She gaped at his forcing her arm.

'Night.' He turned at the door, and called over his shoulder. 'And good luck with your mum.'

CHAPTER 24

Daisy dawdled on the way home, stopping for chips and sitting on a wall to eat them, rather than rush back. She was awash with emotions: annoyance at Finn for strong-arming her into talking to her mother, but also feeling obliged, after all, he had forgiven her, and she did value his opinion. There was a mix of anger and confusion at her mother's behaviour too, and the news she'd been back in the Country and not contacted her or Gran, at a time when her presence could have made a real difference. Daisy didn't want to talk to Lizzy, but she did want answers from her. Perhaps Finn was right, and she should open the door to communication with her mother, even if it was hard.

When Daisy walked into the house, Lizzy was sitting cross-legged in the middle of the room on a gym mat, a glass of wine placed strategically out of reach on one side and an open share-bag of crisps on the other.

'What are you doing?' Daisy asked.

Lizzy smiled. 'I'm off-setting indulgent treats with well-being and health promoting activity.'

'You're what?'

Lizzy sighed. 'Doing yoga in front of the TV. It makes me feel better about filling my body with crap. I saw an article about it in a magazine and thought it was worth a try.'

Daisy rolled her eyes. 'Whatever.' Then walked into the kitchen in search of snacks, but the Tupperware box her gran had kept for the purpose was empty, except for a soft custard cream and a chocolate bar wrapper. She would have been in trouble for that in the past. *Sorry, Gran, guilty as charged*, she thought, snatching the wrapper out and putting it in the bin. 'There's never anything to eat in this house anymore,' she muttered.

Lizzy spoke from the doorway, having followed her from the lounge. 'We need to do a big shop. I'll get onto it in the morning.'

'That doesn't help me tonight,' she grumbled.

'You're welcome to share my crisps. I've had more than I should already.'

'No, thanks.' Daisy was more fretful than hungry, having downed chips and a fishcake on the way home. She hovered in the kitchen, still conflicted on having a proper conversation with her mum. They'd been living alongside each other like virtual strangers for a fortnight. How did you go from that to a full-on heart to heart in one move? She poured a glass of water, buying time, waiting for inspiration, something to get the ball rolling.

'No Finn tonight, then?'

'No, not tonight.' After today, the one thing she definitely didn't want to talk about was Finn.

'I wondered if he might come back with you as it was such a late one. I thought maybe he'd like to join us for Easter Sunday lunch, I mean, unless he's spending it with family. Is he? I mean, I've never heard him mention anyone, but obviously I've not spent that much time with him, so I guess you're more likely to know than I am…'

Lizzy rattled on while Daisy tried to ignore her, sipping her water, but the talk of Finn still somehow filtered through. It occurred to her that she didn't know if he had family or, in fact, anything about him. It disturbed her that this handsome, young guy she'd allowed into her life at such a difficult time, who made her laugh when she was down, who'd made her cry today at the thought of losing him, was to all intents and purposes a stranger. She thought of the news stories about people being scammed on social media, by people they thought of as friends, but were actually con-artists, creating false personas, building whole fake lives for weeks, months, years even, playing the long game to get what they were really after. But then she thought about how his smile lit up his whole face when she said something that struck him funny. She thought about the breadth of his shoulders when he took his top off for the art class, and how it felt to hug him this afternoon; how it would have felt if he'd hugged her too. Oh no, she was not going there.

Heat rising to her face brought her back to the reality of her mother, spouting inane chatter to fill the awkwardness between them, and she flipped out. 'What are you still doing here? You don't live here, so why don't you go back to the US and leave me alone?'

There was a long drawn out silence as Lizzy absorbed this sudden and unexpected attack. Daisy could almost hear her mother's heart breaking. 'Actually, I do live here now.' Lizzy was looking anywhere but at Daisy. 'And I haven't lived in the US for almost a year.'

'What?' Daisy couldn't comprehend what she was hearing.

Lizzy shrugged.

'What?'

'I didn't know how to tell you.'

'You didn't know…' Daisy shook her head in disbelief. 'What the hell?'

Lizzy breathed deeply, as if steeling herself for what was to come, her face pale, her hands trembling. 'My contract… ended. My relationship had ended. I had nothing left there, so I came home, or as close to home as I had the courage to come.'

There was a pause, and Daisy guessed Lizzy was waiting for her to say something, but she had nothing to say.

'When it all imploded, I got the first flight back to London, but when I landed I didn't know what to do. England was home, but not home anymore. I suppose I'd been heading here, but as I got closer, I just couldn't do it.'

A Reason To Be

Daisy stared at her mother, gripping the edge of the worktop, because if she loosened her grasp she was afraid she might fall over.

'I suppose I didn't feel there was a place for me here. There was no room for me.'

Daisy still couldn't speak.

'I know what you guys thought of me. When I came to stay, I could see the looks passing between you. I was the extra cog in the wheel, which interfered with the smooth running of the household. And, on top of that, I had to come back and tell you I'd failed.' She huffed and shrugged again, finally cleansing herself of the secret she'd been keeping. 'I didn't know how to tell you I'd cocked everything up, and I knew I'd be in the way, so I stayed in the city. To start with it was only going to be for a few days, until I got my head together, but I guess I never did, quite, get my head in the right place.'

'I can't believe you.' Daisy had the strange feeling she and her gran were somehow getting the blame for Lizzy's behaviour, and she wasn't about to accept it. 'You're not serious.'

Lizzy looked ashamed. 'I was hiding. I can't deny it. I couldn't face you, or Mum. I couldn't bear to tell you I'd failed, knowing how you'd look at me. My career was the only thing I'd done right since the day you were born and now I couldn't even do that right. Whereas here, everything just fitted together perfectly. Audrey was the proper stay at home, constantly organised parent you'd always longed for. And you were the clever, creative, sweet little child that she'd always wanted me to be. And me, I was a square peg that didn't fit anywhere, let alone in this household.'

'That's a big pile of crap and you know it. You're making excuses for your own selfish choices. You chose the high flying international career; you chose to park me here with Gran, and you chose to move thousands of miles away, abandoning me, abandoning Gran, so you could live the high life, without any awkward baggage holding you back. It had nothing to do with you not fitting in.'

'It was never as simple as that,' Lizzy begged for Daisy's understanding. 'I admit I was selfish at times. I did want to be a young woman with a freedom which wasn't available to me as a young mum. I'm sure a lot of young mothers feel like that from time to time. But, it was more than that. I needed to prove something to my own mother because I'd let her down. She brought me up to be strong and independent, to take on the world. She told me I could be so much more than she'd been, I could have a career, a family, when the time was right, I could have it all. Then I let her down, by getting pregnant with no man to support me, and quitting college. So then I had to rebuild and show her, that although I'd made mistakes, I could still be what she had intended me to be. I had to be more than she intended, do better, so I did all the hours. I went to all the conferences to rub shoulders with the people who mattered, I kissed all the arses which needed kissing to get on, I moved to wherever the promotions needed me to be, but it still wasn't enough.'

'It wasn't like that. She wasn't like that.'

'If I put everything into my career, I was neglecting you. If I stepped back to spend more time at home, I wasn't setting a good example to you. I couldn't win. And, before I knew it, you'd grown away from me and you didn't need me anymore, because you had her. Whenever I came back, I was in the way, which wasn't good for you, for her or for me.' She closed her eyes, breathing slowly, the purge over. 'So, I stayed away.'

They stared at each other for a long while, letting the air settle around them. Then, Daisy leaned forward until her eyes were only inches from her mother's, ensuring she could look nowhere else, would take in every syllable of what she had to say. 'Poor you. I feel sorry for you.' She stepped back and chuckled. 'Oh, no, wait a minute. I don't. Because none of that is true. It's just excuse, after excuse, after excuse, and you're never to blame.'

Daisy pushed past her mother to stomp out of the kitchen, across the lounge to the stairs, where she paused to throw over her shoulder. 'I'm done with you. If I wasn't before, I am now.

Completely and utterly done!' Then she ran upstairs to her room, slammed the door and threw herself face down onto the bed.

So much for Finn's wisdom. She'd set him straight when she saw him.

*

'My girls! They need their heads banging together, they really do.' Audrey turned to the ombudsman. 'Fancy Lizzy being back in England and not telling us. I'm not surprised Daisy's upset, but talking to her mother like that... She wouldn't have done it when I was alive. I feel so helpless up here. I wish I could go down and give'em what for.'

The ombudsman tipped his head to one side in sympathy. 'I'm sure you do, Audrey, but it's impossible. You do understand that, don't you?'

'Yes. I know. But I feel like I've let them down. I should be there or, more to the point, I shouldn't have let it get to this. How could I not know what my own daughter was up to? I should have known.' Audrey shook her head. 'I should have made it my business to know. Then it would never have come to this.'

'Oh, Audrey, hindsight is a cruel judge. You couldn't control everything. You were only human, after all, and you had quite a lot on your plate towards the end.'

'Well, I appreciate your efforts to try and make me feel better, but when I've made a mistake I'm the first to admit it. I can't deny I've made mistakes with those girls and if I had my time again I'd do things differently, I don't mind telling you.'

He nodded sagely. 'I understand that and applaud your honesty, but although you're no longer with them, you may still have some influence. Remember, they both grew up around you, and learnt a great deal from you and, from what I can tell, set great store in what you had to say. I'd be surprised if your opinion on recent events didn't trickle into their thoughts once they've had time to cool down.'

Audrey thought about this for a moment, then beamed a smile at him. 'You're alright, you are. Do you know that?'

The ombudsman pursed his lips at the compliment and returned his attention to the footage. 'I do my best, Audrey. I do my best.'

CHAPTER 25

Daisy took so long deciding what to wear for her TV appearance that she was still finishing getting ready when the doorbell rang to announce Finn's arrival. She quickly opened her bedroom window to let him know she was on her way, but Lizzy was already opening the front door. Daisy groaned in frustration and slammed the window closed. Of course her mother would be right there, probably sharing her sob story, getting him on side. She grabbed her belongings and ran down the stairs to extricate herself and Finn from Lizzy's clutches as quickly as possible. She'd managed to avoid being in the same room with her for the last twenty four hours and had no intention of sharing the same air with her for a moment longer than necessary now.

She arrived in time to hear Lizzy inviting him to Easter lunch "if his family could spare him" and Finn replying he had no other plans. Daisy stalked straight out of the house, grabbing Finn's sleeve and pulling him after her. She turned long enough to yell, 'You're unbelievable, you are,' then switched all her attention to the route in front of her.

'What was all that about?' Finn asked, trotting to keep up. 'Or shouldn't I ask?'

'No, you shouldn't. Let's just say your idea of opening lines of communication with that woman was a huge mistake, and I won't be making it again anytime soon.'

'I guess Easter lunch is off the cards then?'

She glared at him. 'Let's get to where we're going, yes?'

'Absolutely.' He held his hands up in submission. 'The three o'clock bus to the town centre gets us a five minute walk away, with twenty five minutes to spare.'

'Great. Then let's do this.'

They spent the journey going over what needed to be said about the youth club and the project. Chris had provided Finn with some key phrases he could use and facts about the set up, and Finn rehearsed them on Daisy to make sure he had them down pat. Daisy was to handle questions about the project itself and assured Finn that she didn't need to practice, and would play it by ear, to ensure she sounded as natural as possible.

It was all going swimmingly until they hit traffic, the bus coming to a standstill and their twenty five minute contingency almost disappeared. When they finally approached their destination, they both stood, clinging to a pole, desperate for the doors to slide open, way before the bus rolled to a stop. Finn constantly checked and rechecked his watch.

'How long have we got?'

He checked again. 'Eight minutes and counting. We're going to have to go like the clappers. Are you up to running?'

'Who, me?' Daisy shrugged, determined to stay cool, calm and collected for the interview. 'I was born running.'

The bus pulled up.

'No, you were born unable to walk, let alone run, like the rest of us.' His voice raised over the squeak of the brakes. 'Can you run?'

'Yes, I can run.'

'Good. In that case, I'm going for it. Follow me and try to keep up.'

'Not a problem,' she shouted back. As the door opened, Finn was off like a greyhound, but Daisy got stuck behind a passenger trying to get on with a shopping trolley and had to leap over to get out. Panic kicked in, but then she spotted Finn, who'd paused down the street to look for her and was waving her on.

'Come on.'

'I'm coming. I'm coming.'

They arrived at the studio, red, breathless and flustered. An assistant was waiting for them by reception, shuffling foot to foot and rubbing his hands together as he waited for them to be issued passes.

'Come along. Come along. You're cutting it fine,' he urged. 'It'll be straight through to the studio, no time for hair or make up.' He led them into a lift and pressed the appropriate button. Glancing over his shoulder at the pair behind him, he winced. 'I'll make sure someone's on hand with a comb though. We might only be regional, but we have standards.'

Daisy's mouth dropped open at his bluntness and she looked at Finn who simply grimaced and shrugged. Now was not the time to complain, when they'd arrived late and dishevelled for what amounted to free promotion.

The doors opened and they were ushered out. The assistant paused to speak to a young female receptionist as they passed her desk. 'Can you get Trudy to studio three for a quick damage control exercise? And tell her, I mean quick.' He took a step forward, then stopped again. 'How's Craig? Do I need my flak jacket?'

The receptionist was already dialling and had no time to reply before double doors swung open and a smartly dressed, middle aged man with silver fox hair emerged. He glared at the assistant.

'Ah, Craig. This is the couple for the youth club mural segment,' the assistant explained.

The older man's face transformed into a charming smile as he turned to them. 'Lovely, lovely people. Great to meet you. Would have been even greater five minutes ago so we had a chance to prep.' He glared again at the assistant, before slipping an arm each around Finn and Daisy's shoulders and leading them back the way he'd come. 'But these things happen and we're professionals and can cope with tiny schedule changes. We're nothing if not adaptable, but thank goodness for pre-records on the wonders of nature, that's what I say. It's not the first time three minutes of waffle about the preservation of bat habitats has saved the day and I daresay it won't be the last.'

He led them to a bright blue straight backed sofa and gestured for them to sit, while he settled in a bright pink chair of a similar style a short distance away. A glamorous blond woman appeared and began to brush Daisy's hair with viciously efficient strokes.

'Ah, Trudy, my love. A life saver as always.'

Finn chuckled at Daisy's dismay at being manhandled, until the same woman abandoned Daisy's hair and padded Finn's nose with powder instead.

Someone shouted, 'forty five seconds,' and Craig leaned forward, referring to typed notes.

'Time's short so we'll keep this simple. Finlay is it?'

'Just Finn,' Finn said.

'Ok, just Finn it is. I'll do an intro to the topic, then introduce yourself and Daisy. He took a moment to smile at her alone. 'Then, I'll direct a couple of questions to you, followed by a couple more to you, Daisy. Keep the answers to the point – nobody wants a monologue, and please wait your turn. We don't talk over each other. All clear?'

Someone started counting down from ten and Craig gave all his attention to a camera with a light on top.

'Wasn't that fascinating? Who knew that bats were such interesting creatures?' His face was plastered with a syrupy smile. 'Now, to local news and an ambitious project being undertaken by a youth group, to get their building back into a usable state, after a terrible attack of vandalism left it unfit for purpose. But, this inspiring group of teenagers are not taking the attack lying down.

No, they're fighting back and, rather than merely fixing the damage, they're making it into a work of art. Here to tell us all about it are youth leaders Finn and Daisy.'

Craig turned to Finn, the smile replaced with a deep, concerned frown. 'Finn, tell us about the attack. It must have been very traumatic.'

Finn described what had happened and explained more about the history and function of the club.

'So, what is it you're planning to do to prevent the loss of such a vital resource to the area?'

'Well, Daisy came up with a great idea. Didn't you, Daisy?'

Craig turned his attention to her. 'Tell me, Daisy. What was your idea?'

Daisy opened her mouth to speak but, as she glanced at the camera, the knowledge that she was being watched by thousands of people popped into her head, and everything stopped. She couldn't remember the question, she couldn't think, let alone speak.

Craig waited, his eyebrows gradually rising skyward as the silence grew, Daisy's mouth opening and closing like a goldfish, but nothing coming out.

'There is a plan, isn't there?' He prompted.

Daisy, unable to string two words together, squeezed Finn's knee in a silent plea for rescue.

'Yes, there's a plan,' Finn piped up, and the growing look of horror on Craig's face ebbed away. 'Daisy's been helping out at the club for a while, sharing her art skills, and she came up with the idea that rather than repainting the building white, and making it a blank canvas for graffiti, she would cover the entire front of the pavilion with a mural.'

'A mural? How interesting. But creating a piece of art of that size will be challenging, surely? How on earth are you going to achieve that?'

Daisy's mouth opened and closed again, with the same result.

Finn chipped in. 'It is a huge challenge, especially as it's all going to be planned and created by Daisy and a few of the teenagers from the club, relying on donations of paint and equipment from the public. And it has to be finished in three weeks, or we'll have to vacate the premises.'

'Three weeks? My goodness! Is that even possible?' His shocked and dubious gaze fell briefly on Daisy, as if he was doubtful her creative skills were any better than her interview technique.

'It has to be, or the youth club loses the premises and has to find a new base, or cease to exist,' Finn explained.

Craig's face became very grave, his tone serious. 'And what a dreadful loss that would be to the community – all those teens with nowhere to go but the streets. Is there anything the public can do to help?'

At last, they'd reached the whole point of their appearance. Daisy was determined to pull it back and actually say something, and concentrated all her efforts into finally making a sound, but all that came out was a squeaky, 'Paint!'

Craig's head shot back in shock. 'Sorry?'

Finn jumped in. 'We need more exterior paint, Craig. We're hoping the public will kindly donate any leftovers they have, particularly bright colours, as we already have lots of neutral colours, so the mural can be as vibrant and interesting as possible, something that anyone who passes by can enjoy.'

'Well, I'm sure that lots of our viewers will want to get involved with such a worthy cause. Where should they take their leftover paint, Finn?'

Finn gave the details, then Craig wound up. 'I wish you all the best with the project, and perhaps we could talk again when the mural is finished, to show our viewers what's been achieved with their generous donations. Will you come back, Finn? Daisy?'

They both nodded.

'Oh, and Daisy. I forgot to ask. What's the mural going to be of?'

A Reason To Be

Daisy had lost all hope of ever speaking again. She looked at Craig, smiled weakly and gave an exuberant Gaelic shrug.

Finn saved the day again. 'It's a surprise, Craig. All will be revealed in three weeks.'

'Well, we'll look forward to that, then.' He changed the topic, the camera moved in to cover Craig alone, and the assistant reappeared, removing their microphones and waving them out of the studio.

The assistant looked at Finn. 'And the gold star goes to you. Well done for keeping that interview afloat.' He turned a sympathetic gaze to Daisy. 'Never mind, it happens.' He stepped back and looked at his watch. 'Anyway, just hang on a couple of minutes. Craig will want to have a couple of words before you go, while the next segment's running.'

The door swung open and the man himself appeared. 'Thanks, guys. That was great. I hope you get what you need from our viewers, and I meant what I said, it would be marvellous to do a follow up piece once the mural's complete.' His attention flicked to the assistant and he pointed to Finn and Daisy, and the assistant, and back again. 'Can we schedule that in now? Can we?'

The assistant nodded enthusiastically. 'Yes, Craig, I'll see to it, right now.'

'Good, good.' He shook hands with both Daisy and Finn and made to leave, but turned back briefly. 'Oh, and you will be coming, won't you?' His attention was all on Finn.

'Yes, I'm sure I'll be able to make it.'

Craig breathed a sigh of relief. 'Good.' He stared at the assistant and pointed at Finn again. 'Make it happen.'

'I will. I will.'

The assistant herded them away, but behind them they heard Craig talking to himself. 'Such a lovely couple.'

Daisy's ability to speak clicked back into place and she called over her shoulder, 'Thanks, Craig, but we're not a couple.'

Craig stared at her, then pushed through the doors back into the studio, shaking his head. 'Now, she speaks,' he muttered.

Outside, the pair looked at each other and Finn chuckled. 'What happened?'

Daisy cupped her face in her hands and shook her head, unable to believe what she'd done. 'You're my absolute hero, Finn. Do you know that? My absolute hero.'

CHAPTER 26

Daisy slept poorly, waking several times in the night, her stomach clenching as she dreamt herself back in the studio hot seat, her lips mystically sealed together, leaving her unable to scream for help.

She and Finn had had a debrief on the bus ride home – in other words, he'd had a good laugh at her expense, in between bouts of commiseration – but it was cut short as he was working an early shift at the hospice the following day and had to decline her offer of coming in for a cup of tea. It was probably just as well, as it wasn't a pleasant place to be right now for anyone. Morag had popped around in the evening, full of excitement over seeing Daisy on the television, but had soon left again, with a tut, and an 'Audrey would have had a wee thing or two to say about this carry on. She would have banged your heads together, so she would'.

Daisy's mind swam with worry about what she was going to do about the mural when she set off for the pavilion the next morning. She had nowhere near enough paint, or time, or even the slightest idea of what the design would be. This is what came from looking for a purpose, a reason to be, she fretted, nothing but stress. Inwardly, she had come round to the idea that although that secret childhood event had been momentous, there was a possibility of more good things in the future which, even if they didn't live up to what had gone before, would still be worth hanging around for. She hadn't admitted as much to Finn, because she was afraid he might feel his work was done and withdraw from her life, and she realised that returning to her comfort zone would no longer be as comfortable without him featuring in it.

As she turned into the path to the front door of the pavilion, a man in a suit, a beige Mac flapping behind him in his hurry, brushed past her in the other direction. He did a double-take and greeted her with a 'Good morning, Daisy', before striding away. She politely returned his greeting, but frowned in confusion as she didn't recognise him, though he clearly knew her.

As she pushed past the door, she was halted again by a couple laughing and chattering as, again they greeted her. She nodded and smiled, but was even more puzzled. Turning back into the hall, she pulled up short. It was half-filled with a crowd of people.

Chris stood on tip-toe on the far side hollering over the noise. 'If you've brought paint, please take it to the stage area. Thank you.' He waved in the right direction. 'Anything else, brushes or equipment or cloths to Joanna, at the other end. You're all so kind. We're very grateful.'

He spotted Daisy, open-mouthed in the doorway. 'Ah, here she is - our hero artist.'

A spontaneous round of applause broke out and Daisy blushed and smiled, but otherwise didn't know how to respond.

Chris made eye-contact with her through the hubbub and spread his arms wide to take in the whole room. 'Look at this. See how much people care.'

Daisy was dumb-struck as people pushed past in both directions, wishing her luck and congratulating her.

A woman she recognised, a mother of one of the regular teenagers, grabbed Daisy's hand. 'Thank you so much for what you're doing for our children. You don't know how grateful we are. It means so much.' She made as if to leave, but paused. 'Oh, and we can't wait to see the end result.' She shivered with excitement. 'It'll be totally amazing. I know it.'

A Reason To Be

The woman moved on and Daisy felt her chest grow tight as her anxiety bloomed under the weight of everyone's expectations, and she suddenly wished the ground would swallow her whole.

'Oh, Gran,' she whispered, so only she could hear. 'What have I done?'

Only when the crowds diminished as people left to get on with their days, did Chris have the chance to explain. 'I thought I'd get in early, in case your interview prompted a response. I didn't want loads of paint left out front to give passing vandals ideas, but when I got here there was already a pile, and a queue forming. I didn't catch the recording because we can't pick up this region's programmes where Joanna's parents live, but whatever you said must have really struck a chord.'

Daisy felt her cheeks glowing. 'I honestly don't think it was anything I said.'

'Oh, you're too modest.' He waved her protests away, his concentration on the stage, lined end to end with paint pots, chuckling and shaking his head in disbelief. 'So much. So many colours.'

Another couple walked in with boxes full of pots and Chris turned to them. 'Come on in. Yes, anywhere there's room. Bless you. Thanks. You're so kind.'

Daisy watched as he organised everyone and everything around her, unable to think of anything but the immense thud, thud of blood pounding in her ears, sure her heart would stop at any moment from sheer panic at the situation.

Chris glanced at her and his tone became very serious. 'Daisy? Daisy, are you alright?'

The thunderous heartbeat drowned out all other sound and Daisy found she was unable to move except for her hands, clenching and unclenching with the speeding rhythm.

Chris stepped forward and placed a hand on her shoulder. 'Daisy, what is it? What's the matter?'

His touch broke through the mental cocoon she was trying to wrap around herself and she looked at him in terror. 'It's real,' she said. 'This is actually happening.'

Twenty minutes and a hideously sweet tea later, Daisy found herself shut away in the kitchen, the hatch firmly closed against intruders. She sat on a stool, grasping the now empty mug like a life belt. Chris and Joanna were facing her, leaning down to her level.

'Is that better?' Joanna's brow was furrowed. 'Are you ok, now?'

'I think I zoned out for a minute there. Sorry.'

'Don't apologise.' Chris's gaze was equally concerned. 'I thought you were going to pass out. Are you under the weather?'

'No, I'm fine. It's just a bit overwhelming, isn't it?'

'What, the response? Yes, I know. All you hear about these days is people being awful to each other, but there is still kindness in the world. And people really want to get behind us, for all sorts of reasons: for the sake of their own children; because they care about local community; even because they think keeping the teenagers off the streets will reduce antisocial behaviour in their own areas. Whatever the reasons, they've stepped up for us. Now, we've got to do them proud.'

Daisy tried to take a gulp of tea, as her nerves built again, but was disappointed as the cup was dry. She saw the concern in her friends' eyes grow again and sighed. It was time to come clean. 'That's what's overwhelming,' she said. 'We've got to do them proud. But I don't have a clue what I'm doing.'

They looked at her blankly.

'I came up with the idea when the landlord was here, and it seemed like a good one at the time, but that was it, an idea. But when it actually comes to making it a reality, I haven't a clue what I'm doing. I don't even know where to start, let alone how to finish it in three weeks.'

Joanna's mouth was open. 'But you sounded so confident.'

'I did, didn't I. But I'm not.'

'Oh, dear.' Chris's face went from bright red to deathly pale in moments. 'Oh, dear, dear.'

'What am I going to do?'

Chris stood upright, a hand on his forehead, his breaths coming short and shallow. 'Oh, dear me.'

This wasn't the reaction Daisy had hoped for. She needed reassurance, someone calm and collected to step in. It clearly wasn't going to be Chris.

Joanna recapped. 'So, let me get this straight. You don't know what you're going to paint or how you're going to do it?'

'Not a clue.'

'Oh, dear, dear me.' Chris bent over clutching the wall with both hands as the reality sunk in.

'Chris. That's not helping.' Joanna patted him on the back, but her attention was on Daisy.

'Right, well, let's break this down and try to be logical. It seemed like your group of helpers were full of ideas about what to paint at your last meeting. What happened?'

'That's part of the problem.' Daisy shrugged. 'Too many ideas. They all wanted to do their own designs, none of which would work because we didn't have the right materials.'

'Ok. Well, that might not be an issue now. Do you still have copies of all these designs? Perhaps the donations we've had today will solve the problem by default.'

'You mean let the supplies we have make the decision for us?' Daisy spotted a glimmer of hope among the fog.

'Exactly. So, do you have the plans?'

'Yes. They're in a box in the cloakroom.'

'Then let's take a look and see what we can come up with.' Joanna headed out of the door, with Daisy immediately behind.

Chris was still clinging to the wall, hyperventilating.

'When you feel like being useful again, Chris, come and find us. We'll be out front saving the day, ok?' Joanna threw over her shoulder at him.

Daisy collected her files and spread them on a table for Joanna to see.

Joanna looked at them, then at the supplies on stage, then back at the paperwork, her lips pursed. 'Ok. Step one, let's sort the paint into some kind of order, rather than all piled together, so we can see what's what.'

They set to work, until the platform displayed a spectrum of colours from one side to the other.

'Right, job done. Step two, let's go through the designs and discard any that simply aren't feasible.'

Daisy felt so much better with a voice of reason orchestrating events, but still wasn't convinced she was up to the final challenge. She could however, point out flaws with the designs. 'Not that one – we don't have any metallic paints which you have to have to create the effect they have on paper. Or that one – it's so complicated, it would take months.'

Joanna joined in. 'The landlord would not approve of that one. He wants to get the neighbours on side, not rub them up the wrong way.'

Daisy chuckled. 'No, heads on spikes probably aren't the right vibe. This one's good though, and this one.' Her heart sank. 'And that one: simple but effective. Oh, how do we decide?'

Without them realising, Chris had sheepishly tiptoed up behind them. 'It's a shame we've only got one building to paint. They would all look great.'

Joanna side-eyed him. 'Pulled yourself together, have you?

'Yes, sorry about that. I just needed a moment.'

'More like half an hour.' Joanna looked at her watch.

Daisy listened to the couple bickering, all the while a new and exciting idea bubbling up in her mind until it was fully formed. 'I think I've got it!'

The pair stopped and stared at her.

'Go on, then,' Joanna prompted. 'Don't leave us in suspense.'

Chris was holding his breath, and turning red as a consequence.

A Reason To Be

'You said it, Chris - multiple buildings.' Daisy announced, as if her idea was fully explained in those two words.

'Sorry? I don't get it.'

'We paint a terrace of smaller buildings.' She could see they weren't seeing the picture which was suddenly so clear in her own head, and flapped her hands in frustration. She reached for her mobile phone to search for something. 'I saw a documentary the other day about this town in South Africa. What was it called? What was it called?' She was half talking to the others and half to herself. 'Yes, here it is. Bo-Kaap. Look.'

She turned the phone around so they could see the image. 'Every house is painted a different bright colour and it looks amazing. Doesn't it?'

'Yes, it does.' Chris took the phone to study it more closely. 'But I don't understand.'

'Come outside,' Daisy said. 'I'll show you what I mean.'

He handed her phone back and the three of them went out to look at the front of the pavilion. Daisy's enthusiasm was completely renewed for the project and she was in full flow.

She pointed at one end. 'So, we start here with a fuchsia pink house, with white windows and elements of the first design – flowers around the door, that sort of thing. Then, here…' Daisy stepped further along and pointed with both hands to indicate a new area. 'A primrose yellow house, and elements of the second design – a rainbow going from the top of the downstairs window to the edge of the wall. Then, here…' She moved further along again. 'We have, I don't know, a lime green house, with elements of the third design – oversized leaf fronds framing the door and windows. Then, we have the sky above and can incorporate the birds from one of the other designs and so on. What do you think?'

Chris and Joanna were staring at the blank wall in silence, as if they were trying to envisage her description.

'Don't you see? It's perfect. The buildings themselves are simple blocks of colour which should be quick to get done, and everybody's happy because their ideas are included to a certain extent, even if only a little bit, and... and... it will look totally amazing.'

Chris turned to Joanna, shaking his head in happy disbelief. 'She's only gone and done it.' He stepped back and drew both Daisy and Joanna closer to him. 'You're right, Daisy. That is perfect. Absolutely blooming perfect.'

Daisy glowed as the wave of relief and happiness washed over her, pictures still popping up in her mind of how the finished creation would look.

Joanna glanced around Chris to speak to Daisy. 'Now, all you have to do is paint it.'

Daisy's heart fell, but she was still too buoyed up by the image in her head to completely lose the positive vibe. 'Yes, that's all we have to do.'

CHAPTER 27

Daisy pulled a table out into the gentle sunshine and laid out a cobbled together sketch of her plan. Then, she sorted through the supplies, lining up the colours for each segment by the wall where it would be appear, to ensure she had what was needed to complete it. When the design crew arrived, after lunch, they crowded around her, eager to know what they were getting started on.

'So, what do you all think?' She chewed her nails as she waited for their reactions.

Lewis was first to speak. 'It's alright, I suppose.' His response was begrudgingly positive. 'I'm not painting them poxy flowers though.'

'You don't have to. The idea is we get the main block painting done first and then get stuck into the detail. Everyone can work on their own favourite elements.'

'Hmm.' He nodded, placated.

'You've hardly put in any oriental lilies though. It's going to be a bit boring if that's all we do.' Harley was next to speak up.

'This is only a really brief mock-up.' Daisy explained. 'Something I've thrown together to show you the general idea, that's all. The amount of detail we actually include will come down to time.' She shrugged. 'You all know we're on a deadline. We need to get as much done as we can by then, so it looks finished enough for the landlord to be satisfied. But we can always add finishing touches later – assuming the landlord says it's good enough for us to stay on.'

The reminder that the club was in jeopardy was timely and any further grumbling was replaced by a general rumble of discontent with the landlord.

'Is everybody reasonably happy?' Daisy realised this was a dangerous question, but felt she had ask, given that the young people were committing hours of their time to the project.

There was a reassuring hush and she breathed a sigh of relief. 'Ok, good. Then I think the best way to go about this is to mark up some guiding outlines, so we can see exactly what's going where and then start filling them in. Sound like a plan?'

She allocated tasks to them all, being careful to spread them out so they weren't falling over, or out, with each other. They had a huge amount to fit into the tight timeframe and knew enthusiasm was likely to wane as the novelty wore off and tiredness set in. It was up to her to make sure that didn't happen, and keep the project afloat, and it was going to take everything she had to do it. The clock was ticking.

Two hours in, they'd settled into a steady pace, taking turns to refill paint trays and hold ladders, and Daisy was impressed. Chris and Joanna had disappeared for a good part of the day, to get on with their day jobs, but reappeared in the late afternoon to refresh flagging spirits with cake and juice. Reticent to slow momentum, Daisy sent the helpers for breaks in twos, while the others carried on.

As the last pair climbed down for their breaks, Daisy stepped away to gauge progress. She sighed, large sections of outline had been marked out and there were patches of paint on the wall, but there was clearly a long way to go, and the challenge didn't seem any less overwhelming.

'Looks alright, miss, doesn't it?' Harley stood alongside her.

'It's coming along.'

A Reason To Be

Daisy's lacklustre reply wasn't fooling anyone, let alone Harley. 'I reckon if we keep this up, we'll have it sorted with time to spare.'

'Hmm, you're probably right. Rome wasn't built in a day.'

Harley glanced at her sideways. 'You know what we need?'

'No, tell me.'

'More manpower, miss. Where's Finn got to? I thought he'd be here helping out, or have you two fallen out again?'

Daisy looked at Harley. 'I've told you, we're just friends.' She said this clearly and concisely, to be sure there could be no mistake. 'And, we haven't fallen out. He's working today. He said he might come by later if he's not too late finishing, but he'll come to help out later in the week, when he's off.'

'Yeah, yeah. I know, friends. Whatever.'

'No, Harley. Not whatever. Just friends.'

Harley's face remained neutral as she looked at Daisy. 'All the best relationships start out like that apparently. I read it in my Mum's magazine the other day.' Her mouth broke into a grin. 'I'm going in to get my cake. See you later.'

Daisy sighed. She may never convince Harley there was nothing going on between her and Finn, but there wasn't. There absolutely, positively, irrefutably wasn't. She heard her Gran's voice inside her head. 'Who are you trying to convince?' Daisy worried at her lip. Was there more between them than friendship, after all? She thought back over the time they'd spent together, from Finn's kindness when Audrey had passed, his support, his encouragement, getting her involved with the youth club, and the WI. Her heart dropped as she remembered the WI. She'd almost ruined it then, embarrassing him, making him take his clothes off in public, not that he had anything to be embarrassed about in the slightest. In fact, if anything, he should be proud of having a body like that – the broad shoulders, the manly chest, the strong, muscled biceps, the…

'Joanna says, do you want cake, miss?'

Daisy blushed as Harley interrupted her thoughts. 'Yes, thanks. I'll be there in a sec.' Where had her mind been going? Honestly, anyone would think she did want more from Finn than friendship, but she didn't, did she?

She took a sharp intake of breath as the realisation hit that, yes, given half a chance, she absolutely did. Why else would she have been so distraught when she'd upset him? Why else did her stomach turn to hot metal when she pictured his bare torso? And, why did it hurt so much when she realised that, in all the time they'd spent together, he'd shown absolutely no romantic interest in her. She gulped. She was in love with Finn. And that was a complication she really didn't need right now.

*

'Don't say I didn't tell you.' Audrey shook her head at the scene. 'Didn't I tell you she had a soft spot for him?'

The ombudsman stroked his chin, in thought. 'Not in so many words, Audrey, not that I can remember.'

She looked down her nose at him. 'Sometimes the actual words aren't necessary, but I certainly implied it, back at my wake, back when he was encouraging her with her art. I told you he was up to something.'

'Oh, I see.' The ombudsman nodded as if beginning to understand. 'You're saying that all the while, Finn had an ulterior motive. He wasn't acting in her interests at all. He was luring Daisy in, plotting to make her fall in love with him.'

'I wouldn't put it past him. He is a man, after all. And now, you see, I was right to be suspicious. Wasn't I?'

'Hmm.' He fell into silent contemplation.

Audrey allowed him a few moments, but could wait no longer for him to admit her superior wisdom. 'If by "hmm" you mean, yes, Audrey, you've got him sussed, then, thank you very much and you're welcome.'

He turned and looked her straight in the eye. 'Actually, Audrey, by "hmm" I meant, what a shame a person can be so suspicious of someone who has given them no reason to be, apart from being a thoroughly nice young man, carrying out the final request of a dying lady, exactly as he agreed to do. I meant, perhaps he's given the girl every reason to fall in love with him, purely because he is a pleasant, honest, thoughtful, kind and, may I say, extremely patient young man. I meant, not everything is a plot, masterminded by a clever, evil villain. Sometimes things simply are.' His voice had begun stern, and became moreso with every sentence.

Audrey was taken aback by his vehemence, but was not of a mind to back down. Her wariness of mankind had been ground into her over her long lifetime and wasn't to be wiped out by one passionate speech from him.

She returned her eyes to the screen. 'It's amazing what some people can pack into a single "hmm", isn't it?'

CHAPTER 28

Luckily, the next few days were so busy, Daisy didn't have time or energy to spare for mooning over the Finn conundrum. On the days he helped out, she cast him a few glances, studied him a little in her rest periods, testing her feelings and trying to read his, but otherwise put it to one side. She was pretty sure nobody noticed.

Other helpers came and went, splitting their time between the mural, revision and downtime as it was school holidays, and the design moved on, slowly but surely. Harley and Lewis had given more time than anyone, and Daisy was impressed by their dedication and effort.

Five days into the project, on an overcast afternoon, threatening heavy showers, only the four of them had steadfastly stuck to the work. Finn and Lewis went inside to mix up a particular shade for the last of the terrace of houses in the design, while Daisy and Harley stood back and admired what they'd achieved so far.

'It looks good, doesn't it, miss?' Harley had her head tipped to one side, studying the section she'd just finished working on.

'Yes, I'm really pleased with it. If we can finish the main colours before the weekend, it means I can mark on some of the detail outlines and we can start filling them in next week.'

'See, I told you.' Harley grinned at her. 'Three weeks is loads of time. I knew we'd do it.'

A Reason To Be

Daisy was more cautious. 'There's a long way to go.'

'My nan says Rome wasn't built in a day.'

'Yes, my gran used to use little nuggets like that as well, to make me feel better.'

'They're old.' Harley shrugged. 'So I guess they probably know best. She definitely knows more than my mum. She's made a right mess of her life.'

Daisy was taken aback by the girl's frankness and didn't know how to respond. 'Oh, Harley, I'm sure she hasn't.'

'She has.' Harley confirmed. 'Ask her. She tells me all the time, especially when she's been on the gin. Apparently my dad was the man of her dreams and she should never have let him go. Joel's alright, but he's not my dad, you know? He was a bit special.'

Remembering what Finn had said previously about how important it was to let the teens off-load, Daisy tried to be open to Harley's woes, though she seemed to be merely stating fact rather than upset about the situation. 'Do you get to see him at all?'

'Who? My dad? I never met him. I'm just going by what my mum says, but it sounds like it was one crazy weekend.'

'Oh, right.'

'Anyway, the point is, miss, that if you think you've found, you know, the one, you should hold on to him.'

Daisy rolled her eyes as she suddenly cottoned on to what Harley was getting at. 'Harley, I've told you…'

'Yeah, right. I know, you and Finn aren't a couple. But I'd need a white stick if I couldn't see you want to be. You were all Shakespeare's tragedy when he was blanking you last week, and I should know, I've been revising Romeo and Juliet non-stop for the last three months, ready for my exam.' She faked a bored yawn.

'I was not…'

'Save it for someone's listening. You've got the hots for him and, what's more, he's got the hots for you.'

Daisy's mouth dropped open. 'He has not.'

'Why else does he look at your bum every time you go up the ladder?' Harley left a gap for Daisy to argue, but Daisy was struck dumb.

'See. I told you.'

A rattle behind the pavilion door suggested the guys were coming back out.

'Anyway, stop all that talk now.' There was no way Daisy wanted Finn to get wind of what Harley had been saying. She was embarrassed enough already, embarrassed, and intrigued, and a little bit flattered and excited at the prospect. Finn had been looking at her...

'It's alright. I'll say no more, except... if you fancy him, don't let the fact he's got another girlfriend put you off. He's worth fighting for.

Daisy's teeth banged together in shock, her stomach clenched and every positive feeling which had started expanding within her melted away. Finn had a girlfriend? 'No.' The response was automatic and overly emphatic and she immediately tried to pull it back with a more gentle, 'I don't think he has.'

'Well, that's not what Lewis says, and he had that photo in his wallet, don't forget, but hey, you know him better than we do.' The girl shrugged, but then fell silent as the door swung open and the others emerged, laden down with paint and fresh equipment.

'Quick, somebody take some of this.' Items tumbled out of Finn's arms, as Daisy stepped up to catch them. He wiped his brow with his palm, then squeezed the back of his neck, pulling the collar of his t-shirt and revealing a brief glimpse of his collar bone. 'Sorry, I should have been sensible and made two trips.'

Daisy realised her eyes had instantly dropped to the exposed patch of skin and that Harley, who was standing to one side grinning at her, had spotted it. Heat rose to her cheeks and she gave Harley a glare, as Finn turned his back on her and bent over to pick up a roller which had fallen and bounced behind him. She couldn't stop her eyes from glancing at his rear and Harley let out a guffaw before walking away with Lewis and returning to work.

Finn stood upright, quizzically watching the girl's retreat. 'What's up with her?'

She shook her head and turned her attention to the equipment she was holding. 'I have no idea. Now, where do you want this?'

Daisy was relieved Finn let the matter drop, but for the remainder of the day, she found herself studying him on more than one occasion, wondering. Could he have a girlfriend he'd never mentioned? Could he be squeezing in a complete other life when he wasn't with her? She didn't think so, but how much did she really know about him? Not a lot.

Until now, their relationship had had a certain dynamic, their conversations almost always about Daisy and her life. It would be difficult to alter that, without seeming strange or nosey? It wouldn't be easy, but she was going to make it her mission to rectify the situation, as soon as she possibly could

Finn walked her home, but little conversation passed between them. Daisy was preoccupied and suddenly conscious of every word that came out of her mouth. Everything sounded contrived in her head, everything manufactured to delve into Finn's life and past. She wasn't going to be able to do this alone. She needed to call in the big guns, even though it would personally cost her a great deal. Lizzy?

They stopped at her front door and Finn looked at her, frowning. 'Daisy, is everything alright tonight? You seem a bit quiet.'

'Who, me?' She shook her head. 'I'm fine.'

He wasn't convinced, but shrugged as she clearly wasn't going to say any more and turned to leave.

'Finn?' She called after him.

'Yes?' He stopped and looked at her.

'Are you still up for lunch on Easter Sunday? My mum was asking.'

His eyes widened. 'Really?' He took a step back towards her. 'Are things ok…?' He jerked his head towards the door to indicate he meant in the household.

She grimaced. 'Not exactly. But I'm working on it.'

'Good for you.' He placed an encouraging hand on her shoulder. 'It'll be worth it in the end.'

'So, Easter Sunday? Will you come?'

'You want me too?'

She nodded and forced a smile.

'Then tell your mum, I'd love to.'

Daisy walked into the house, closed the door and leaned back against it with a sigh. Operation Finn was under way.

Lizzy looked up from the sofa. 'Are you alright, Daisy?'

Daisy opened her eyes, looked at her mother, shook her head and stalked past her to the stairs and her bedroom. Now, there was just the small matter of rebuilding a bridge with Lizzy, so that Easter Sunday lunch would do its work. But not tonight. That wasn't going to be easy either. Oh, why was life so complicated?

CHAPTER 29

Sunday had been allocated as a day of rest from the project. So many people had generously offered up their time and toiled tirelessly to get as much done as possible but, as Chris pointed out, everyone needed a break, and they didn't want the crew to burn out when the deadline was in sight.

Daisy spent the day planning, working on sketches for the detailed sections of the mural they'd be painting next, but also working out how to bring up the subject of Easter Sunday lunch with her mum, without having to eat humble pie. Twice she walked to the door of her bedroom to talk to her, having heard Lizzy banging around downstairs, but twice she chickened out. She wasn't confident she could keep her temper, and it wasn't the time for another row. In the end, she settled on leaving a note on the table when she left for the pavilion on Monday morning. She'd worry about how she was going to cope with sitting at the table with her for the meal, later.

Note left – a cursory "don't forget you invited Finn for lunch on Sunday" – Daisy headed off, drawings safely tucked under her arm. Her mind was broiling with thoughts of Finn and the mystery girlfriend, if she even existed, and planned to make use of Harley and Lewis as undercover spies. It probably wasn't the right thing to do but, hey, she was desperate, and had a feeling that Harley at least would be a willing participant. The more Daisy thought about Finn, the more she realised how important he was to her, and how much more important she'd like him to be.

It was lunchtime before either teenager arrived, Lewis first by a full hour. Daisy was champing at the bit and had to hold herself back from cornering Lewis to tell her everything he knew, but she needed to be more subtle than that. Instead, she carefully talked him through the technique she wanted him to use on a cloud section of the mural, then climbed onto the platform erected for work at height (kindly provided by a friend of Joel's – he really was a man with connections) next to him, under the excuse of checking he understood her instructions.

She watched him apply the stipple brush with a level of attention far beyond that required, willing up the nerve to start the necessary conversation. 'So, Lewis, I hear you're quite the life saver.'

'Huh?' He grunted, deep in concentration.

'You found Finn's wallet,' she prompted. 'He would have been completely lost without it.'

'Oh, yeah.'

Daisy had to give it to him. When he was focussed on a task, Lewis was really focussed. 'Yes, we carry our whole lives around in our wallets, these days, don't we? Not just money - cards, receipts… appointment cards… stamps.' She ran out of steam.

'I keep everything on my phone. It's easier.'

'True, true. Yes, I suppose phones have replaced wallets, haven't they?' She was going to have to be more direct. 'Even photos. And you can keep hundreds of photos on your phone, whereas in a wallet, you can only keep one… or a couple, at most. So, yes, phones are better, in that respect too, I suppose. Unless you only want to keep one photo, like, a particularly special one, I mean, which is there every time you go to get money out, or your card, or…'

Lewis stopped working and stared at her, a smile hidden behind his eyes. 'Stamps?'

'Yes, stamps.' She'd been rumbled, she was certain of it.

A Reason To Be

Lewis sighed. 'He had a single photo of a girl, older than me, maybe about your age. She had red hair, I mean, like, dyed in-your-face red, not ginger, and a nose stud.'

Daisy felt her face glow with embarrassment, and used sarcasm as a defence. 'You only got a brief look then.'

'And she looked sassy, you know, like, trouble. And she was pretty. Very pretty.'

The wind blew out of her sails in an audible sigh. 'Oh.'

'I don't know if it was his girlfriend – I've never heard him mention one - but I definitely would, if you know what I mean.'

'Lewis!'

He chuckled and returned his attention to the cloud he was creating. 'Do you want me to find out? Ask around?'

'No.' Her lips said one thing, but her brain said something else entirely.

'Yes, she does.' Harley's voice came from the platform behind Daisy, and Daisy jumped, a hand flying to her chest. 'It's alright, miss. Don't have a heart attack. It'll be our little secret.'

'No, honestly, Harley. It's none of my business. I shouldn't be nosey.' Daisy was so conflicted, but knew it wasn't a good idea to hand this much power to a couple of bolshie teenagers.

'Course not. Understood. We won't do a thing.' Lewis leaned back and winked at her. 'For example, I won't speak to my mate who lives in the same street as him.'

Harley giggled. 'And I won't talk to my aunty who runs the launderette he uses.'

Daisy's mouth opened in denial, but nothing came out.

'And I won't quiz Chris when I go in for cake later, either.' Lewis was enjoying Daisy's discomfort.

She gasped. 'No, definitely don't do that.'

'Oh, we won't.' Harley laughed aloud. 'Anyway, what about the hearts and flowers?'

'What?' Daisy stared at her.

'The hearts and flowers on the pink house. Where do you want me to start?'

Oh, yes, the mural. 'Right, yes. Come down and I'll show you the plan.'

Daisy climbed down the ladder, pausing at the bottom for a couple of soothing deep breaths to get herself back on track, but she had an uncomfortable feeling she'd set something in motion which she had no control over. She hoped she didn't live to regret it.

It was three days before the teenagers fed back what they'd discovered. Finn had left early for a shift at the hospice and Daisy wouldn't see him again until Sunday lunchtime, as work on the mural was ramping down for the Easter weekend.

Harley had hinted they had news as soon as she arrived but, even though Daisy was desperate to hear what that news was, it was agreed they wouldn't discuss it until there were fewer people around, and less chance of being overheard. Daisy would have been mortified if Finn found out about the snooping.

She tried to play it cool, but so wasn't. 'Did you have anything to tell me? Her face revealed no emotion, but inside, every atom was crying out "please let there be no girlfriend", though she had no clue what she was going to do next even if there wasn't.'

Lewis leaned against a scaffold pole, arms folded, his demeanour deadly serious. 'There's good and bad news.'

Daisy wanted to grab him, and shake it out of him, but held back. 'Ok.'

'I spoke to my mate who lives on Elm Tree Close and he said there might be a girlfriend, or there might not.'

'Elm Tree Close? Where's that?'

'The street where Finn lives,' Harley piped up. 'You did know that, right?'

Daisy was too embarrassed to admit she hadn't until that moment. Finn had always called at her house, or met her elsewhere. 'Yeah, of course. But what does that mean? Might, or might not?'

A Reason To Be

'He said there is a fit girl, who goes into the same building, but he's never actually seen them together, so she might live in one of the other flats, and she doesn't have red hair. He's not sure, but he's going to see if he can find out, go through the recycling and stuff.'

'What? No, he mustn't do that. It's illegal, well, it probably is.'

Lewis sniggered. 'That's never bothered my mate before and, besides, I'm not sure he's doing it just for you. I think he has his own reasons.'

'Seriously, no. Tell him not to. Absolutely not.' Daisy was adamant. 'But was that the bad news, or the good?'

'Both,' said Lewis. 'He might have a girlfriend which is bad, but then he might not, which is good.'

'Oh.' Daisy was disappointed.

'But it's not all the news.' Harley had been waiting her turn. 'My Aunty Glenda says he uses the launderette on a regular basis and, although he's left an odd sock behind once or twice, they've always been men's socks. Nothing girly, no bras or anything like that.'

Daisy wasn't sure their detective skills had served any purpose whatsoever.

'I did have a quiet word with Chris. You know, man to man, like.' Lewis nodded his head to one side as if he expected some credit for using his initiative.

'Oh, dear.' Daisy didn't like the sound of that. 'And? What did he say?'

'He said Finn was married with four children, a German shepherd and a barn-load of hens, but I don't think that's true.'

Daisy grimaced. 'Of course it's not.'

'No, I mean why would he need a shepherd if all he has are hens and no sheep?'

Harley tutted. 'A German Shepherd is a dog, silly. Chris was just telling you to mind your own business in a complicated way, like he does.'

'I knew that.' Lewis scowled and stared at his feet.

'Well, thanks anyway. I appreciate your help.' Daisy didn't think she was any further forward. 'But I think Chris is probably right and we should mind our own business. If Finn wanted us to know about his life, I guess he'd tell us.'

'Not necessarily.' Harley nodded wisely. 'My Aunty Glenda did say one other thing.'

Daisy waited. 'Well? What?'

'Have you considered he might have a criminal record? Aunty Glenda says there's only one good reason why somebody is that shifty about his past and that's because he's been inside.'

There were several seconds of silence as Daisy absorbed that suggestion. 'I'm sure Finn hasn't …'

'He's not going to advertise it, is he?' Harley scoffed.

'He had to be DBS checked to help out at the Youth Club.'

'I'm only saying.'

'Nah, Finn's sound.' At least Lewis was on the same page as Daisy.

'Anyway.' Daisy felt it was time to bring things to a close. She wished she'd never started it, for what good had come of it. 'Thanks for your input. But I really do think we should leave it there. No more delving into Finn's private life. After all, it isn't any of our business.'

'You were the one who wanted to know.' Harley was scowling.

'Yes, I did. But I was being nosey, and shouldn't have. It was wrong of me, so no more. Yes?'

Lewis shrugged and threw his jacket over his shoulder. 'Whatever, but I'm off. Things to do.'

'I'd better be going too. Joel's taking us out for dinner tonight.' Harley rolled her eyes and walked away, but paused after a couple of steps. 'You sure about this? No more private detective stuff? I've got plenty more sources where Aunty Glenda came from.'

'Absolutely sure, but thanks.'

'Shame.' Harley disappeared down the path, leaving Daisy to finish clearing away and lock up. She did so on automatic pilot, her mind elsewhere. Was there a girlfriend? Wasn't there a girlfriend? Who was the fit girl with red hair and piercings? Could Finn have a criminal record he was keeping hidden? She thought not. At least she was confident he wasn't married with four kids. Wasn't she? The only hope she had of finding out now was Sunday lunch with her mother. Joy!

*

'I knew that boy was hiding something.' Audrey's smile was smug. 'Didn't I tell you?'

'To be fair, Audrey, you've cast aspersions of one sort or another about most of the people we've observed so far, so I would have been surprised if he'd escaped scot free.'

Audrey considered denying the accusation but, after some thought, nodded in agreement. 'Well, I think most people are hiding something or up to something, but in Finn's case, he strikes me as particularly suspicious.'

'Hmm, and what exactly do you think he's hiding?'

She pursed her lips, eyes narrowed as she studied the young man's figure on the screen. 'A criminal record, I reckon. He'll have done time in juvie.'

The ombudsman looked down his nose at her. 'Audrey, my dear lady, you watch far too much television and, from the sound of it, most of it is American trash drama. Juvie!' He shook his head at the term.

They continued to watch the footage, but after several moments, the ombudsman broke the silence. 'So tell me, Audrey, what was it that you were hiding when you were down there?'

Her eyes widened at the suggestion and she pressed a hand to her chest. 'Me? I was an open book, I was. What you saw was what you got.'

The ombudsman let out a loud guffaw, but didn't comment.

She frowned at his mirth, but any offence she felt soon passed. A little while later, she nudged the ombudsman with her elbow. 'I tell you what the lad shouldn't be hiding.'

He glanced away from the screen at her. 'Oh, yes? What's that?'

'That six pack of his.' She winked. 'While there's nothing much going on, I don't suppose we can watch the art class at the WI again, can we?'

'No, Audrey. We absolutely cannot. This is not a peep show.'

'Ah, well, can't blame a girl for trying.'

CHAPTER 30

Daisy had eased herself into spending a whole meal in Lizzy's presence by pausing in the lounge a couple of times as she passed through, and exchanging a couple of verging on civil sentences with her, like "what time is Finn to come here on Sunday?", and "I don't suppose you've seen my pink hoodie?'. She hadn't let those interactions develop, because she couldn't deal with any more of the ridiculous accusations about her gran not making Lizzy feel welcome when she came home, and didn't want to create an even darker atmosphere as backdrop to Finn's visit. Merely thinking about what crazy allegation her mother might come up with next, made Daisy angry.

It hadn't escaped Daisy's notice though, how grateful Lizzy seemed for even the briefest, most impersonal interactions. Lizzy spent most of her time huddled on the sofa looking miserable and sad. Her hair didn't look as if it had been brushed, she'd been wearing the same outfit for days, and Daisy was dubious whether she'd bothered showering either. Daisy experienced moments of guilt about the part her own actions played in creating such a pitiful tableau, but then remembered their last row, and her heart hardened again.

When Sunday morning arrived, Daisy sat on the edge of the bed to steel herself for the day. It was going to be challenging, but hopefully rewarding too. She would have to be polite to Lizzy – Finn wasn't going to open up about his life if Daisy and Lizzy were at each other's throats – in fact she was going to have to be the model daughter for this short period. Yes, it was going to be hard, biting her tongue, but she could do it.

'You are strong. You are brave. You are true to yourself. And you are enough.' She'd found a mantra online to use in preparation for the day. She had a feeling she was going to need it.

Daisy walked downstairs with purpose. Lizzy was banging around in the kitchen, and mouth-watering smells wafted through to the lounge.

'Can I do anything to help?' Daisy hovered in the doorway to the kitchen, rubbing her hands together. It was a begrudging offer, but an offer nonetheless.

Her mother crouched next to the open door of the oven, steam damp on her pink face. 'Huh?' She looked up at Daisy in shock, but soon recovered herself, closed the oven door and stood up, gripping the tea towel she'd been using with both hands. She studied her daughter's face like she expected more, some kind of backlash maybe, but forged on regardless. 'I think I'm all good here, but you could lay the table? If you don't mind?'

Daisy couldn't help noticing Lizzy was wearing the same outfit yet again, and her hair hung limp about her face. 'Yeah, sure.'

The woman's sigh of relief, as Daisy turned to get on with the job, was audible, and Daisy felt a little jolt in her heart that her behaviour had made her mother feel such tension, but then anger flared again at the idea she'd been made to feel guilty when it was all Lizzy's fault in the first place. 'You are strong. You are brave. You are true to…'

'Sorry. Did you say something?' Lizzy leaned out from the kitchen.

Daisy quit whispering and took a steady breath. 'No. Not a thing.'

'Oh, ok. I'll get on then.'

A Reason To Be

Half an hour later, Lizzy emerged and surveyed the table. Daisy had taken extra care, using Audrey's best cloth and table mats, had rubbed the cutlery until it shone, and the glasses gleamed. 'This looks great, thanks.'

Daisy had been admiring the final result and glanced up with a smile which instantly disappeared as she took in Lizzy's drab appearance fully. She glanced at the clock and realised the time. Finn would be arriving soon. 'You are getting changed, right?'

Lizzy looked down at herself. 'I suppose I should. I expect I can find something else to put on.'

'With your wardrobe? Yeah. I'm sure you can.'

Lizzy scratched her head, distracted. 'Yes. Probably. I've got a bit behind with the washing, that's all.'

Daisy's eyes narrowed. 'And you're going to shower? Do your hair?'

Glancing in the mirror on the wall, Lizzy's bottom lip wobbled, either at what she saw or Daisy's scathing tone. 'I guess so. I don't want to show you up.' She walked to the bottom of the stairs, paused and turned to Daisy again. Her face was a picture of misery. 'But the veg. I need to…' Her voice broke.

Daisy felt her temper straining at the bit. 'Don't do that,' she ordered. 'I can see to the veg. I'm not an idiot.'

'No, of course you're not.' Lizzy sniffed.

'Go and sort yourself out before he gets here. Go on.'

Lizzy did as she was told and Daisy stalked into the kitchen. Placing both hands on the worktop to brace herself, she took two deep, calming breaths. She had a horrible feeling lunch was going to be a disaster, for all the fancy food and expensive wine already in the cooler, unless Lizzy pulled herself together. There was only one thing for it. As hard as it had been for Daisy to be civil, she was going to have to up the ante. She was going to have to be nice.

She exhaled slowly through pursed lips. 'You are strong. You are brave. You are a flipping miracle worker if you can pull this off.'

She grabbed the tea towel and looked around. 'Right, asparagus, I'm coming for you!'

Finn was as true to time as ever, and Lizzy was yet to reappear. Daisy had called up the stairs twice already before he arrived, her anxiety growing by the minute.

Daisy ushered Finn in with a welcome and a smile, and offered him a drink, on her best behaviour, then called up again. 'Mum? Finn's here.' Then waited, nerves on fire.

'I'll be right there.' The call came back, and Daisy relaxed slightly. At least Lizzy wasn't refusing to come down, making a scene. She could get through this.

Sitting opposite Finn, on the sofa, Daisy made small talk. 'So, Finn. How have you been?'

'Yeah, good.' His brow sported a small frown at her unnatural behaviour. 'I only saw you on Thursday.'

'Yeah, well, I was just checking in on you. You know, making sure.'

He leaned forward, confidentially. 'What about you?' He tipped his head at the stairs. 'Are you guys working things out?'

She shrugged and was about to reply, when her mother came down and stopped in front of them, hands clutched in front of her body.

Daisy was pleased to see she was clean at least, but her hair was still damp and her face red and blotchy from crying. She was wearing no make-up, and her outfit was an astonishing mismatch of grey tracksuit bottoms with a formal blouse and jacket. Daisy's mouth fell open - this was so unlike her permanently well turned out mother, but Finn didn't notice, or, if he did, was too polite to show it.

'Hello,' he said. 'Thanks so much for inviting me.'

Lizzy's smile was a watery affair. 'You're welcome.' She sidestepped towards the kitchen. 'Anyway. I'd better get on. Won't be much longer.' She disappeared into the kitchen and pulled the door to, in effect sealing herself off from them.

Daisy watched her go, and when she turned back to Finn, he was staring right at her, eyes narrowed. 'What's going on?'

She tried to be flippant. 'Oh, nothing. Everything's great. Everything's fine.'

'Daisy?'

'Ok,' she admitted. 'Things aren't perfect, but it will be fine. Trust me. I'm trying, ok?'

Before he could reply, Lizzy carried steaming dishes in to the table. 'Right,' she said. 'It's as ready as it's going to be. Come and take a seat.'

They did as instructed, but Lizzy didn't reappear. After a few embarrassed moments, Daisy called. 'Mum? Do you need me to help?'

'No, no. Everything's under control. I'll be right there.' Lizzy's voice was broken and tremulous.

'Daisy,' Finn whispered. 'It's not fine.'

'It is. It is.' She jumped up. 'I'll go and help and it will be great, honestly.' She ran to the kitchen and closed the door behind her. 'What are you doing? Are you trying to make this a disaster?'

Lizzy stood in the corner of the room, crying into a piece of kitchen roll, and jumped when Daisy entered. 'Sorry. No, I'm ok.' She shook her head. 'I just can't seem to get my head together.' She moved to the sink, ran the cold tap and splashed her face. Coughing to clear her throat, she visibly straightened her back and shoulders and grabbed two more dishes. 'Ok. I've got this.'

Before Daisy could say any more, Lizzy pushed her way back into the dining area and slid the dishes onto mats, without making eye contact with Finn, as if that would stop him noticing how upset she was. 'Tuck in, Finn. We don't stand on ceremony here. Help yourself.'

Finn looked from Lizzy to Daisy, as if he expected her to step in and do something other than place the roast potatoes on the table, but what was she supposed to do? What was she supposed to say? She ignored Finn's silent entreaties and said. 'Yum. These look soooo good.'

He continued to stare at her.

Lizzy sat down but almost immediately stood up again, slapping her forehead with a palm. 'I forgot the mint sauce. How could I forget the mint sauce?' A forced and obviously fake laugh. 'You can't have lamb without mint sauce. That would be a travesty.' There was a lot of banging and crashing in the kitchen and muttering and, finally, a single stifled sob. She reappeared in the doorway. 'I forgot to buy it. I'm really sorry.' Her voice was cracking.

Finn was clearly horrified by her distress, Daisy mortified. 'For goodness sake, sit down and eat, Mum. Nobody wants mint sauce anyway. It's rank!'

Lizzy did as she was told, as far as sitting down was concerned, but merely stared at her empty plate, gripping the table with her hands.

Finn once again turned to Daisy with an accusatory glare, but when she continued to ignore Lizzy's suffering, he reached out and rested his hand on one of Lizzy's, closest to him. 'Lizzy, are you alright? Look, if it's a bad time for me to be here, I'll go.'

'No, no,' she managed. 'I'm all good. Let's eat.'

'No. You're not. You're far from it. What's wrong?' When she didn't reply. 'Have you two quarrelled again? Is that it?'

'Don't blame me. I haven't done anything.' Daisy sighed. Her plans for the afternoon were completely ruined thanks to her mother's histrionics. 'Finn, she said she's fine. Can we not just forget all this nonsense and get on with it?'

He was still studying Lizzy. 'I know what she said, but it's not true, is it? Lizzy, what is it?'

Lizzy looked up and shrugged. 'It's all so sad.'

His tone was gentle, a tone Daisy remembered well from Audrey's last hours in the hospice, when he'd talked with her endlessly about

Audrey, Daisy's feelings, her fears and the future. 'What is? What's sad?'

'Life.' She shrugged. 'Everything, I suppose. My life, anyway.'

Daisy tutted but, without looking at her, Finn held his palm out to her, silently warning her to stop. 'Why is that? What's sad about it?'

'Everything. This.' She shook her head. 'I thought I'd have time. Things were bad and they had been for a long time, but I thought I'd have time to sort things out, with Mum, and Daisy, but now it's too late and Daisy doesn't even want to know me.'

He briefly side-eyed Daisy before carrying on. 'I thought you guys were talking things out.'

Daisy held her breath. If Lizzy told Finn they hadn't been talking at all, it would make her look terrible. After all, she'd told him she'd been trying. She so didn't want him to think badly of her. She wished she'd made more of an effort.

'I always say the wrong thing. But I don't know what the right thing is. Their relationship, Daisy and Mum, was… special and I… I didn't understand it, and I didn't feel a part of it, so how can I know how to deal with it now? Me and Mum, we were so different. We had different ideas about how things should be. It didn't work with both of us trying to bring Daisy up because we kept contradicting each other, arguing and… She was the grown up and had the experience, so who was I to say she was wrong? But I couldn't sit and watch and not be true to myself either. It was all such a mess, so I ran away.' She looked at Daisy. 'And I'm sorry. I wish I'd tried harder and stayed, and now it's too late and I've lost you forever.'

Daisy's frown deepened. The feelings bubbling up inside of her were uncomfortable. She didn't want to deal with them in the privacy of her own room, let alone here, in front of Finn. But she knew she couldn't shut Lizzy down. Finn would think she was a horrible person if she did. Maybe she was, but she didn't want him to think so and, in fact, she wanted to be better when she was with him. There was a huge knot in her chest, which had been there for so long, and it felt as if it was beginning to unravel. Her breaths were fast and shallow. She had to hold on to her emotions. 'You haven't lost me.'

'Oh, I have. Look at us. We can't talk without yelling at each other, hurting each other. It's been years since we've had a proper relationship, since we've been right together. You hate me.'

'I don't hate you,' Daisy denied, but she couldn't immediately find the words for what she did feel about her mother and had a strong suspicion she might explode with emotion if she delved too deeply. This conversation had been a long time coming: since Lizzy first went to live in America. 'I don't hate you,' she said again.

Finn had been a quiet observer but, as the silence stretched, he broke it. 'You see, Lizzy. Daisy doesn't hate you. You can sort things out. It'll take time but, if you both want to make things right, and you both work hard, it's doable. Yes?' He looked at Daisy for confirmation.

She was clamping down on her bottom lip, trying not to have a meltdown herself. 'Yes.'

'You see?'

Lizzy seemed to think about it for a long moment then nodded.

Daisy exhaled slowly. Maybe this whole nightmare scene was about to be over. Maybe they could put it behind them and move on and, in a couple of hours, she could try and forget it had ever happened. She couldn't deal with all this drama. But no.

'But I'll never get to sort things out with Mum, will I? It's too late. All those years, I could have come back and confronted her about how things were. I could have stood my ground and made sure I had a place here, but it was always "next month", "next year", "next time I grew a spine".' These phrases were spat out in an exaggerated version of her own voice. 'But I never did.' She stopped for breath, and the anger leaked away, replaced with despair and confusion. 'Why didn't she tell me she was dying?' She looked from Finn to Daisy and back again, desperately searching for answers.

The tension in Daisy's chest was so tight, she couldn't speak. She couldn't explain what Audrey had said, the excuses, no, the reasons, when she was first diagnosed, when she fell more and more ill, as she'd lain in the hospice in her final days, because it took Daisy back there. She'd already lived through losing her gran once. She couldn't do it again, even to ease her mother's pain.

Finn saw the fear on her face, recognised the pain she felt and reached across the table for her hand too – he still held Lizzy's in the other. Perhaps he thought it would give Daisy the strength to say what needed to be said, but she was beyond that, so he spoke, filling the gap. 'It's hard… losing someone close. Always hard, even when you know it's coming. You're never prepared, even if you think you are. And if you have no idea, if it comes out of the blue…' He shook his head, exhaling steadily, as if he really knew how that felt.

Daisy studied him as he took time to pull himself together. Of course, she thought, he's seen it all at the hospice, witnessed people's pain on a regular basis. He knew what he was talking about. She hadn't allowed for the shock her mother must have felt when she heard Audrey had died, estranged or not.

'Did the letter Audrey left for you help at all?'

As soon as Finn's words reached Daisy's ears, something shifted inside her, and her free hand flew to cover her mouth. The letter! Lizzy's letter! It was still in the small bag of belongings Daisy had brought back from the hospice that last day. She'd read her own letter the night when Audrey died and many, many times since. It had been a boon to her soul on the days when she ached with loss, when she needed to feel her gran close. But she'd forgotten Lizzy's letter. With everything that had gone on since, it had completely slipped her mind, and now she felt terrible. She'd failed in the promise she made to her gran, and she'd failed to give her mum something which may have helped her deal with the grief now eating her up.

'Letter? What letter?' Lizzy's demeanour instantly changed.

Finn looked at Daisy with question in his eyes.

She stood up and turned to Lizzy. She needed to put this right immediately. 'I'm sorry. I forgot. Gran left you a letter.' What if

Finn thought she'd done it on purpose, to punish her mum? She looked him square in the eye. 'I forgot,' she repeated, then ran up the stairs to her room and rummaged in her wardrobe for the bag. Not even taking the time to locate the letter, she grabbed the bag and ran back downstairs with it.

The others sat in silence, waiting, watching, as she frantically rifled through the bag until she found it, a little bent, but still intact at the bottom. She pulled it out and flattened it against her chest, then held it out to Lizzy. For a moment both had a hand on it. Lizzy stared at her daughter, then down at the envelope, as it was relinquished, as if it was an ancient lost treasure.

Daisy looked at Finn. 'I forgot,' she said again. She had to make him understand it was a mistake.

Lizzy pulled the letter into her chest and held it there. 'I think I'm going to go and read this in my room. Do you mind?'

'No, of course not.' It was Finn who spoke.

'Please stay and eat,' Lizzy said. 'I don't want all this to go to waste.' Then she hurried upstairs. The door of her bedroom banged closed only seconds later.

Finn glanced at the table, then at Daisy. 'I'm going to go. I'm sorry, I don't feel much like eating.' He pushed his chair back and stood up, before pausing. 'You need to be there for her when she comes back down.'

'Yes, I will.' Daisy nodded, ashamed at her omission. 'But I didn't do it on purpose, I promise.'

'I know,' he said, but the pained expression on his face meant Daisy wasn't entirely convinced he believed her.

She followed him to the door.

Suddenly, what he believed wasn't the most important thing. She gazed at him, her lip trembling with emotion. 'Finn, I let her down, Gran, I mean. I promised I'd pass the letter on and I forgot. I let her down.' Tears poured unchecked down her cheeks.

Finn pulled her to him, holding her against his chest, then released her slightly to bend down and look her straight in the eye. 'No, you didn't. You were grieving and you forgot, that's all. You've done it now.' He pulled his sleeve over his hand and wiped her tears away. 'Now, you and your mum need to be here for each other. That's what Audrey would have wanted. Make her proud.'

She nodded sadly. Finn walked away and Daisy closed the door.

*

Audrey's face was a picture of bafflement. 'Well, I don't know what to say?'

'Really? That's unusual.' The ombudsman coughed to clear his throat. 'What is it that's troubling you, Audrey?'

'Everything. Lizzy. I mean, what's got into her? She's usually so... together, so in control. Where's all this come from? And then, there's Daisy. You can tell she's struggling. She must be to forget something like passing my letter to Lizzy. My girls, they're a complete mess. I've never seen them like this before.'

'Well, of course you haven't. They've always had you there before, for support.'

Audrey was quiet as she considered this. 'I had no idea,' she said, at last.

'No idea of what, Audrey?'

'That I made such a difference, I suppose. I thought they were just getting on with their lives and I was on the outside, looking in. I didn't realise I was such a big part of it too.'

'Jenga.' The ombudsman nodded, sagely.

'Beg pardon?' Audrey frowned.

'The game, Jenga?' He tipped his head in question. 'You know, the big tower of bricks. All very stable, but you remove random bricks one by one, and when you remove the wrong one, the whole thing comes tumbling down. Jenga.'

She glared at him for a long while. 'If that was meant to make me feel better, it was a darn poor attempt.'

'I was merely trying to explain the situation. Families are like a big pile of bricks and…'

'Stop,' she ordered. 'Go and do something useful, like putting the kettle on, instead.

He rolled his eyes, but did as instructed.

'And make mine nice and sweet, while you're at it. I need it for my nerves.' She shook her head. 'Jenga, indeed.'

CHAPTER 31

Daisy didn't know how to feel. She still wanted to be angry with Lizzy, because of her earlier accusations against Audrey, about feeling pushed out. But she also felt hideously guilty for not passing on Audrey's letter and denying Lizzy the comfort her own letter had brought her. After all, Audrey was Lizzy's mother, and Lizzy must have felt something when Audrey died. With Finn looking on, Daisy's grudge against Lizzy had felt petty and she was ashamed. She couldn't imagine him ever treating anyone as harshly as she'd treated Lizzy these past weeks. Another voice in her head goaded her though – but you still don't really know him, do you? It was all so draining.

After he left, and Lizzy didn't reappear, Daisy packed away the food and tidied the kitchen, then sat on the sofa, chewing her lip, not knowing what to do. Wondering if she should go and bang on Lizzy's door to check she was alright. Morag rescued her from her over-thinking.

'Cooee!' She called as she let herself in. 'My goodness, I could smell your lunch halfway down the street. What a feast you must have had.'

Daisy glanced up and managed a watery smile. 'Hi, Morag. It's good to see you.'

Morag's eyes widened at the unusually warm welcome. 'Is it indeed?' She took in Daisy's demeanour and patted her shoulder, before lowering herself into the armchair opposite. 'You're missing Audrey. It's on days like these you really feel your losses, the empty seats at the table bring it home.'

Daisy couldn't speak, but nodded.

Morag nodded wisely. 'She's here with you, you know. All the time.'

Daisy coughed a laugh. 'I don't know if I like that idea. She might not like what she sees.'

'Get away!' Morag swiped the idea away with her hand. 'She worshipped the ground you walked on, but was under no illusions that you were perfect, you know, anymore than she was herself, or me, for that matter. The wicked schemes we cooked up together, honestly, we've pulled some stunts in our time. Like when ... No, I shouldn't be telling you about that.'

'Oh, please do. I'd love to hear about her.'

Morag narrowed her eyes in thought. 'Alright, then. I suppose no harm would come of it.' She shuffled in the seat, settling herself in for the telling. 'Your granny once persuaded me to back her up in telling Stella Scunthorpe there was a full gym-wear dress code for the new armchair aerobics class. The poor woman turned up in a spangled leotard, sparkly tights and leg-warmers when everyone else was in normal clothes. Oh, we laughed.' The memory sparked hearty laughter and Morag had to pause her tale until she'd finished slapping her thigh, and got her breath back. 'It made Lester Craddock's year. His eyes were on stalks. Mind you, he had thyroid problems so he always was a tad...' She cupped a hand in front of each of her eyes to mimic bulges. 'And I shouldn't laugh really, because they carried him off in a coffin not a week later and who knows if Stella's knobbly knees didn't have a part to play in that.' The chuckling began again, though Morag placed a palm firmly over her mouth to contain it.

'Morag!' Daisy's tone was scandalised.

A Reason To Be

A low cough drew Daisy's eyes to the bottom of the stairs, and she turned to see a wan Lizzy holding on to the newel-post, no doubt drawn down by Morag's hysterics. She appeared undecided whether to proceed or turn round and go back the way she'd come. Daisy couldn't take any more tension – she needed it to end and this seemed like an opportunity to build bridges. 'Morag's telling stories about Gran.'

It wasn't an invitation as such, but it was enough of a lapse in hostility for Lizzy to take a step forward.

'Come on down, lassie. Cosy up with Daisy and we'll seek comfort in conjuring up the best memories of Audrey we can.'

Lizzy edged forward and sat at the other end of the sofa from Daisy, and pulled her feet up onto the seat, hugging her knees to her chest.

'Tell me another one, Morag.' Daisy was eager for more laughter, to come in and banish the darkness she felt inside.

Morag smiled and tipped her head to one side. 'I have to be very careful here. I can't be incriminating myself, you know?' The fingers of one hand, tapped against the back of the other as she sorted through memories like they were a box of fancy chocolates and she could only choose one. 'Oh, yes. The WI. We had fun there, Audrey and me, but back in the early days it was quite… hmm… straight-laced, I suppose you'd call it. Old Meryl Ramsbottom ruled the roost with an iron rod, she did, God rest her soul. It was all cake sales, here, and knitted tea-cosy patterns there. Not that there's anything wrong with cakes and tea-cosies, I'm rather partial myself, but you can have too much of a good thing. The crocheted toilet roll dollies were a step too far, mind. Anyway, Audrey and me, we were the newbies, the youngsters, so to speak, and Audrey masterminded a plan to liven things up a wee bit.'

'I bet she did.' Daisy was picturing it in her head.

'Meryl had control of the calendar and had done as long as anyone could remember. It was the same routine, year in, year out and everyone was bored stiff with it. So, January came around, as it generally does, and the same old itinerary went up on the notice board and we thought there'd be dissension in the ranks. But they were afraid of their own shadows, that lot, let alone the wrath of Meryl. Anyway, Audrey, having heard the moans and groans, took the bull by the horns and spoke out, but Meryl wasn't having any of it. It'd always been spring bulbs in March, cake making in June, in readiness for the Summer cake sale fundraiser, and wreath making in November and she saw no reason to change it. Of course, no one on the board had the courage to challenge her.'

'What did Gran do?'

'Well, she wasn't one for making a scene...'

Daisy wasn't sure she could agree with that particular sentiment, but allowed Morag to continue.

'So, she nodded away and said "oh, silly me, forgive my ignorance, I'm new here" kind of thing, but I knew she wouldn't be leaving it at that, and she knew how to play the long game. Anyway, a couple of the board retired in the March - one was turning ninety and not as spry as she once was, and the other's husband had a knee replacement and needed round the clock nagging to do his stretches – and Audrey had been carefully toeing the line, backing Meryl on every dull decision she made. You get the picture, "Yes, Meryl. No, Meryl. Three bags full, Meryl" which meant Meryl was more than happy to support Audrey's nomination, which was put forward by yours truly.' Morag proudly patted her chest.

Daisy and Lizzy glanced at each other briefly, both caught up in the tale, both well able to imagine Audrey's ability to avenge, but not the method in which she would achieve it.

'So, in the May, there was a hullaballoo. The usual baker that was supposed to teach us a new sponge recipe in June – as I said, for the cake sale fundraiser - had to go in for an op. Something female...' She dropped her voice for the last two words, and waved a hand to show she would be giving no further detail in that regard. 'And couldn't make it. Well! What were we to do? It was too late to get another one from the authorised list, they were booked up months in advance, but we had to find a baker. Meryl was quite pale with it all, but Audrey sticks her hand up and says "leave it to me. I've a friend of a friend of a friend who bakes amazing cakes, who might stand in, if she's free, but she's so popular, there's no guarantees, but she might squeeze us in, for me, if I ask". And Meryl jumped at the chance, "oh, would you, Audrey. That would be fantastic. You're a lifesaver".' Here, Morag dissolved into laughter, which left her coughing and breathless, so much so that Lizzy had to run to the kitchen for a glass of water for her.

After she'd calmed, Lizzy and Daisy settled back in to hear the end of the story. 'So, what was so funny? Was there a baker?' Daisy prompted.

'Oh, aye, there was. Sandra Toogood, a friend of ours from way back, had hired her to cater her hen do. Honestly, a hen do for a second, no, third marriage, when you're pushing seventy and already had one eye on number four if number three pegged it in the near future, which was highly likely – he wasn't a well man. But that's beside the point. She'd hired this caterer, who specialised in… rude cakes. Of course, you can get away with that sort of thing for a hen do, or one of those naughty knicker parties, but the WI?' She pulled a face and hooted. 'It was sponge cakes in the shape of bums, Madeira bosoms and devil's food cake willies everywhere you looked. You should have seen Meryl's face when the woman whipped away the table cloth to show "these are some I made earlier". Apoplectic, she was.' Morag sounded out each syllable with care. 'That's the only word for it, and the glare she gave Audrey. It would have melted butter.'

'What happened next?' Lizzy was agape.

'Ach, well. There was an emergency board meeting held and Meryl called for Audrey to be thrown off, but the other members had found it funny, mostly, though they did agree the recipes wouldn't be suitable for the cake sale, what with it being officiated by the Bishop and all. But then Meryl made the big mistake of saying that if they didn't throw Audrey off, she'd resign. They said they completely understood and would miss her terribly. Poor woman. I did feel sorry for her, for five minutes anyway. Last I heard, she'd transferred to U3A and was ruling the roost there instead. She was never one to stay in the shadows.'

Daisy bit her lips together. She didn't know whether to be proud of her grandmother or scandalised. 'Gran really was naughty, wasn't she?'

'There was certainly never a dull moment with Audrey.' Morag's gaze rested in the distance and she shook her head at the memories. 'Those were the days. I can tell stories about her all day long.'

'I think we could listen to them, too.' Lizzy smiled a wistful smile. 'Will you stay for tea, Morag? We've loads of food left over. You'd be doing us a favour.'

Morag met her smile. 'Well, why not? My veal and ham pie will keep for another day.'

Morag regaled them with tales until the clock reminded her she needed to get back to catch *The Antiques Roadshow,* leaving Daisy and Lizzy alone. As soon as the door closed behind her, the atmosphere changed, the lightness that had buoyed up the women's moods slipping away. They were cautious around each other, neither wanting a return to the hostile environment of before, but neither could they pretend it hadn't happened.

As they tidied away, it was Daisy who broke the silence first. 'It was nice to talk about Gran like that, wasn't it?'

'Yes, it was.' Lizzy smiled. 'It's easy to focus on the hard times when someone passes away and forget all the other stuff. It takes someone special, like Morag, to bring it all back. She has a good heart.'

Daisy nodded. 'She was good to me, those first few days after… I didn't always appreciate it at the time, but yes, she does.' She paused. 'Did…?' She wasn't sure she was on safe territory, but forged on. 'Did Gran's letter help? I mean, did it bring you comfort at all?' She closed her eyes and swallowed hard. 'I'm sorry I didn't give it to you before. It just clean went out of my head, with all... I didn't do it on purpose.'

Lizzy nodded. 'It's alright, I know you didn't. It's ok.'

'So, did it? Help? Did it explain anything?'

'I think so.' Lizzy frowned as she considered the matter. 'Yes, it did. And I think if I give it a few more days and read it again, it'll probably help even more. But right now, I can't take it in, can't feel it in the way I ought to. Do you know what I mean?'

'I'm not sure. Do you want me to read it? Tell you what I think?'

'No.' Lizzy shook her head. Then, 'Yes. I mean you can read it by all means, in a few days, when I feel calmer about it. It's not that there's anything private in there or anything, it's only, right now it's just words on a page. I just can't absorb it's from Mum to me, how she was feeling and thinking at the end, because it hurts too much. I need time, if that makes sense.'

'I think so.' Daisy shrugged. 'Finn says grief is made up of a great big soup of feelings that can be overwhelming, but they settle down in time, so you can deal with them one by one. Maybe that's what you're going through?'

Lizzy smiled. 'He's a clever chap, your Finn, isn't he? Where did all his wisdom come from?'

'I don't actually know.' Daisy said, aware she was trusting her mother with one of her deepest worries. 'I sometimes think, I don't really know him at all, but I still trust him. Is that wrong? Should I be suspicious about him being so closed off? Like, maybe he's hiding something?'

'What, Finn?' Lizzy grimaced. 'No. He's a lovely boy, through and through. I'd trust him with my life... or my daughter, and that says something.'

'It's not like that, I've told you.' Even so, her mother's comments were reassuring.

'I know. You've told me.' She patted Daisy's shoulder. 'Listen, I've got to get an early night. I don't know what's wrong with me. I'm exhausted.' She walked towards the stairs, then paused, looking back. 'If you ask me, Finn's one of the good ones.' She hauled herself up step by step, as if it was a huge effort. 'Mind you, why would you take my word for it? Look at my history with men. '

Daisy watched her leave, then sighed. Lizzy had a point, her history with men was appalling. Daisy only hoped it wasn't like mother, like daughter

CHAPTER 32

Daisy's sleep had been peppered with random, disturbing dreams, and she woke early on the bank holiday Monday full of restless energy. After an hour of tossing and turning, she got up and pulled on some clothes. Perhaps a walk would make her feel better.

The ground was still damp, but the sky was a vivid, cloudless blue and a few steps and a couple of gulps of fresh air soon raised her spirits. It was going to be a long day with no work on the mural scheduled in, it being a bank holiday with most people having other plans, but that didn't mean she couldn't go and spend some time there, even if it was only to take in what had been achieved so far and plan what needed to come next, to get as far along as possible by the end of the week. She was pleased with the progress, but the more detailed touches would take longer, need more close attention and advancement would slow down. The truth was that they could go on forever, adding embellishments, but she only had to reach a point which would satisfy the landlord, and the heckling neighbours.

When she turned into the path, Finn was already there, overall sleeves pulled up, forearms exposed. He seemed to be erecting some kind of construction around the gateway leading into the yard to the pavilion.

'What are you doing?'

Finn had had his back to her and was startled when she spoke to him. 'Oh. Hi. I'm putting up a barrier so passersby can't see what's going on here.'

'Really? Why?' Over the past weeks they'd been happy to talk to interested onlookers, mustering support for the project, and had even persuaded a few to join the workforce.

'I was thinking about it in the night. It'll have a bigger impact on Friday if we do a proper reveal, rather than everyone seeing it every step of the way. The TV guy's coming along for photos and stuff and he'd probably like that, you know, a grand unveiling. Don't you think?'

'I guess. It sounds like you had as restless a night as I did. Is something up?' Her mind was busy. Was there something keeping him awake? Someone, even? Her heart ached at the idea.

He shrugged off her concerns. 'When I got here, one of the stroppy neighbours was having a good old nosey over the gate. When he saw me, he moved on, pretended he'd been waiting for his dog to walk on, but it made me think. Perhaps we should have a bit of protection from prying eyes.'

'Makes sense, I suppose. Do you think he would have done something if you hadn't come along? Was he trying to sabotage the project?'

'I doubt it, but there can be no harm in removing the temptation, and I wasn't doing anything else.' He ran his fingers through his short fringe and back over the top of his head. 'Anyway, what are you doing here? I thought everyone was having a day off?'

'I was but I woke up early and didn't know what to do with myself. I don't want to be knocking about the house all day with Mum. We'll wind each other right up?'

He frowned. 'How is she?'

'Better, I think. We talked a bit, not much, but it's a start. It's going to take time.'

'Hmm.' He returned his attention to what he'd been doing. 'Families are tricky things.'

A Reason To Be

She waited for him to elaborate. He didn't, but her curiosity was piqued and she couldn't hold back from prompting him. 'I thought you didn't have any family?'

'What made you think that?' He didn't turn to look at her.

'You said you didn't have anywhere to go for Easter Sunday, so I thought...' She left a pause for him to fill.

'I've got family.'

She waited, but he clearly he had no intention of saying any more, all his concentration on the bubble of a spirit level. 'So why weren't you spending Easter with them? Didn't you want to see them?'

'It's complicated.'

'Is it? Why's that?'

'Families are.' He tapped a piece of wood with a hammer. 'You're asking a lot of questions today.'

She sensed she was making him uncomfortable, but she needed to know what Finn was about, who he was, this person she'd let into her life, who she was starting to have strong feelings for. Did he secretly have a wife and kids squirreled away somewhere? Did he have a past he wanted to conceal from her?

'It's not a problem, is it?' Her hand gripped the edge of the stepladder as the tension grew, as she studied him, waiting for a response. 'You've got nothing to hide, have you?' As the silence lengthened, her suspicions ballooned.

He glanced at her momentarily and realised she was watching him. Turning from his work, he shrugged. 'No, it's not a problem. I just don't like to talk about them much. They're not really... relevant, that's all.'

'How can a family not be relevant? Why so top secret?'

'There's no secret, but I don't understand why you're so interested suddenly. Not all families live in each other's pockets. I don't see much of them anymore, so why would you be interested in my past?'

Her mouth dropped open. 'Why? Because I'm interested in you, and the past is never simply the past. It's what makes you what you are today. It's important. Why won't you tell me?'

He shook his head and returned to his work, ignoring her, and she began to wonder if he was going to respond at all, but she continued to watch him and, after a few more seconds, he halted again.

'You've got quite a nerve, haven't you?'

'Me?'

'Yes, you. You expect me to tell you my life story, but you won't even tell me what this huge event was that means "your life is all a waste of time now". Why should I trust you with my personal stuff when you don't trust me?'

Daisy thought about this. She wondered if now was the moment to tell him she wasn't so sure her life was a waste of time, but decided the conversation they were having was tricky enough all ready without adding that into the midst of it. 'I do trust you with my family stuff. You know all about that, but the other thing isn't really my secret to tell.' She chewed on her bottom lip, considering the matter. She had promised never to tell, though a lot of the reasons why it needed to be kept secret were no longer important. On one hand, telling him would be breaking a confidence, but, on the other, she desperately wanted to know about Finn. 'Ok, then. I'll tell you mine, if you'll tell me yours.'

Finn chuckled in disbelief. 'Yeah, right.' He shook his head again and rifled through a pot of nails. As he straightened and made to hammer it into a piece of wood, he realised she was still watching him, waiting. 'Seriously? You're like a dog with a bone, you are.'

She nodded. 'Seriously! We either trust each other, or we don't. So, tell me. And I promise I'll tell you what happened to me.'

He dropped the hammer on the ground and stood with his hands on his hips, his eyes fixed on his feet, as if he was weighing it up. Eventually, he shrugged. 'Ok. If it's that important to you, but not here.' He began to strip off his overalls. 'You never know who's going to turn up, and I don't want the whole world knowing my business. Let's go for a coffee.'

She didn't need telling twice and hurried to catch up, falling into step beside him as he marched out onto the pavement toward the town. He didn't say a word, but strode on until they reached a run-down little café with a couple of two-seater bistro tables huddled on the pavement. He bypassed these and went inside, settling into a booth on the left-hand side. Daisy slipped into a seat opposite him. A waitress appeared from a door at the back and took their order, then they sat in a brooding silence. Daisy sensed this was a momentous occasion, that Finn was struggling with letting her into something very private, and bit her tongue, waiting for him to be ready. Whatever this was, it could be the make or break of their future relationship, whatever shape it would take.

Only when the waitress returned with their steaming mugs did he meet her eye.

CHAPTER 33

'The reason I don't talk about my family, or spend time with them, is because to all intents and purposes, I no longer have one.' Finn was fiddling with the handle of his cup.

Daisy struggled to hold back her impatience. 'What does that mean? "To all intents and purposes"?'

His knuckles turned white as he gripped his coffee mug, staring at the tiny undulations in the liquid as it reacted to a slight tremor coming from his body. 'They don't want to have anything to do with me anymore. They disowned me.'

Daisy's mouth fell open. She and her mother weren't on great terms, but she couldn't imagine a scenario where she was disowned by her. The rumour that he'd done time sprung to mind. 'Finn, what did you do?'

His mouth worked a little, as if he was trying to control his emotions. 'It was more what I didn't do.'

The urge to reach out and take his hand, to offer comfort, was strong, but she held back. She needed to know more about the situation first. What if it was something so bad, she couldn't forgive. What if it hurt her too.

'I didn't save my sister. That's why I'm no longer welcome back there anymore.' He coughed to cover his emotions then sipped at his hot drink, buying time, the cup and saucer rattling together with the clumsiness of his actions. 'I let her die.'

Daisy felt helpless. She didn't know how to help him through this, but she needed to know the full story. 'Tell me.' Sod it, she needed to touch him. Reaching out, she stroked his hand briefly then, conflicted, pulled her own back. 'Tell me everything.'

He pulled a juddering breath into his body, released the air back out, and began to tell his story. 'Becky was a year younger than me, actually, not quite. She was a school year below me but there was only really eleven months between us. She was always there, you know? I can't remember a time without her, until…' He wiped his brow before carrying on. 'And, because I was the oldest, I was supposed to look after her – first day at primary school, then high school. Mum always used to say, "Finn, you're in charge. I'm relying on you to show Becky the way." And I did, most of the time. Not that she always wanted my help.'

'She didn't like you watching over her? Did she resent it?' Daisy was trying to build a picture.

'No, nothing like that. We were really close, but if I tried to pull the big brother card, she would just laugh and ignore me. I was a stick in the mud trying to spoil her fun. She had a reckless streak I never had, that's for sure, and Mum and Dad both knew it, but they thought I'd keep her on the straight and narrow when they weren't around.' A smile crept onto his face as he remembered events of the past. 'It was a job and a half sometimes, I can tell you.'

'So, what went wrong?'

The smile vanished. 'She wanted to go travelling after her A-levels with a group of friends. Mum and Dad weren't keen, for obvious reasons. I'd never had the same travel bug and had taken a dead end job for a year to finance going to university, but Becky came up with a plan. Why didn't I take another year out, go travelling with her for six months, to keep the folks happy, then come back to top up my funds for uni? I wasn't really interested, but she worked on me non-stop for months, every conversation was about how you're only young once, why I should go out and see the world, how we'd have an amazing time, how I'd be making her dreams come true and she'd be forever grateful and, in the end, I gave in. That was my first mistake.'

Daisy observed him across from her, his body hunched over the table. She felt mean forcing him into retelling a story which clearly caused him so much pain, but at the same time, the need to understand what made him tick was overwhelming.

'My second mistake was thinking I could keep her in line, thousands of miles from home, with so many outside influences getting in the way. At home, sober, and with the backing of the folks was one thing. On the other side of the world, with the temptation of all sorts of substances readily available, and mixing with people as hot-headed as she was, I didn't stand a chance.'

Daisy inhaled sharply. 'Drugs?'

'She was taking stuff here and there and, when I caught her, I told her that that was it, I was taking her home, but she wasn't having any of it. It got to the point, I felt so out of my depth, I threatened to call Mum and Dad, but before I could, the worst happened. We'd had a row and I'd given her an ultimatum. Then suddenly she gave in and was, like, "ok, I get it, I'm sorry, I won't do it again. Let's start fresh tomorrow and put this all behind us". I thought I'd talked her into an early night for once. I saw her back to the female dorm and stupidly went to bed, thinking I'd won, but when I got up in the morning, that's when... That's when...' His voice failed him.

'What happened?' Daisy croaked.

'I walked out of my dorm to go and get her up, we were booked on a boat trip, but there was a cordon blocking the path to the other building. There were police everywhere and medics and I just knew. Before they even told me, I knew something had happened to Becky.' He closed his eyes as the final words left his mouth. 'She'd drowned in the pool. She'd waited until I'd gone to bed, then gone back out, drank herself unconscious and somehow ended up in the water. Her so-called friends pleaded ignorance and it was marked down as an accident. That phone call to my parents was the hardest thing I've ever had to do.'

'But it wasn't your fault. Didn't your parents understand that?'

'It's not like they threw me out. I came home, back to my old room, but it was never the same. They were never the same. The atmosphere was terrible. Nobody talking, just so much... silence. It was unnatural.'

'It must have been awful, but surely that was grief, wasn't it? And would pass?'

He shrugged. 'Grief, guilt, blame, anger, disappointment – the whole caboodle. I couldn't face the thought of uni anymore, but didn't know what I wanted to do with my life otherwise. I couldn't stand being in the house though, so I started volunteering, tried a few different things, but the hospice somehow felt right, peaceful. I don't know why. Maybe it was about accepting I couldn't stop Becky dying, but at least I could help others to have as good a death as possible. Is that weird?'

'No, Finn. It's not weird. You really helped Gran, and me. That's a good thing.'

He rolled his eyes. 'My mum didn't think so. I was spending more and more time at the hospice and, one night, I got home in the early hours and found Mum propped up at the kitchen table, drunk and in a right state. I'd never seen her like that before. She accused me of abandoning them, said I preferred spending time with dying strangers than in my own house and, I don't know, maybe because I was exhausted or simply tired of tiptoeing around, I was honest with her. I said I did prefer it. I said I felt she blamed me, that they hated me for not saving Becky, that they wished I'd died instead, and she just sat there staring at me until I'd finished. Then, she got up and walked out, didn't say a word. She might have at least tried to deny it, but she didn't.'

'Oh, Finn.' Daisy didn't know what to say. She couldn't imagine how that had made him feel.

'The next day, Dad cornered me and suggested perhaps uni would be a good idea after all, so we could have space,' Finn made speech marks around the word space with his fingers. 'From each other. I was upsetting my mother, apparently. What he meant was she couldn't bear to look at me.' Finn scratched his head, his eyes searching the air as if looking for some missing piece which would make it all make sense.

Daisy felt helpless. She watched him, not knowing what to say to make him feel better.

'I packed a bag and went to a hostel for a few nights, knowing my funds wouldn't last long. Then, I knew the hospice had a couple of staff bedrooms which weren't being used, because they were earmarked for a refurb, but they were warm and dry, good enough for me, so I sneaked in for a couple of nights. Until one of the maintenance guys caught me. I got marched off to the Superintendant's office and thought that was it, I'd be out on my ear, from both the room and my volunteering post. But the maddest thing happened.' He laughed softly.

'Tell me.'

'She said she'd had her eye on me for a while, the Superintendant, that is. That I fitted right in, and would I be interested in a job – zero hours to start with, until a full-time space came up? On top of which, she happened to have friends whose lodger had given notice, and had a spare room, if I could use it. Those friends were Chris and Joanna. The rest, as they say, is history.'

'Wow! What an amazing woman.'

'I know. It could have so easily gone a different way altogether. And Chris and Joanna were amazing too. They let me stay at a ridiculously low rent until I sorted myself out financially and could afford a bedsit of my own. I think I was one in a long line of hopeless cases they rescued. They're good people.'

'I've come to see that for myself.' Daisy nodded. 'But what about your mum and dad? Hasn't time healed the rift?'

'Not really. I phone home now and again to let them know I'm still alive.'

'And you haven't been able to sort things out at all?'

He paused. 'I only phone when I'm sure they'll be out, and leave messages.'

'Finn!' This shocked Daisy more than anything else he'd said.

'Mum picked up once and I put the phone down. I couldn't handle it. Does that make me a terrible person?' He was studying her face, trying to read her reaction.

'No, it doesn't. It makes you human. But, someday, you're going to have to face it. You can't spend your whole life avoiding them.'

'Hmm.' His response was non-committal.

The silence stretched.

Daisy glanced across at him, a slow grin spreading across her face as she remembered the stories she'd been making up in her head about him prior to this conversation. 'So, you haven't got a wife and three kids tucked away somewhere, then?'

His head shot up. 'What? No! I'm twenty four! I'd have been going some to fit all that in by now.'

She shrugged. 'No criminal convictions for GBH or twocking?'

A lightness slowly returned to his face. 'I've never even stolen a chocolate bar, let alone taken a vehicle without consent. Who's been filling your head with all these ideas?'

'The thing is, Finn, you're a man of mystery, and when people don't know a person's story, they make up their own. I even heard one where you were a Russian hacker hiding out from the authorities.'

'Really? Hmm, I actually quite like that one. I might drop a couple of Russian words into conversation to give it some fuel.'

Daisy chuckled. 'Where did you learn Russian?'

He winked. 'If I told you, I'd have to kill you. I'm a man of mystery, remember?'

'Yeah, right.' She thought for a moment. 'Finn?'

'Yes?'

'Did Becky have dyed red hair?'

He shrugged. 'Sometimes. Or blue. Even green once. Why?'

'Oh, nothing. It was just something someone said once.' A lightness filled her heart. The photo in Finn's wallet had been his sister, she was sure of it.

He frowned at her response but let it go. 'Anyway. I've told you my story. Now it's quid pro quo time. Come on, what's your big secret?'

Daisy breathed deeply. She'd never told anyone the story, but the time had come, and she trusted Finn, especially now he'd shared his with her. As a teenager, it'd seemed vital not to let anyone find out, both for her own and someone else's sake. As an adult, those reasons were probably no longer relevant, but a promise was a promise and it went against the grain for her to break it, and she wouldn't have with anyone except Finn.

'Ok. I'll tell you, but you understand, right? That it mustn't go any further?'

'Who am I going to tell?' He shrugged. 'This is between you and me.'

'Right, well it was about eight years ago…

CHAPTER 34

EIGHT YEARS EARLIER

Daisy scampered down a lane between caravans, past chalets, pausing briefly to check each way before exiting onto the main promenade along the sea front. Not that she was up to no good exactly, but her mother had been adamant about homework being completed before going out to enjoy herself. But the homework was getting longer, and the evenings shorter, by the day. Besides, her mother rarely made an appearance before eight, that is, if she wasn't on one of her frequent business trips abroad anyway. There was always a meeting or a conference or a video call, so Daisy should be able to search for the sea-glass she wanted for her craft project and be home again, with her mother none the wiser. Gran kept out of it, letting daughter and granddaughter fight it out between them, though Daisy could always rely on her for back up when she needed it most.

Daisy loved the tidal pool. It nestled below the sea wall, among craggy rocks, freshly washed and refilled with the tide twice a day. None of those awful chemicals, which made your eyes water, at the swimming baths. Of course, generally, collecting sea-glass didn't require a wetsuit, but Daisy had put it on, just in case. The fact it made a quick dip in the lido possible while otherwise going about her business was a bonus.

The sea was way out, but the waves were wild after last night's winds and the rhythmic roar was music to her ears. She was torn. Really she should search for the glass first and see if there was time for a swim, but her heart sent her straight towards the pool, overriding her conscience. She tiptoed around the pockmarked sand, dips and troughs left by the last tide, pausing here and there to examine interesting bits and bobs rejected by the ocean. A sudden sound caught her attention, but the wind was still a little high down here on the shore and she couldn't make it out. It came again, and she stopped what she was doing, straightening up, ears pricked like a meerkat. Something was off. She couldn't see anyone around, but the lido was just round a corner and she was drawn to it, urgently.

Climbing over a rock, she was now above the pool and, looking down at it, she could see a girl, in trouble. There was a woman lying on a towel to one side, completely ignoring the child's cries. Daisy stood tall and shouted, gesticulating wildly, to get the woman's attention, but the woman was engrossed in something she was reading on her phone and the wind whipped Daisy's words in the opposite direction. Frustrated, Daisy scrambled down and took the quickest route to get close to where the child was flailing, her head disappearing under the water before bobbing back up. When Daisy reached the concrete edge, she picked up speed, racing around the perimeter, knowing the pool wasn't deep enough to dive in and it would be quicker to run to the other side than wade through the water.

At last, she had the woman's attention, who dropped her phone on the towel and leapt to her feet. Daisy reached the spot first, launched herself off the side, landing only a metre or so away from the girl. She grabbed the child from behind, as she had learned in lifesaving classes, pulling her up so her face was no longer submerged and dragged her to the edge, where the shocked woman hovered, a hand covering her mouth as if unable to believe what was happening.

A Reason To Be

'Quick! Help her out.'

Between them, they manhandled the coughing child out, and the woman enveloped her in a fluffy towel. Daisy climbed out behind her.

'Thank you.' The girl spluttered. 'Thank you so much. I slipped and couldn't get back up.'

'That's ok.' Daisy didn't know what to do now the drama was over and looked to the woman, who had a strange quizzical expression on her face and was studying the child intensely, but otherwise didn't appear to be taking any action. 'Should we... should we call an ambulance or something? If you've breathed water in it can be serious.'

Again, the child was most vocal of the pair. 'Oh, no. Thank you, but I'm alright now.'

'Are you sure? It might be a good idea to get checked out, just in case.'

'No. Thank you, but no, honestly, I'm ok and anyway, it's probably best nobody finds out about this. Don't you think so, Mum?'

The woman stared into the girl's eyes for a moment before replying. 'Yes, actually, yes, it probably would. I mean, I should have been watching more closely. I'm really sorry.' She turned to Daisy. 'And sorry to you, too, to have put you to so much bother. Please, don't report this. I promise I'll pay more attention in future, but it's quite important I don't get into trouble, what with the divorce and everything. If her father were to find out...'

The girl piped up. 'Yes, please don't say anything. That social worker might split us up and that would be horrible. I want to stay with my mum.'

The girl's eyes were wide with fear, and the idea the child and her mother might be separated hit Daisy hard. Having only ever lived with her mother and grandmother, she couldn't imagine what it would be like to be taken from them. Also, she'd realised that if the emergency services were to become involved, it would probably get back to her own mother that she'd been at the beach instead of doing her homework, and then she'd have hell to pay.

'Well, I suppose. If you're sure you're alright.'

'I am. I promise you I am.'

The woman stepped forward. 'And can we rely on you to keep this to yourself? You won't tell anyone? Please?'

Daisy shook her head. 'No, I won't.'

The girl grabbed her hand and stared into her eyes. 'Cross your heart and hope to die?'

Daisy smiled. It was a childish phrase she'd used in the past and knew how serious it meant the situation was to the girl. She couldn't let her down. 'Well, I won't hope to die, because that would be horrible, but I do promise with my whole heart. Will that do?'

The girl seemed to think deeply about it. 'Yes, ok.' She turned to the woman. 'Can we go home now, Mum?'

The woman slipped an arm around the child's shoulder. 'Yes, darling, I think that would be a good idea. Let's get going.'

They gathered up their belongings and suddenly Daisy didn't feel like swimming anymore, or collecting sea-glass. She wandered away, but, as she was about to jump from the rocks, to the low sand, the girl piped up. 'Goodbye, and thank you. And don't forget your promise.'

Daisy waved a final farewell. 'Don't worry. I'll never tell a soul. Bye.'

EIGHT YEARS LATER

'So, you see why I couldn't tell anyone? I guess it doesn't matter anymore because I'm grown up and the girl would be too - she could only have been a few years younger than me. I couldn't let them be split up and, of course, I didn't want to get into trouble either. But now do you see why when I read Gran's letter the future seemed so bleak to me? When am I ever going to do anything as important as saving a life again?'

'But when Audrey said she'd done what she was put on earth to do, she wasn't talking about a single event, on a single day. She was talking about something much bigger – a lifetime of small things which, when clumped together, amount to more – being your gran, being Lizzy's mum, being a friend to Morag. Each day she did those things seemed ordinary, insignificant in their own right, but if you step back and look at her whole life, that was very special, wasn't it?

'I hear what you're saying, Finn, and I'm trying to get my head around it. I know logically you're right but I'm not sure I'm in the right place right now to think that way. There's a massive hole in my life where my gran used to be and, on top of that, the most significant event of my life has been and gone. It's over, and everything else I ever do will be measured against it.'

He was getting frustrated. 'By who? Who's doing the measuring?'

'Me! I am.' She waited for this to sink in. 'Look, that doesn't mean I'm going to give up, or lose the will to go on. I'm too stubborn for that, but I do have to accept the fact that the rest of my life is less, will be less than it once was. It's a shame but I can accept it.'

'Well, I can't accept it, because I think you're wrong. Life can't be all about one moment in time. What about families? What about friendships? What about love? They're what life is really about, surely?'

She felt her cheeks redden. If one thing had helped to make her more positive about the future, it was her growing attraction to him, but she certainly wasn't about to tell him that. Not yet, anyway. Besides, she didn't want him to think she didn't need him helping her to find her purpose, not when things were going so well.

'Maybe,' she said. 'I'll let you know if it ever happens.'

He sighed. 'Come on, drink up. I've got things to get on with before the rain comes in.'

They walked in silence back to the pavilion and each got on with the jobs they had gone there to do, and later went their separate ways. What Finn had said was trickling down in Daisy's thoughts, and an idea was beginning to form.

Audrey held her hands out in a wide shrug at what she'd witnessed. 'I don't know what to say.' Dropping her arms to her side, she continued staring at the screen.

'Wonders will never cease.' The ombudsman muttered under his breath.

'I mean, that poor lad. What he's been through, bless him. How a mother could turn on her own child like that and… oh, I just don't know.' She shook her head. 'And as for Daisy, how on earth did she keep that to herself? Such a trauma, and she's never told a soul, not even me. Can you imagine that? Not telling her own grandmother.'

'I thought it was too good to be true,' he muttered.

'Sorry? What's that you're saying?'

'Nothing, Audrey. Nothing at all. I'm as speechless as you are.'

CHAPTER 35

Her brain bubbling with ideas, Daisy went straight to the kitchen when she got home and downed a half pint of cold water, refilled her glass, and leaned her back against the worktop, trying to get her thoughts in order.

Lizzy walked into the room. 'Hello. I heard you come in. Have you been working on the mural?'

'Not really. I went down to give it the once over and work out what to do next.'

'How's it looking? I bet it's great.'

Daisy shrugged. 'It's ok, but it's a bit basic. We've got so much detail to add. I don't think we'll get it all done in time, but I want to be sure we do enough to pass the landlord's inspection.'

'I'm not a fantastic artist like you are, but I can wield a paintbrush if it would help. And it would give me something to fill my days until I find another job.'

Tempting though the idea was, Daisy wasn't sure spending too much time with her mother would be a good plan, when their relationship was so fragile. 'I'll think about it, maybe make a schedule of work, and let you know. Thanks.'

'Ok.' Lizzy unloaded the washing machine into a basket on the floor.

Daisy watched her and decided this was progress. At least Lizzy was making an effort, if nothing else she would have clean clothes to put on. 'How are you feeling today... about everything?'

Lizzy stood up and wiped her hair back from her face. 'Alright, I suppose. Every time I read Mum's letter I pick out something new to fixate on. On the whole, it's all good, but I wish...' She shook her head.

'What?'

'I wish she could have said it to my face, you know? Not waited until it was too late for me to ask questions, or make things right.' Lizzy's eyes swam.

'I'm sorry. I didn't mean to upset you again.'

'You haven't. It's the situation which upsets me. I keep reading the same sentence and one minute I think she's being nice and then I think it's criticism. It's enough to drive you mad.'

'But you know Gran. She had a funny way of putting things sometimes but it's just her way.'

'I don't think I did know her, not like you. I'm second guessing everything.'

Daisy rested a hand on her mother's shoulder. 'I know it's private, but shall we read it together, so I can give you my take on it?'

'It's probably a good idea. And, it's not that private. We weren't close. You know that.' Lizzy reached up and patted Daisy's hand, acknowledging its presence, accepting it. 'I'll go and get it.'

While she waited, Daisy sat on the sofa and steeled herself for hearing her gran's voice again.

Lizzy returned, stood for a moment grasping the letter in both hands, as if reticent to let go of it, then passed it over in a rush and sat next to her daughter.

The paper trembled in Daisy's fingers. She smiled at Lizzy, then read aloud. *Dear Lizzy. It's been a while, hasn't it? Too long, and I can't imagine what's going through your mind considering the circumstances or how you're feeling. Shocked and angry, I expect. Sad too, I hope, because we were important parts of each other's*

A Reason To Be

lives once upon a time, even if not so much recently. I think it's fair to say we both had a part to play in that. You may not agree, but then, we agreed on less and less as we got older. I suppose I took it too personally that you had your own opinions, and didn't always fall into line with mine. Perhaps I could have been more open to what you had to say, especially about how to bring up your own daughter. What can I say? I'm set in my ways.' Daisy looked up at Lizzy to gauge how she was feeling. 'You alright?'

Lizzy nodded, so Daisy continued. *'I didn't mean for you to be left out, at the end. I kept thinking I was going to get better, feel stronger and, when I did, I'd call you up and tell you what was going on and we'd sort things out between us once and for all, but that day never came and suddenly it was too late, and I didn't have the strength to say what needed to be said. Besides, I didn't want all your memories of me to be nothing but bad ones – us at odds for years and then of me withering away and dying. Try and remember the good days we had, when it was you and me taking on the world, rather than each other. Please.'* Daisy dropped the hand holding the letter down to her side. 'I did tell her to let me ring you, but she wouldn't. She didn't want you to give up everything in America to come back, when there was nothing you could do anyway.'

'I should have told you I was back in England.' Lizzy frowned deeply. 'I should have let you know, then I could have been here for you, even if she didn't want me.'

'But you see, it wasn't about not wanting you.' Daisy waved the letter. 'It wasn't about that.' She sighed and continued. *'Daisy's going to need her mother now she doesn't have an old granny to call the shots. Thank you for sharing her with me, and I'm sorry if I was greedy. I loved her firstly because of who she was in herself, and secondly because I loved her mother too, though I was terrible at letting that show. It's the two of you taking on the world now, but don't worry, I'll be keeping any eye out for you both. Your grumpy and loving battleaxe of a mother. P.S. I may have rued the day I met your father, but I never regretted what came from that meeting, even for a minute.'*

Lizzy was sniffing back tears. 'It's a good letter, isn't it? It means nice things?'

Daisy had been absorbing the contents, particularly the bit about Audrey being greedy, and it reminded her of what Lizzy had said about feeling pushed out, and she realised there may have been some truth in it. 'Of course it is.' Her heart ached with unspent tears. 'Gran did love you. She was always telling me stories of things you'd done together, in the old days, and she'd have this dreamy look on her face.'

'I know she did, but I wish… oh, I don't know what I wish. Just that things had been different, I suppose.' She wiped a tear from her cheek with the heel of her hand. 'But it's too late now, isn't it?'

'I don't know. I think this goes a long way to setting things straight.' She waved the letter before handing it back. 'She's acknowledged things weren't right, that she felt a good part to blame and she wanted to put it right. It's up to you now, isn't it? And how you choose to remember her? Gran could be…' Daisy chose the word carefully, not wanting to be disloyal to her beloved grandmother. 'Tricky, but underneath, she had a good heart, and that's what we should remember.'

'Yes, you're right.' There were several seconds of silence before she continued. 'But I wish I'd had the chance to give her one more hug, you know?' Her voice disappeared.

Daisy's eyes were full of tears too. 'I know. But maybe you could hug me, instead?'

They held each other tight and Lizzy cried. When she finally pulled back, she wiped her face and shook the emotion away. 'Let's make a pact that you and me will always talk about our problems and keep the lines of communication open, even if we're pains in the bums. Yes?'

Daisy laughed. 'Yes. Ok.'

Lizzy stood up and exhaled slowly. 'I need to wash my face. Fancy a film and a takeaway?'

'Yeah, why not.' She watched her mother slowly walk up the stairs, but her mind was elsewhere. If this experience had taught her anything, it was how important it was to build bridges and put an end to disagreements. She shouted up the stairs. 'I've got to pop out for a bit, Mum. I've got a couple of things to do, but I'll be back later. Ok?'

A disjointed voice came from above. 'Ok. See you later.'

CHAPTER 36

Daisy stared at the phone number she'd added to her list of contacts. The less said the better about how she'd got hold of it, but now that she had, she still wasn't sure whether she should use it or not. In a certain light, it could be seen as a betrayal of trust, but wasn't it the end result that really mattered? And, Finn had done so much for her, starting even before her Gran had died and, since that terrible day, he'd continued to be a rock. She wanted to do something for him in return. Besides, what could go wrong?

Clenching her teeth, Daisy clicked on the number before she could chicken out. It rang several times, and she was about to give up, when a small voice spoke at the other end. 'Hello. Kennedy residence.'

Daisy's tongue tripped itself. 'Oh, hi, um, hello, um.' She took a deep breath, mentally urging herself to pull herself together. 'Hello. Is that Finn's mum?'

Silence stretched out, until Daisy thought the woman may not have heard, but eventually, 'Yes. This is Finn's mother. Is he... Is everything alright?'

The woman sounded petrified and Daisy kicked herself for not planning her words more carefully. The family had already lost one child. No surprise if his mother's first thought was that something disastrous had happened. 'Yes, sorry. Finn in fine, everything's ok.

It's just, I'm a friend of his and I thought... I don't know what I thought. I suppose I was hoping I might be able to do something, help in some way, to bring you all back together. He's been kind to me and I wanted to do something for him, because I know he's hurting right now, and I'm guessing you are too...' She ran out of steam and a long pause followed.

'Is he? Hurting?' There was a tremor to the woman's voice.

This was her one chance and Daisy didn't want to get it wrong, but neither did she know what was the right thing to say. 'Yes, but, I mean, he's ok. He's getting on with life, you know? But it would be better if he could find a way back to being closer with you and his dad again.'

'Did he say that?'

Daisy's conscience pricked. 'Yes, well, no, not exactly, but I know it's true, whether he said it outright or not. He misses you terribly, both of you... and Becky.'

'Of course. They were so close. We all miss Becky.' There was another pause. 'And we miss Finn, too. He can come back any time.'

That wasn't going to be enough to convince Finn. He was so hurt, Daisy was convinced he would never have the courage to take the first step, for fear of being rejected again. She had to go further. 'He feels so responsible, for what happened, and he thinks you hold him responsible too.'

'I know he does.' The woman sighed. 'And I suppose I did, for a while anyway. We were all in a great deal of pain and that doesn't always allow you to see a situation clearly. I needed someone to blame. I've been seeing things differently for a while now. I got some help. It still hurts, but I know the pain isn't caused by Finn.'

'He could really do with hearing that from you.'

'Believe me, if I had the opportunity to tell him, I would. But he hasn't spoken to us for months, years it is now. And we have no way of contacting him. His number changed and we don't know where he's living. My husband said we should give Finn space, that when he was ready to talk to us, he would. Trust me, it's not been easy waiting, but I feel responsible for the situation we find ourselves in and, because of that, I've respected his choice to be away from us. You know? If he needs space, I owe him that much, don't you think?'

Daisy wondered if the woman was right, that it should be up to Finn to take the first step towards reconciliation. But no, he hadn't chosen to walk away, he thought he had no choice but to go, and he needed to be invited back in. It was time to bridge that distance. 'Maybe he needs you to reach out. Maybe it's something he can't handle himself.'

'If I thought that was true, I'd move heaven and earth...' The woman's voice broke momentarily, but she coughed to cover it up and took that time to regain control. 'What do you suggest? You clearly know our son better than we do these days. What should we do?'

Now they'd arrived here, Daisy's resolve faltered. It was the point of no return. 'We've been working on a project together - painting a mural on a building used by a local youth club that we help out at. There's a grand unveiling on Friday. Maybe you and Mr Kennedy could come along? I'll text you the details, if that's ok?'

'Alright. I'll talk to Roger and wait to hear from you. ' She paused. 'I'm trusting you here, to know what's best for our family. I take it you're his girlfriend?'

'Oh, no. Nothing like that.' Daisy was quick to jump in. 'We're just friends, that's all, good friends.'

Daisy ended the call and sat in quiet contemplation. The Kennedy family reunion was an awfully big deal. If it went wrong, it could be the final straw for the family, and the end of her friendship with Finn too.

CHAPTER 37

Daisy and her helpers worked as long as the light would allow each day to get the mural as far forward as possible, and she was pleased with the progress. She didn't see much of Finn as they were on opposing shifts, he overseeing Lewis and a couple of others, while Daisy supervised Harley and her band of friends. Each day, they shared a smile and a quick chat as they handed over to each other, but Daisy felt there was a change in atmosphere between them somehow wasn't so easy, she didn't feel as free. She didn't know if this was because of the secret she was keeping, or the feelings she had for him, but something had definitely shifted.

The day before the unveiling, Chris came to talk to them, during changing over. 'Good news,' he said.

The hustle and bustle paused as they stopped to listen.

'Sorry to interrupt, but I've had a call from Joel – you probably already know about this Harley, so apologies – but he wanted to let me know that the TV studios are sending a film crew to the grand unveiling tomorrow evening, so it's turning out to be quite an event. It would be lovely if we could gather a crowd, so if you'd like to invite friends and family that would be great, for about six in the evening.'

Daisy was nervous. 'Do you think we're ready, Chris? There's still lots to do.'

He stood back and gestured at the wall. 'We're close enough. I think Mr Cahill will find it difficult to refuse us continuing use of the building – it's been completely transformed from what it was. Besides, that's partly why it's good the TV crew are coming. It makes it very hard for him to turf us out without coming across as a total scrooge, but don't tell anyone I said so. But to be honest, any small advantage we can grab hold of is of value, for the youth club to live on for another day.' He looked around to take everyone in with his smile. 'You've all worked so hard. You should be proud of yourselves. Thank you.' He paused. 'Anyway, I'll let you get on.'

Daisy turned to Finn. 'There's no way I'm going to sleep tonight. I know Chris is Mr Optimistic, but what if it goes wrong?'

Finn slipped one arm around her shoulder, pulling her close to his side, waving at the mural with his other hand. 'The only way it could go wrong now would be if the wall fell down or something massive like that. If we had to do the unveiling now, it's close enough to done to pull it off. Look at what you've achieved, Daisy.'

She did look, but all she could think about was the feel of his body pressed against hers. She cleared her throat. 'I suppose it's ok.'

'Ok?' He looked down at her with raised eyebrows. 'It's fantastic.' He dropped his arm. 'Is Lizzy coming along tomorrow?'

'I haven't mentioned it to her yet, but I'm sure she will, if I ask her.'

'You should. She'll be so proud of you. It'll be good to have your mum there to support you.'

Her stomach twisted at the plan she'd put together. She was almost as nervous about what she'd planned with Finn's family as she was about the mural itself. There was still time to turn things around. 'Perhaps you should invite your family too?' She tested.

'Now, *that's* not going to happen. Let's not even go there.' He chuckled, shaking his head, and held his palm up to her as he walked away. 'I'll see you for the great event.' He paused. 'Do you want to get together for something to eat after? There's something I wanted to talk to you about.'

A Reason To Be

She tipped her head to one side in question. 'Sure, what's up?'

'It's nothing to worry about.' He smiled. 'It'll keep until then.'

'Ok. See you there then.'

Daisy worked on the mural right up to the last ten minutes. Tarpaulin's had been rigged up, ostensibly to be whipped away for the unveiling, but it also gave her somewhere to hide while she added a leaf here and flower there, trying to create wow factor. Tension had been building all day, both for the reaction to the painting, and for Finn's reaction to his parents' surprise appearance. She'd have ducked out from behind the sheet and run for the hills until it was over if she thought she would get away with it, but she knew she wouldn't, and besides, too many people were relying on her.

Joanna appeared from one side. 'Daisy. Time to pack away. Chris wants to start soon, and there's someone here to see you.'

Her first thought was that Finn's parents had arrived already. 'I'll be right there.' She gathered her tools up in a bucket and sidestepped to the end of the screening and out. Lizzy stood there, hands clasped tightly in front of her, as if she was as nervous as Daisy. 'Oh, Mum, it's you.'

'Yes, it's me. How are you feeling? Are you all set?'

'As ready as I'll ever be, I suppose.' She rattled the bucket. 'Let me stow these away and I'll be right with you.' Daisy nipped into the pavilion and placed the bucket in the kitchen to wash up later.

Finn was in there already, rubbing his cheek with a damp cloth. He glanced at her and grimaced. 'Apparently, I've still got gloss paint on my face from yesterday. How the heck do I get it off? Sandpaper?'

'I'm sure it won't come to that.' She moved in closer for a good look and laughed at the smudge next to his nose. 'Hang on, I've got some turps somewhere.' She opened a cupboard and reached down a bottle from the top shelf, tipped a little onto a cloth and turned her attention back to him. 'You're too tall, crouch down so I can see what I'm doing.'

He did as he was told. 'That cloth's filthy. You're not going to make it worse rather than better, are you?'

She pulled back a little so she could meet his eye, one hand still holding his cheek. 'Finn Kennedy, don't you trust me?'

He met her gaze and held it a moment longer than was strictly necessary. His voice had a husky quality. 'I'm not entirely sure I do.'

Her mouth went dry under his scrutiny, and her belly did a flip. Was he thinking about kissing her? She was most definitely thinking about kissing him, but now was not the right time.

'The film crew's here, guys. Stations, please.' Chris's voice came from the main hall.

Finn took the cloth from Daisy's hand and wiped his own face, but maintained the proximity and the eye contact. 'Are you still coming out with me after this?'

'Umm, yes. Yes, I am.'

'Good.' He turned his face slightly. 'Am I fit to appear on camera?'

She smiled shyly. 'You'll do.'

Chris ushered them out to face the crowd which had gathered. Finn nudged Daisy in front of him, shielding himself from too much attention. Daisy scanned around for familiar faces, and a particular couple of unfamiliar ones. She spotted her mother near the front, talking to Joanna, with Morag alongside, too. Harley was in a huddle with her friends, ignoring her own mother's calls to join her and Joel with a man wielding an enormous video camera. Chris darted around, checking everyone was ready to go, then stood with Daisy and Finn to deliver his speech.

'Hello, everyone. Thanks for coming, particularly Mr Cahill, our generous and long suffering landlord - thank you for your patience, and the local residents, who have put up with all the comings and goings over the last few weeks - I hope you'll be pleased with the result. Also, thanks to all the young people who have worked with us to get us to this point and, of course, to Daisy our designer/artist and Finn, one of our youth leaders, who's been helping to coordinate the efforts.'

He rubbed his hands together and nodded at Lewis, who was waiting to one side, ready to pull the cover away when instructed. 'Ok, Lewis, let everyone see what we've done.'

Lewis pulled one end free of its hook and ran across the yard to reveal the front of the building.

There were gasps as the crowd reacted to the artwork of a colourfully decorated terrace of miniature houses, complete with gardens, on a backdrop of blue skies and wispy white clouds. A spontaneous round of applause broke out, and Daisy felt her cheeks glow with bashful pleasure.

'Thank you, everyone.' Chris acknowledged the appreciation. 'Daisy, do you want to explain a bit about what's been done here?'

Given the option, she would have rather not but, following an encouraging. 'Come on, Daisy,' from Chris, realised it was a rhetorical question.

'Umm, yes. Well, we wanted to use lots of colour to brighten the place up, and the design is based on Bo-Kaap in South Africa, where they decorate their houses in vibrant colours. Then, each of our helpers added their own personal touches to make a part of the mural their own. I hope you like it.'

Morag hollered from the crowd. 'It's a bobby dazzler, so it is.' More applause followed the comment.

Chris waited for the noise to drop. 'We like it, and it sounds as if you do too, but the most important opinion here is Mr Cahill's, and whether he thinks it's good enough to let the youth club stay here a while longer.'

Mr Cahill looked very serious and coughed into his hand before speaking. 'Yes, well, it has been suggested to me on many occasions that perhaps it's time to redevelop this land and put houses here instead of an old pavilion. But, I must say, the huge amount of effort that has been put in to transform the building speaks volumes of how much these young people value the premises. And, seeing the fantastic result, I can only say what an absolute travesty it would be to see it torn down. Bravo, team. Bravo.' He clapped.

Daisy's heart swelled with pride and feeling tears gathering in her eyes, she turned to share the emotion with Finn. But, rather than joining her in her joy, his face was frozen in shock. She followed his line of sight to see what had affected him so intensely, and realised it was a smartly dressed middle-aged couple, standing on the edge of the crowd. His eyes were fixed on them and she could see the rapid rise and fall of his chest as his breathing increased.

Chris continued to speak and the audience continued to react, but Daisy was oblivious to everything but Finn. At last, there was another rapturous round of applause, and Chris placed a hand briefly on her shoulder as he stepped away to go and mingle. Chatter filled the air, but Daisy felt as if she was in a bubble of muffled sound.

'Finn?' She questioned.

He looked at her, but didn't move.

She reached out and touched his arm. 'Is it ok? Did I do the right thing?'

His mouth fell open. 'You?'

She nodded. Finn stared at her for a moment longer, then stepped away, allowing her hand to drop down, and walked towards the couple she assumed to be his parents.

A voice broke through the fog – Lizzy. 'Well done, Daisy. It's wonderful. Are you happy?'

She turned and smiled, but was distracted by the interaction taking place on the other side of the yard. The woman was dabbing her face, the man talking earnestly, while Finn stared at his shoes. Then, as a group, they walked towards the gate and out.

'Daisy?'

'Sorry, what?'

'I said, shall we go somewhere to celebrate? What do you fancy? Italian?'

Daisy figured she was no longer going somewhere with Finn, but it was something they could rearrange for another time. At least, she sincerely hoped so. 'Yeah. Italian is good.' The last thing on her mind was her stomach.

*

'Oh, I was afraid of that.' Audrey held her face in her hands as she watched events unfold. 'If only I could have warned her against it.'

'You don't think Daisy should have tried to bring Finn's family back together?' His head was tipped to one side as he studied her.

'Well, when you say it like that, of course it sounds like the right thing to do, but mark my words, nothing good ever came from sticking your oar in where it wasn't wanted.'

'Hmm, possibly. That remains to be seen.'

'I completely agree,' Audrey jumped in quickly. 'I was afraid you might try and hurry me along on my journey, but I absolutely have to see how this pans out, even if I do have my suspicions it's going to come back and bite my Daisy on the bum.'

The ombudsman pursed his lips as he stared at her, then shook his head. 'You don't miss a trick, Audrey, do you?'

'Not me.' She chuckled. 'I've had too many years of practice, and I'm not ready to give up quite yet.'

He breathed deeply for a few moments, then turned to her with a serious expression. 'You do know this has to end though, don't you Audrey?'

The smile dropped from her face and she bit her lips together before answering, composing herself. 'I'm no fool. Of course I do. But not yet, eh? You can spare an old lady a bit more time, can't you?'

He reached across and patted her hand where it rested next to her empty tea cup. 'I've nothing pressing, right now. I expect there's time for one more.'

'That's the spirit.' She smiled as he headed for the drinks machine once again. 'And if there are any Custard Creams squirreled away back there, I wouldn't say no to one of those either, for medicinal purposes.'

'There's nothing medicinal about a Custard Cream.'

'You're a doctor as well now, are you? Along with all your other skills?' She tutted, and gave him no time to reply. 'No, I thought not, and until you've got your medical certificate, I'll decide what's good for me and what's not, alright?'

'You're the boss, Audrey.' He sighed. 'You're the boss.'

'Yes, and don't you forget it.'

CHAPTER 38

Despite numerous texts to him, Daisy heard nothing from Finn, but Chris rang her to say that Finn was 'under the weather' and wouldn't be able to go with her to do the follow up interview at the TV studio. Instead, Harley would be attending with her, and Joel had arranged a car for them.

Daisy chewed her lip as she thought about it. Perhaps Finn wasn't well, but surely not so ill he couldn't even message her. After all, he'd managed to let Chris know. She had a horrible, gut wrenching feeling she'd really stuffed it up with Finn, once and for all. Ironic that he'd put up with all sorts of diva behaviour from her since her gran died, even tried to help her find her reason to be, but it was when she tried to do something nice for him in return that it should all go so wrong.

She wondered what had happened at Finn's reunion with his parents. It clearly hadn't been hugs all round – she'd witnessed that for herself - but surely it had been a chance to talk, to clear the air. That's what she'd been trying to achieve, but what if she'd only made things worse? Finn may never forgive her.

Daisy had been told to be ready for her trip to the studio, and had dutifully done so, but she wasn't prepared for the limousine which pulled up outside the house.

A door at the back swung open and an overly excited Harley leaned out. 'Come on, miss. We've got champagne and everything in here. Let's go.'

Daisy glanced up and down the street, aware of curtains twitching. This would give Morag something to talk about, she thought, as she climbed in. 'What's all this? It's only two minutes on local TV, not a world premier.'

'I know but Joel says a girl should make the most of her five minutes of fame, and if he wants to flash the cash, who am I to stop him. Besides, he owes me, because he's booked us a trip to Disneyland, Florida, and it clashes with my prom night. I wasn't going anyway, but no need for him to know that.'

'Harley!'

'What?' She shrugged dramatically. 'There's got to be some advantages to being part of a blended family or what's the point?' She pulled open a mini-fridge and handed a champagne flute and miniature bottle to Daisy, before opening one for herself with a loud pop and a giggle.

'Are you even allowed to drink that? You're only sixteen.'

Harley adopted a gruff voice. 'Go easy on the booze, young lady. You can have one and not a drop more. No stepdaughter of mine is appearing in front of the great unwashed half cut. Got it?' She grinned and took a sip before grimacing. 'Yuck, that's rank. One'll be more than enough. Come on, miss. Get it down you.'

Daisy considered it. 'I'm not sure I should. Last time I went to the studio I completely froze. I need all my wits about me to get through this, particularly without Finn backing me up this time.'

'All the more reason to have a drink. It'll loosen you up. Anyway, I'll be right there next to you, so what's to be afraid of?'

Daisy shrugged. 'I think it was seeing Craig Allbright in the flesh. I watched his evening show every week with my gran. It was a bit overwhelming meeting the man himself.'

'What? You're worried about Craig?' At Daisy's nod, Harley continued. 'He's nothing special, even if he thinks he is. We went to a pool party at his last summer. He's got a swish pad, I'll give him that, but by halfway through the evening he'd had one too many sherbets. He went to dive off the diving board, slipped and his shorts got caught and were dangling off the end, while he fell in, absolutely starkers.' She shuddered. 'Completely put me off my prawn vol au vent.'

Daisy couldn't help but laugh at the image.

'Remember that if you start getting star struck. You'll soon get over it.' There was a pause, before Harley continued. 'So, what's up with lover boy, anyway?'

Daisy frowned in confusion.

'Finn,' Harley let her frustration show. 'Why isn't he here?'

'I told you he's not my lover boy.'

'Yeah, yeah, whatever!' Harley batted Daisy's comment away. 'Come on, spill. What's gone on?'

Daisy huffed in annoyance, then sighed, realising Harley wasn't giving up any time soon. 'I don't know.' She shrugged. 'But I did something I probably shouldn't have. And I haven't heard from him since.'

'Wow, miss. Did you do the dirty on him? I didn't know you had it in you.'

'What?! No! Nothing like that. Honestly, Harley, I don't know where you get your ideas from. I tried to do something nice and I guess it didn't go the way I'd hoped. I shouldn't have stuck my nose in to his business.'

'Oh, well. He'll get over it and I happen to know he is going to be at the youth club party on Tuesday, so you'll have a chance to sweet talk him them. Anyway, don't sweat it. My mum says that as long as you act with good intentions it'll all work out in the end…'

Daisy nodded, happy to accept any words of comfort, wise or otherwise.

'And if it doesn't, that's their loss, so stuff the lot of them.'

'Oh…'

'Hey. We're here. Brilliant. Come on. Let's go.'

Before Daisy could digest Harley's last words, she was whisked out of the limo and through the rotating doors into the studio building.

Daisy had been waiting in the green room with Harley for what seemed like an age, and nerves were starting to get to her – and the tall macchiato she'd treated herself to in the studio canteen earlier was pressing on her bladder. The runner who'd told her where to wait rushed in to collect another guest, and Daisy felt she had no choice but to waylay him.

'Excuse me. Would it be ok for me to pop to the loo? Is there time?'

He glanced at his huge wristwatch and pursed his lips. 'We're running a couple of minutes over so, yes, if you're quick.' He waved her to the door and pointed. 'End of the corridor, through the doors and on the left, halfway down. You can't miss it. Sorry, I'd show you, but I need to get Norman on.'

She hurried into the corridor after him so she could follow his directions. 'Ok. Thank you.'

'Straight back, though. No wondering off. Criag'll have my guts for garters if you're not ready on cue.'

She reassured him she'd be as fast as she could and quick stepped down the way he'd indicated, but was pulled up short by Harley's voice.

'Hang on, I'm coming too.'

A couple of minutes later, they exited the toilets to find a corridor which looked identical in both directions. Daisy took a step to the right, then stopped. 'This is the right way, isn't it?'

Harley looked both ways. 'I'm not sure now.'

Daisy turned back the other way, marched a few steps and stopped again. She'd completely lost her sense of direction and the pressure of being against the clock only made it worse. 'Let's wait here a minute. Maybe somebody will come by who we can ask.'

A Reason To Be

They both hovered, craning their necks in either direction every time there was a sound, but no one appeared.

'Oh, heck. We're going to be in such trouble if we're not ready when they call us.'

'Don't worry, miss. It was only through one set of doors. Let's just run down and peek through at that end. If it doesn't look right, we can turn right around.'

Daisy was dubious, but didn't want to delay any further. 'Go on, then. Let's have a look.'

They both jogged to the double doors and pushed through. Daisy immediately realised it was the wrong way. Instead of a sign for the green room being on the other side, there was another set of double doors marked up with the words "Studio 4" and a red glowing electronic sign above it saying "Recording in Progress".

'Come on,' Daisy said. 'We'd best get back.'

'Hang on.' Harley was peering through small glass slats in the upper half of the doors. 'I want to see what's recording. Somebody famous might be in there, an influencer or someone.'

'I doubt it.' Daisy was impatient to get moving. 'It's only local TV remember, not national.'

Harley sighed. 'I suppose,' but kept peering, then gasped audibly. 'Hang on, I think that's…' She stood on tiptoe and leaned so close her nose was touching the glass of the door. 'It is.'

'It's who?' Daisy took a step closer.

'Thingy.' Harley shook her head in frustration. 'You know, that actress from Weird Dimensions. The young one. She's, like, a superstar. You must know of her. I wonder what she's doing here?'

'I don't know who you mean.'

'You must have seen it. It's on, like, its third season or something. It's huge.'

Daisy shrugged. Audrey had always refused to pay for subscription TV, so if the show hadn't been on terrestrial, she was unlikely to have seen it. 'I must have missed that one.' She checked her watch and glanced over her shoulder to where they should be heading. 'Come on. They'll be looking for us in a minute.'

She heard the doors in front of her swish softly open and Harley's harsh whisper. 'I'm going in.'

'What? No! You can't go in there.'

But it was too late. Harley had already disappeared inside.

Daisy stood open-mouthed for a few seconds. 'Oh, Harley.' She put her hand to her forehead. What was she to do? The teenager was in her charge. She had no choice but to go in after her.

Inside was a different atmosphere altogether. Only a section in the centre of the room was brightly lit – two turquoise sofas set at angles, so the two occupants were half facing each other, but were also facing the cameras, which circled the area a few metres away. Behind the sofas, were fake walls, which looked very odd to Daisy, as they seemed to stop abruptly at normal room height, whereas the studio itself was cavernous. The celebrities being filmed – Daisy recognised the middle-aged man on the left as a well-known chat show host, but although the trendy young girl looked familiar, Daisy couldn't quite place her – were chatting animatedly, in what gave the appearance of quite an intimate setting. They were surrounded however, not only by cameras, but by at least twenty technicians, operating equipment, holding booms and clipboards and directing lighting.

Harley had snuck around the edge to a particularly shady area, where she could see everything while not being seen herself, and was staring wide-eyed.

Daisy waved to get her attention, but Harley either didn't notice or chose to ignore her, so she pressed herself close to the wall and side-stepped towards her young charge.

'Harley,' she hissed. 'We need to go!'

'Shush! Two minutes. I want to hear the end of the story. She's a legend.'

Canned laughter drowned out what the celebrity was saying and she paused for it to end.

A Reason To Be

The interviewer prompted her when quiet returned. 'So, tell me, how exactly *did* your private rehearsals get you into trouble? I've got to hear this.'

The actress looked around the space, biting her lips together as if loathe to reveal her story, but then looked back at the interviewer and rolled her eyes. 'Oh, I suppose I can tell you, but it's so embarrassing. It'll go no further, right?' Her accent was a strange combination of upper class English and American.

The interviewer looked straight at camera and wiggled his eyebrows, faking a small cough, before saying, 'Of course, anything you say will stay strictly between us.'

More canned laughter.

She straightened her shoulders in readiness to tell her tale. 'You must remember, I was only young.'

'Whereas now you're clearly getting on a bit.'

More laughter.

'No, I mean really young, like twelve or something, and I'd just got the part in Mixed Emotions. You know, the one I got my first Best Supporting Actress nomination for.'

'We all remember that one. You were phenomenal, absolutely phenomenal.'

She put a modest hand to her chest. 'Thank you. But anyway, I'd been sent a pile of pre-filming notes, so I could prepare ahead of time, and I was between roles, so my mother, my agent and I took a short vacation. We all need a little R & R from time to time, right?'

'Especially when you put so much of yourself into each role, I'm sure.'

'Exactly. So, my agent had a little apartment, not far from here actually, so we came on down for some chill. But, of course, I just had to have a few run throughs of my scenes. I mean, the writing was so strong, so powerful, how could I not, right?'

'I completely understand.'

'So, this one afternoon, I'm out with my agent, right? And, we're down on the coast, taking in the waves and the sun and, my, it's a beautiful place. And then we come across this kind of outdoor pool, surrounded by rocks and there's virtually nobody around and I'm, like, struck with how it's the perfect spot to practice one particular scene. So, I say to my agent, like, are you thinking what I'm thinking? And, you know, she's known me so long, she can just read me.'

'A great relationship to have.'

'Oh, yeah, we're tight. So, she says, "Billie, go for it girl". So I did… really…go for it.' She shrugged.

The interviewer's mouth was agape. 'What did you do?'

'Well, there was this scene – it actually got cut before production, so I never got to use what I rehearsed – but it was a near drowning scene. So, picture this: I'm in the water, shouting, coughing and spluttering, my arms flailing, my head slipping under now and again, giving it my all. My agent is on the side, half watching, half catching up on her emails, shouting directions at me now and again, but generally just letting me do my thing. Then along comes this girl.'

'A girl? Who?'

'To this day I have no clue, but she came running from nowhere, shouting at my agent, and dived right in and pulled me out onto the side.'

The interviewer slapped one of his knees, clearly enjoying the tale. 'Oh, no, she didn't. I can't believe it. What did you do?'

Billie held her face in her palms briefly, shaking her head. 'Well, you can imagine what a shock it was, for me, and for her, and, you know, on a different occasion she would have been a real hero and I, sort of, couldn't let her down. So I pretended she had really, genuinely saved me, and my agent, well, she just followed my lead. In fact, she pretended to be my mother and, of course, we couldn't let a story like that get out. I mean, the paparazzi would have been all over it, would have hounded me to find out what I was working on, and it was all still top secret right then, so we couldn't take the risk. My agent begged the girl to keep it to herself, said she'd be in so much trouble if the authorities had found out she wasn't paying proper attention while looking after me. I think there was some mention of Social Services and I could tell, the girl, she bought every word. She promised never to tell a soul and to the best of my knowledge, she never has.'

The interviewer was laughing. 'Oh, that's so good, that's such a good story. Thank you for sharing that with us.' He paused. 'Tell me, Billie, if you were to come across that girl again, what would you say to her?'

'Gosh, I don't know.' A frown formed on the girl's forehead. 'I guess I'd thank her again, because she may not have been a lifesaver, but she certainly saved my bacon and my career.'

Daisy watched, stunned as the girl retold Daisy's own story, the story which she had replayed in her mind time and again since reading her gran's letter on the day she died. A barrage of emotions rushed through her: she felt embarrassed, not to have recognised what was obviously a very famous actress; angry and mortified that she'd been played in that way and had fallen for it hook, line and sinker, but also relieved that the event which had hung over her as the biggest achievement she could ever hope to reach had, in fact, been a fake.

Before she could decide which emotion won out or react, a hand grasped her shoulder and she turned to see the runner scowling at her, and whispering harshly. 'I've been looking all over for you. What are you doing… Oh, never mind. Come on, you're on, now.'

Daisy grimaced and apologised, grabbing Harley's hand and dragging her through the doors, behind the disgruntled assistant. She couldn't wait to get their segment over with, so she could go home and digest what had happened.

The TV interview went well. Harley was a natural in front of the cameras, only leaving Daisy to fill in a few gaps, and Daisy was more than happy with that – her mind was too full with what she'd learned at the studio and she needed time and space to process it fully. The limo dropped her off first and Harley had offered up some final wisdom before being driven away.

'If I were you, miss, I'd give him a call to break the ice. It'll all blow over, you'll see.'

'I'll think about it.' Daisy managed a weak smile. 'Harley, do you think there's a chance you might drop the "miss" and call me Daisy instead?'

'I don't know, miss.' Harley grinned. 'I'll think about it.'

The door slammed and the car pulled away, leaving Daisy alone at the end of her path. She suddenly felt lonely. Ever since her gran died, if she was feeling low, if she needed someone to talk to, Finn had been there. This new lack of certainty was uncomfortable and disturbing. If she'd lost her gran, and now lost Finn, how was she going to cope?

She walked up the path and pushed open the door, only to be engulfed in a huddle of arms - Lizzy and Morag.

'Well done, Daisy. You were absolutely amazing.' Lizzy stood back to look at Daisy from arm's length. 'I'm so proud of you.'

'Aye, you and Harley both put on a fine performance.'

Daisy couldn't help but laugh at their exuberance. 'It was only a five minute interview. Nothing special.'

'Nothing special?' Morag was incredulous. 'Go on now. It was terrific and I'll tell you what, Audrey would have been proud too, you mark my words.'

The attention was a little overwhelming, but welcome too in the confusion she was feeling, and the hollow left by Finn's absence. 'Ok,' she said. 'Well, it's done now. I don't suppose anybody's put the kettle on? I'm dying for a cup of tea.'

*

'Aah, Morag! Now there's the best friend an old woman could have. She knows me as well as I know myself and she's right, I am proud.' A small frown settled on Audrey's brow. 'I hope Daisy knows that, even if it turns out she didn't save that young lady's life.'

'I'm sure she does, Audrey. I know there's been some crossed wires, with the letter and you asking Finn to look out for her, but that's all down to the tangled emotions of the occasion.' He patted her hand. 'It seems to me the two of you are on pretty much the same wavelength most of the time.'

'I'd like to think so.' Audrey was quiet, contemplative. 'It's almost time, isn't it?'

'It's certainly heading that way, yes, particularly now we know the event which Daisy has been fretting about all this time wasn't genuine.'

She nodded and sighed. 'You know, it breaks my heart to see her upset over that lad, though I must admit she's no one to blame but herself if he does run a mile. She has a tendency to be a little… rash on occasion.'

'Impetuous, yes, but well intentioned, Audrey, and that counts for a lot.'

'Yes, she doesn't have a malicious bone in her body, and he's a good lad for all I might have said earlier, so hopefully he can see that in her. What do you think? Do you think he'll forgive her? That they can work through this? Even if it's only as friends, I'd like to know before I go.'

He smiled softly at her. 'I don't know, but I think we should have faith that, whatever happens, Daisy has the wherewithal to face it, and with Lizzy and Morag as backup.'

'I'm glad they've made amends. It's not right the two of them being at odds, and I'm afraid I might have played a part in that, or at least I could have done more to stop it getting to where it was.'

'We're none of us perfect, Audrey.'

'You're right, there.' She paused for a moment, then looked up at him grinning. 'Though Alan Titchmarsh comes pretty darn close.'

'Alan Titchmarsh, indeed.'

She laughed and reached out to pat his arm. 'A little bit more and then I'll be off. If I could just see how the Finn thing plays out, it'll put me out of my misery and I'll be able to rest in peace. Can you do that for me?'

'Oh, I suppose so, but only because it's you, Audrey. For anyone else, I'd be moving them along tout suite.'

She clasped her hands in her lap and turned her attention to the screen, but leaned a little towards him for a moment. 'I knew you had a soft spot for me, all along.'

CHAPTER 39

Daisy picked up her phone to call Finn a hundred times over the next two days, but talked herself out of it every time: he might be working; he needed space; she didn't know what to say and, finally, she'd be seeing him at the party in the evening anyway so maybe it would be better to talk face to face. The party itself loomed large and scary as it came closer, and when Tuesday evening arrived she was a nervous wreck.

She paid particular attention to her outfit, pulling on her best jeans and a girly, floaty pink top, and applying a touch of make-up too. It had to be practical, after all it was a youth club party, not some swish do at a grand venue, but she also wanted to look her best, so that when Finn saw her he would... What? What would Finn think, say, do? Would he even speak to her? She sighed. In a couple of hours her questions would all be answered.

'You look nice.' Lizzy looked up from the sofa as Daisy crossed the lounge to get her jacket.

'Thanks,' she said. 'The youth club are having a party, so I thought I ought to make an effort.'

'That colour looks good on you.' Lizzy pushed a magazine away, giving Daisy all her attention. 'Is Finn calling for you?'

Daisy shook her head. 'The pavilion's only a few minutes away.'

'That's never stopped him before.' Lizzy's words were slow, as if chosen carefully. 'I haven't heard anything about Finn for a day or two. Is everything alright with you two?'

'We're not an "us two".' She shrugged. 'I expect he's been busy, that's all.'

'Oh, well. Absence makes the heart grow fonder, and his eyes'll pop out when he sees you dressed up like that.'

'Is it too much?'

'Absolutely not.' Lizzy stood up and took Daisy by the shoulders, straightening her up tall. 'In fact...' She ran upstairs. 'I've got just the thing.'

'What? Mum...' Daisy shouted after her. 'I've got to get going.'

'One minute.' The call came from above, in the midst of rattling and shuffling, followed by hasty footsteps across the landing and back downstairs. Lizzy held out a delicate chain with a small silver flower pendant in both hands. 'Mum gave me this when I turned eighteen, not long before you came along. See? It's got a daisy on it and I thought it was so beautiful. It's how you got your name, or one of the reasons I chose it anyway. It only seems right that you should have it now.' She offered it up.

Daisy nodded. 'If you're sure. It's lovely.'

'Here, let me.' Lizzy moved behind Daisy and did up the clasp, then stepped around to look her in the eye. 'Go on.' She smiled and winked. 'Knock that boy's socks off.'

Daisy thought for a moment about refuting the comment but stopped and smiled shyly. 'I'll do my best.'

Daisy approached the pavilion with a heavier heart than should have been expected, considering the evening was to celebrate the success of the project she'd imagined and brought to fruition. Every time she turned a corner en route, she hoped to catch sight of Finn heading towards her, running late, smiling and pleased to see her. Every time, she was disappointed.

When she got there, Chris was standing in the doorway, facing outwards. His face lit up when he saw her. 'Here she is, hero of the hour.'

She smiled back. 'Hi.'

'I was thinking as it's so warm and sunny it might be nice to set tables up in the yard, so we can admire the mural while we eat. What do you think?'

'Sounds good to me.' She peered past him to see if Finn was there.

'Great. Come in then, and you can help shift the tables.' She followed him inside. 'Here, Finn, grab an end of this, will you? We're going al fresco.'

So, he was there. Daisy looked across the room, where he had his back to her and waited for him to turn, to smile, as he usually did when he saw her.

He turned alright, but his focus stayed entirely on Chris. 'Ok. I'm coming.'

'Hang on. Can I borrow you, Chris?' Joanna called from the kitchen.

'Anything for you, my love.' He winked at Daisy. 'Sorry. Help Finn with this one and I'll be right back?'

'Sure.' Moment of truth. He definitely wouldn't be able to avoid noticing her now.

He came and grabbed an end, but didn't make eye contact and didn't speak.

'Hi. Are you ok?' Act normally, she urged herself, picking up her end of the table. Don't read more into his distance than is there.

'Yep, fine.'

He wasn't fine. This was going to take work. 'How've you been since the unveiling?'

'Fine.' He frowned. 'Mind the step.'

She glanced behind to traverse the steps down to the yard, her mind on finding a safe topic of conversation to break the ice with him. 'Where shall we put this?'

He nodded towards the far corner, still avoiding eye-contact. 'Best start that end and work back, so we don't have to dodge tables with all the others.'

She walked backwards to where he'd indicated. 'That seems like a good id...'

He dropped his end of the table and walked back towards the door before she'd finished speaking. This was turning into a nightmare, but at least he was talking to her, even if it was purely functional. She followed him inside to find him waiting, already clutching one end of the next table to be moved. She lifted the other end.

'Have you been working? At the hospice?' She inwardly kicked herself. She hadn't needed to add that – he knew where he worked.

'Yes.'

She waited for him to expand, but that was it. This was excruciating.

'Watch your back.'

Daisy looked over her shoulder to see Lewis and his mates coming through the doorway, and stopped.

'We need another three of these outside. Do you want to get stuck in, lads?' Finn addressed the group.

There was a scramble as they scuttled to help, and Daisy was relieved of her burden, set adrift, not knowing what to do next. Finn had carried on, still holding a table end. Someone mentioned chairs and she jumped to attention – she couldn't stand there all night like a lemon, she needed to do her bit too. She unhooked a couple of chairs from a stack and scurried outside. Finn was supervising the organisation of furniture in the yard.

'Where do you want these?' She asked, feeling lame but wanting to engage his attention any way she could.

'Anywhere. We'll sort it in a minute.'

She was dismissed, and dismayed, as he turned his back, and an urge to cry rose up in her. He was clearly angry with her, so why didn't he just say so, give her the chance to apologise, move on? This coldness, this detachment was so cutting. Well, she wasn't going to stay here and make a fool of herself getting upset. She'd rather go home.

Daisy back-stepped to the path and turned to leave as Harley and her friends entered.

'Hi, miss. How's it going?'

Daisy shrugged, too slow in making her escape, but too full of emotion to speak.

Harley stopped, studying Daisy's expression, then spoke to her friends. 'Go on in. I'll be right there.'

The chatter of the girls moved away, leaving only the two of them standing on the path.

'What's up?' Harley's gaze was intense.

Daisy shrugged again and controlled her breathing. She needed to pull herself together. 'I'm alright. Honestly.'

'No, you're not. As my Nan says, "you can't kid a kidder". What is it? Is it him?' She tipped her head to where the boys were setting up. 'Shall I?'

'Don't do anything, Harley. That's an order.' Daisy had visions of her young friend making a huge scene, confronting Finn in front of everyone. She leaned in confidentially. 'This is my doing, my fault, and I need to sort it out, but not now, not here.'

Harley dipped her head to one side, studying Daisy. 'Are you sure? Because I don't mind having a word…'

'Absolutely not! I'm a grown up and I can handle it myself.'

'Like being grown up means you have all the answers.' Harley was sceptical. 'Alright. But I'll be watching, both of you, and if puts a foot wrong… We women stick together, right?'

Daisy didn't speak.

'Right?'

'Yes, ok, but please don't do anything.'

Harley tutted and walked away. 'I'll be watching,' she threw over her shoulder, before disappearing inside.

The evening crawled forward and the harder Daisy tried to break through to Finn, the more frustrated she became. There was always something in the way, or Finn was determinedly looking the other way. While Chris made speeches and snacks were devoured, they were polar ends of the yard. When they split into groups to play ridiculous but hilarious games, they were on opposing teams. Even when there was clearing up to be done, Finn was back on furniture moving detail, while Daisy was allocated washing up.

As time ticked on she resigned herself to the fact she wasn't going to get to speak to him properly tonight, and the torture of waiting stretched out before her like a carpet of nails.

She sighed heavily as she dunked the last of the plates into lukewarm suds.

'You don't have to dry them with your breath, miss. I've got a tea-towel for that.'

'Sorry, what?'

'All that damsel in distress stuff. The sighing?' Harley clarified at Daisy's blank look. She huffed and leaned back against the counter, looking straight at Daisy. 'You need to get this sorted. You know that, don't you? Enough is enough.'

Daisy had given up all pretence of keeping her feelings to herself. 'Of course I know that. I have tried, but it's driving me barmy. I can't get close enough to him to have a private chat. I guess I'll just have to message him again later. Maybe he'll reply this time. And if not, there's always next week.'

'Next week? You'll have given yourself an ulcer by that time.'

Daisy held her palms wide. 'What else can I do? I can't get a minute alone with him.'

A slow smile spread across Harley's face. 'Sometimes, miss, you've got to take the bull by the horns. Anyway.' She glanced at her watch and threw her tea-towel onto the worktop in front of the hatch, then thought better of it and picked it back up, making a big performance of folding it carefully and replacing it neatly. 'I've got to get out of here. Places to be. Are you alright to finish off?'

A Reason To Be

Daisy looked at the pile of dishes still to be dried and stacked away but knew she had no choice. If Harley had to go, she had to go. 'Yeah, sure. See you next week?'

'Yeah, see you.'

The door slammed shut behind her, leaving Daisy alone to contemplate her situation. The longer she was away from Finn, the more it hurt – not the sharp, deep pain like losing her gran, but a dull, constant, empty nagging pain. She needed to apologise, and she needed to tell him how important he was to her, that he was a good friend, a really good friend, a really, really good friend, but she so wanted him to be more. But what could she do, if he didn't want to play ball? She couldn't force him to listen, and she certainly couldn't make him feel the same way about her, and he clearly didn't. He could barely look at her.

As she continued working, the general hustle and bustle of other busy bodies floated through to her via the loosely closed hatch, gradually reducing as people filtered away, but suddenly the hatch slammed shut with a bang and a click, as it automatically locked. She jumped, jolted from her reverie assuming someone had accidentally leaned against it, or knocked it, and carried on drying cups but, within moments, raised voices came from outside.

'Quickly, yes. It's in the kitchen and it's huge, isn't it Lewis?' Harley's voice and, to Daisy, she sounded frantic.

'Enormous. I haven't got a clue what it is, but it's got gigantic fangs.' Lewis agreed.

Another voice sounded confused. 'Fangs? What do you mean, fangs?' This was Finn.

Daisy only had a moment to steel herself for what was to come as the door swung open and Finn was pushed through. His eyes widened as he came face to face with her, and he turned as if to leave, but his retreat was curtailed as the door slammed shut and the sound of the key turning removed any possibility of escape.

'Now, then, you two. You need to talk and you're not coming out until you've sorted things out.' Harley's tone from outside was steely and reminded Daisy of Audrey when she had meant business. 'Me and Lewis are going to keep Chris and Joanna busy for ten minutes. Ten minutes, you hear me? So, no wasting time.'

Heavy footsteps pounded away from the kitchen, the outside door creaked as it opened and closed, and silence fell. Daisy and Finn looked at each other, Daisy gripping a cup in her hand like a lifebelt.

'Did you put them up to this?' Finn was scowling.

'No, of course I didn't.' She didn't know what to say, although she'd been mentally debating precisely that topic only moments before. 'You know Harley and Lewis. They've got minds of their own.'

Finn grunted an acknowledgement. He rattled the door in its frame, despite having heard the key turn. Stepping back, he put his hands on his hips. 'Ah! I know.' He turned to the hatch and pushed it and, when it stuck fast, reached round the side to turn the latch which released it, only to find it empty. He gave her an accusatory glare. 'Who's taken the key?'

'Not me.' She held her hands up defensively. A memory of Harley taking a great deal of trouble folding up her tea-towel, which still lay there now, came to mind. 'Harley,' she said. 'She must have planned this.'

He huffed. 'So, now what are we going to do?'

Daisy shrugged. This was exactly what she'd been saying she needed, time alone with him, where he couldn't avoid her. Well, not exactly like this: she hadn't meant taking him prisoner against his will, though it did achieve the desired result. How did she say what she needed to say?

'I suppose we could... talk? Like Harley said?'

He shook his head. 'Talk about what exactly?'

Bull by the horns, Daisy. Bull by the horns. She took a deep breath and let the words flow. 'That I'm sorry.'

He was staring at a far corner of the room. 'Oh, yeah? Sorry about what?'

A Reason To Be

She bit her lips together, forming a list in her mind. 'Loads of things. I'm sorry about interfering in your business without permission. I'm sorry about contacting your parents without telling you, and them turning up when you weren't expecting, because that clearly didn't go as well as it did in my head. I'm sorry for being really horrible to you at times over the last couple of months, when all you've done is try to help me.' What else was there? 'Oh, and I'm sorry for making you strip off in front of a load of feral women. I'm sorry.'

He glanced at her momentarily at the last comment, before returning his attention to the wall. 'Ok. So you're sorry. I hear you. And, are you sorry for invading my privacy by accessing my phone to get my parents' contact details? Because that's the only way you could possibly have tracked them down.'

'Ah, yes, that wasn't me. It was Lewis… but it was at my request, and yes, I'm sorry about that, too.'

His lips were pursed, head nodding in comprehension. 'That makes sense.'

The quiet stretched until Daisy had to fill it, feeling in her bones that more was needed. 'I shouldn't have done it, but I wanted to do something for you. You've done so much for me, being with me after Gran died, making me sort things out with Mum. You've been such a good friend, even if I didn't always fully appreciate your methods, and saying thank you didn't seem enough. I wanted to give you something, and healing the rift between you and your parents was the only thing I could think of that would even come close.'

He tutted. 'It'll take more than bringing us face to face to do that.'

'I know that now, and I should have seen from the start, but you know what I'm like. When I get an idea in my head, nothing can change it, except hindsight.' She bit her lip. 'Sorry. Was it awful? Have I made things worse between you and them?'

'No. I mean, yes, it was awful, but no, you haven't made things worse.' His eyes dropped to his toes. 'We've actually spoken a couple of times since, but as for healing the rift, it's not going to happen overnight. A lot of water has flowed under the bridge, you know?'

'Yeah. I know.' She tipped her head, sensing a softening in him, trying to meet his eye. 'I want you to know, I might have done a bad thing, but it was for the right reasons. Someone once told me that if you do a wrong thing for the right reasons, it should all come good in the end, that friends can rebuild their friendships.'

His shoulders lifted in a chuckle, and he finally looked up at her. 'That sounds like Audrey style wisdom. Was it?'

'No. Not this time.' She grimaced at him. 'It was Harley.'

His chuckle turned into a guffaw. 'Harley? You're taking relationship advice from Harley, now?'

A smile spread across her face and she shrugged. 'Hey, when you're desperate, any port in a storm.'

'Good grief. It must have been a force ten tornado to take cover in that port.'

Seeing the humour in his eyes, feeling the hope of him forgiving her, that everything might actually be alright after all, filled her with emotion. She wanted to laugh and cry at the same time. Tears gathered in her eyes despite the smile on her face. 'I was pretty desperate. I thought I'd lost you.' She realised what she'd said and backtracked. 'I mean I thought I'd lost our friendship and it's… it's so important to me.'

His brow furrowed as he studied her. 'Yes, Mum said. She said, I was lucky to have such a *good* friend, that you'd assured her that's all we were – *friends*.' He said the word like it was lead balloon.

A spark ignited in Daisy's chest. His tone suggested disappointment. Did he want more? She had started to suspect it the night of the unveiling, but now she was happy just to have him speaking to her. Could he still be interested in her? Maybe, if she was lucky, he'd ask her out again in a few weeks, months even. Could she wait? A voice in the back of her mind said 'take the bull by the horns, miss', and Daisy felt the spark travel from her chest to her gut. It was time to be true to herself and end the misery of not knowing.

'Of course I did. I couldn't exactly say "yes, Mrs Kennedy, we're friends now, but I'm just waiting for the first opportunity to snog his face off", could I?'

His head shot back in surprise and he stared at her without speaking.

Her courage faded and she was garbling. 'I mean, she'd have thought I was a right weirdo, wouldn't she? Some girl she'd never met, never even heard of, phoning her out of the blue saying she fancied the pants off her son. She'd have thought... I don't even know what she would have thought but...'

Finn's hand reached up to cup Daisy's cheek and he leaned in to stop her jabbering with a kiss on her lips, before pulling back to gauge her reaction, still close enough for his breath to whisper across her face.

Daisy inhaled sharply in surprise and closed her eyes, waiting for him to kiss her again. When he didn't, she opened them again to see him studying her. She wondered if she should say something, to reassure him, to encourage him, but decided actions spoke louder than words. She stepped towards him, lifted her face and kissed him like she'd never kissed anyone before. It took only a moment for his hand to drop and his arms to wrap around her and pull her even closer, so neither of them had any doubt about how they felt.

*

'STOP!' Audrey hollered, placing her hands over her eyes.

'Whatever's the matter? I thought this was what you wanted to happen.'

Keeping her eyes averted, she waved at him frantically. 'Stop it. Stop it now, I said.'

'Alright, alright.' The Ombudsman fiddled with the controls, turning the screen back to the blank wall it had originally been. 'There. Is that better?'

She glared at him. 'That's quite enough, thank you. There are certain things a grandmother has no business seeing, and shenanigans of that nature's one of 'em. Good gracious me.' She pressed a hand to her chest.

'I suppose you're right.' The ombudsman smiled. 'Does this mean you're ready to move on now?'

'All good things come to an end.' She sighed. 'So, I suppose I must.'

He nodded sagely, as he pulled out his tablet computer and tapped at it. 'Indeed they do, but perhaps you could look at this as more a new beginning than an ending. There are exciting things in store for you, I'm sure.'

'Excitement is one thing I haven't been short of recently. Rest, on the other hand.' She tipped her head.

'There'll be plenty of that too. Grace or Blessing will be along to collect you in due course. ' He put the tablet down and smiled at her conspiratorially. 'Before you go, is there anything else you want to ask me before they arrive? Now's your chance to solve some of life's great mysteries. We've got a minute or two to spare.'

Audrey pursed her lips as she considered the matter. 'There is one thing…'

'Go on, then. Fire away.'

'What, anything?'

'The world is your oyster, Audrey.'

'Alright, then. I've always wondered, is the Loch Ness monster real? I had no end of nightmares when I was growing up and it would certainly ease my mind if I knew it wasn't.'

The ombudsman laughed out loud and long, holding his stomach as if he thought it might explode.

'Well I never!' Audrey glared at him. 'You said anything.'

A Reason To Be

He pulled himself together, but his face was still alight with mirth. 'Indeed I did, Audrey. I'm sorry, but you took me by surprise, that's all. I was expecting something deep and mysterious, like the answer to life, the universe and everything, not the Loch Ness monster.'

'I'd say Loch Ness is pretty deep and mysterious, if you ask me.'

'True, true.' He coughed to clear his throat and returned to a serious tone. 'Well, I can assure you, Audrey, you will not be troubled by the Loch Ness monster where you're going.'

She nodded slowly. 'That's good enough for me.'

There was a knock at the door and Grace walked in. 'Client ready for dispatch, I understand.'

'Yes, indeed, Grace. Perhaps you could see Audrey on her way.'

Grace eyed Audrey with suspicion. 'You're not going to give me any trouble, are you?'

'Me?' Audrey's eyes were wide. 'I wouldn't say boo to a goose, me.' She lowered herself carefully from the stool and made to follow her guide, but paused in the doorway. 'Oh, just one more thing.'

The ombudsman looked at her in query.

'Having watched Daisy and Lizzy sort out their differences, I'm wondering if maybe me and my old mum should have had a chat while we still had time. The things we rowed about don't seem like much now, you know? Where I'm going, is there any chance I might... run into her?'

His face softened into an understanding smile and he winked. 'Stranger things have happened, Audrey. Stranger things have happened.'

She studied his face a moment longer, then nodded to indicate she was finally done. 'I'll be away then. Thanks for your time... and everything.' And with that, she was gone.

CHAPTER 40

The key turned in the lock and the kitchen door opened. Daisy and Finn jumped apart. Harley grinned through the opening. 'Look lively, Chris and Joanna are coming your way. Oh, and…' she dived into the room and replaced the key to the hatch, before heading out again, stopping only to engulf the pair of them in a brief but exuberant hug. 'Didn't I tell you it would all be alright, Daisy? Didn't I?' She rushed out without waiting for an answer.

Daisy and Finn stared at each other for a moment before collapsing in a heap of laughter. 'She finally called me Daisy.' Daisy chuckled.

Chris's booming voice reached them through the door as he approached. 'I'm glad to hear people happy in their work.' He leaned in. 'Are we done? My bed's a-calling.'

Finn winked at her as she turned to stack the final dishes in the cupboard. 'Almost. We'll be right there.'

'Marvellous, see you out front in five.' Chris withdrew and his cheerful whistle could be heard as he retreated across the hall and outside.

Daisy checked the worktops, folded up the tea-towel and hung it on the hook where it belonged.

A Reason To Be

Finn pulled her to him again. 'I don't suppose you want dinner after all that party food, but shall we go somewhere for a drink, where we can... talk?'

Daisy pressed a quick peck on his lips. 'Yes, please.'

'Good, because we need to come up with the next step in the plan to prove you have a purpose.'

Daisy's eyes stretched wide. 'Of course, I haven't told you.'

'What?'

She explained what she'd found out during her visit to the studio, Finn staring as she told the story.

'So you thought you'd saved Billie Harper-French from drowning, and she was acting? That must have been quite a performance for you to fall for it hook, line and sinker.'

'I was only a child myself remember.' She blushed. 'But I still can't believe I fell for it. What an idiot I am.'

'No, you're not. You're still a hero, because whether she needed saving or not, you put yourself on the line without a second thought.'

She shrugged. 'I suppose.'

'But more to the point, it means you're off the hook. You can let yourself enjoy the rest of your life without measuring it against that one event. The best is still to come. You still have time to find your reason to be.'

'Yes, and about that, I'm sorry for being so... so melodramatic. I think it was just everything getting on top of me, feeling so serious and dark, losing Gran. I was confused and lost but I know now, I've got plenty of good stuff to look forward to, and I intend to make the most of every moment, including this one.' She leaned in and pecked him on the cheek.

Smiling, he held out a hand for her take, and they walked towards the exit together, but he paused before opening the door, gazing into her eyes. 'You know, we'll always have Audrey to thank for bringing us together. What would she think if she was looking down on us now?'

Daisy moved in closer and kissed his lips, long and hard, then pulled away, chuckling. 'Let's hope she isn't, eh?'

ABOUT THE AUTHOR

Sharon Francis

Born and bred in beautiful North Devon, Sharon is married with two grown up children. She studied creative writing with the Open University, completing her BA in 2017. A Reason To Be is her third romantic comedy novel in the Limbo series, following the debut, Girl Plans, God Laughs and What Might Have Been. She also writes crime fiction, including Bloodline and Twisted Roots from her series, Hidden Histories.

For more information about Sharon, or her books, go to:-

Facebook.com/Sharon-Francis-Author-110933057304441/

OR

www.foursirenspress.co.uk/authors/sharon-francis

KEEP UP TO DATE

If you have enjoyed this book, please remember to leave a review on Amazon, so other readers can have the benefit of your thoughts.

You could be the first to know when Sharon's next novel is available to purchase and receive free additional content by signing up for the Four Sirens Press newsletter at:-

www.foursirenspress.co.uk

ROM-COM BOOKS BY THIS AUTHOR

Girl Plans, God Laughs

The choice between life and death is usually a no brainer, but Violet Harper has her own reasons to head for the afterlife. She needs to make a complaint.

In a drunken haze she made a deal with God to meet the man of her dreams. With her eyes on the prize, she's carried out good deeds galore, but her love life is still a mess and she can't help feeling let down.

When a freak accident leaves her hovering between life and death in Limbo, Violet raises her grievance. The Spiritual Ombudsman agrees to examine her case, but she may get more than she bargained for.

Sometimes it takes a bolt from the blue to see what's right in front of your nose.

ROM-COM BOOKS BY THIS AUTHOR

What Might Have Been

Life and love can be a rollercoaster, except for Lily Armitage, so far it's been more of a train crash. Perhaps it should be no surprise that she's decided to get off the ride and watch from the sidelines.

However, if Lily is to finally connect with her soulmate, she has no choice but to face whatever ups and downs life has to throw at her.

Can divine intervention give her the courage she needs to get back on the ride?

CRIME BOOKS BY THIS AUTHOR

Bloodline

Tony Viscount is a widower, a father and a restaurateur but has no idea where he came from, so helping his young son, Jamie, complete a family tree could be fun for both of them.

But Tony doesn't expect the tale of terror he uncovers, or that it could have followed him into the present.

What he discovers will change his life forever.

Assuming he gets to live it...

CRIME BOOKS BY THIS AUTHOR

Twisted Roots

When Emily agrees to handle her late uncle's estate, it seems the perfect escape from her troubled marriage and her father's ill health. But as she delves deeper into her uncle's history, a troubling pattern of broken relationships and mysterious disappearances are revealed.

Driven to unearth the truth, the shocking revelations she uncovers are more sinister than Emily could ever have imagined.

What is the truth, and who can she trust?

Printed in Great Britain
by Amazon